Trapnel was not at all appeased. In fact he became more heated than ever, striking his stick on the floor.

'How one envies the rich quality of a reviewer's life. All the things to which those Fleet Street Jesuses feel superior. Their universal knowledge, exquisite taste, idyllic loves, happy married life, optimism, scholarship, knowledge of the true meaning of life, freedom from sexual temptation, simplicity of heart, sympathy with the masses, compassion for the unfortunate, generosity – particularly the last, in welcoming with open arms every phoney who appears on the horizon. It's not surprising that in the eyes of most reviewers a mere writer's experiences seem so often trivial, sordid, lacking in meaning.'

Trapnel was thoroughly worked up. It was an odd spectacle. Bagshaw spoke soothingly.

'I know some of the critics are pretty awful, Trappy, but Nicholas wanted to talk to you about reviewing an occasional book yourself for *Fission*. If you agree to do so, you'll at least have the opportunity of showing how it ought to be done.'

Trapnel saw that he had been caught on the wrong foot, and took this very well, laughing loudly. He may in any case have decided some apology was required for all this vehemence. All the earlier tension disappeared at once.

A Dance to the Music of Time

A Question of Upbringing
A Buyer's Market
The Acceptance World
At Lady Molly's
Casanova's Chinese Restaurant
The Kindly Ones
The Valley of Bones
The Soldier's Art
The Military Philosophers
Books Do Furnish a Room
Temporary Kings
Hearing Secret Harmonies

*All the books in the series
are available from Mandarin Paperbacks*

ANTHONY POWELL

Books Do Furnish a Room

Mandarin

A Mandarin Paperback
BOOKS DO FURNISH A ROOM

First published in Great Britain 1971
by William Heinemann Ltd
This edition published 1991
by Mandarin Paperbacks
Michelin House, 81 Fulham Road, London SW3 6RB

Mandarin is an imprint of the Octopus Publishing Group,
a division of Reed International Books Limited

Copyright © 1971 by Anthony Powell

A CIP catalogue record for this title
is available from the British Library

ISBN 0 7493 0648 3

Printed and bound in Great Britain
by Cox & Wyman Ltd, Reading, Berkshire

For Rupert

A DANCE TO THE MUSIC OF TIME

★ ★ ★ ★ ★ ★ ★ ★ ★ ★ ★

BOOKS DO FURNISH A ROOM

1

REVERTING TO THE UNIVERSITY AT forty, one immediately recaptured all the crushing melancholy of the under-graduate condition. As the train drew up at the platform, before the local climate had time to impair health, aca-demic contacts disturb the spirit, a more imminent gloom was re-established, its sinewy grip in a flash making one young again. Depressive symptoms, menacing in all haunts of youth, were in any case easily aroused at this period, to be accepted as delayed action of the last six years. The odd thing was how distant the recent past had also become, the army now as stylized in the mind—to compare another triumphal frieze—as the legionaries of Trajan's Column, exercising, sacrificing, sweating at their antique fatigue, silent files on eternal parade to soundless military music. Nevertheless, shades from those days still walked abroad. Only a week before, the peak of a French general's khaki képi, breaking rather too abruptly through the winter haze of Piccadilly, had by conditioned reflex jerked my right hand from its overcoat pocket in preparation for a no longer consonant salute, counterfeiting the gesture of a deserter who has all but given himself away. A residuum of the experience was inevitable.

Meanwhile, traditional textures of existence were lab-oriously patched together in an attempt to reaffirm some sort of personal identity, however blurred. Even if—as some thought—the let-up were merely temporary, it was no less welcome, though the mood after the earlier conflict —summarized by a snatch Ted Jeavons liked to hum when in poor form—was altogether absent:

> 'Après la guerre,
> There'll be a good time everywhere.'

That did not hinder looking forward to engrossment during the next few weeks amongst certain letters and papers deposited in the libraries here. Solitude would be a luxury after the congestions of wartime, archaic folios a soothing drug. War left, on the one hand, a passionate desire to tackle a lot of work: on the other, never to do any work again. It was a state of mind Robert Burton— about whom I was writing a book—would have well understood. Irresolution appealed to him as one of the myriad forms of Melancholy, although he was, of course, concerned in the main with no mere temporary depression or fidgetiness, but a 'chronic or continued disease, a settled humour'. Still, post-war melancholy might have rated a short sub-section in the great work:

THE ANATOMY OF MELANCHOLY
What it is, with all the Kindes, Causes, Symptomes, Prognostickes, and severall cures of it. Three Maine Partitions with their severall Sections, Members and Sub-sections, Philosophically, Medicinally, Historically, Opened and cut up by Democritus Junior. With a Satyricall Preface, conducing to the following Discourse. Anno Dom. 1621.

The title page showed not only Burton's own portrait in ruff and skull cap, but also figures illustrative of his theme; love-madness; hypochondriasis; religious melancholy. The emblems of jealousy and solitude were there too, together with those sovereign cures for melancholy and madness, borage and hellebore. Burton had long been a favourite of mine. A study of him would be a change from writing novels. The book was to be called *Borage and Hellebore*.

As the forlorn purlieus of the railway-station end of the town gave place to colleges, reverie, banal if you like, though eminently Burtonesque, turned towards the relatively high proportion of persons known pretty well at an earlier stage of life, both here and elsewhere, now dead, gone off their rocker, withdrawn into states of existence they—or I—had no wish to share. The probability was that even without cosmic upheaval some kind of reshuffle has to take place halfway through life, a proposition borne out by the autobiographies arriving thick and fast —three or four at a time at regular intervals—for review in one of the weeklies. At this very moment my bag was weighed down by several of these volumes, to be dealt with in time off from the seventeenth century: *Purged Not in Lethe . . . A Stockbroker in Sandals . . . Slow on the Feather . . . Moss off a Rolling Stone . . .* chronicles of somebody or other's individual fate, on the whole unenthralling enough, except insomuch as every individual's story has its enthralling aspect, though the essential pivot was usually omitted or obscured by most autobiographers.

However, nearly all revealed, if not explicitly in every case, a similar reorientation towards the sixth climacteric, their narrative supporting, on the whole, evidence already noticeably piling up, that friends, if required at all in the manner of the past, must largely be reassembled at about this milestone. The changeover might improve consistency, even quality, but certainly lost in intimacy; anyway that peculiar kind of intimacy that is consoling when you are young, though probably too vulnerable to withstand the ever increasing self-regard of later years.

Accommodation was in college. The place looked much the same as ever. Only one porter, his face unfamiliar, was

3

on duty at the lodge. After studying a list for a long time, he signified a distant staircase for the rooms allotted. The traditional atmosphere, tenuously poised between a laxly run boarding-school and seedy residential club, now leant more emphatically towards the former type of institution. The rooms, arctic as of old, evidently belonged to a fairly austere young man, whose only picture was an unframed photograph of a hockey team. It stood curling on the mantelpiece. In the bookcase, a lot of works on economics terminated with St John Clarke's *Dust Thou Art*, rather a recondite one about the French Revolution, which might be pleasurable to reassess critically. I pushed on into the bedroom. Here a crisis declared itself. The bed was unmade. Only a sombrely stained blue-grey mattress, folded in three, lay on the rusty wires of the frame. Back at the porter's lodge, the inconceivable difficulties of remedying lack of bedclothes at this hour were radically discussed. Later, in hall, a few zombie-like figures collected together to consume a suitably zombie-sustaining repast.

This was the opening of a routine of days in the library, nights collating notes, the monotony anodyne. One became immediately assimilated with other dim, disembodied, unapproachable entities, each intent on his own enigmatic preoption, who flit through the cobbled lanes and gothic archways of a university in vacation. It was what Burton himself called 'a silent, sedentary, solitary private life', and it well suited me during the middle of the week. For weekends, I returned to London. Once Killick, a hearty rugby-playing philosophy don of my college, now grunting and purple, came bustling up the street, a pile of books under his arm, and I accosted him. There were explanations. Killick issued an abstracted invitation to dinner. The following week, when I turned up, it was to be told Professor Killick had gone to Manchester to give two lectures. This oversight hardly came as a surprise. In a city of shadows, appointments were bound to be kept in a shadowy fashion.

At the same time something very different, something perfectly substantial, not shadowy at all, lay ahead as not to be too long postponed, even if a latent unwillingness to face that fact might delay taking the plunge. A moral reckoning had to be discharged. As the days passed, the hypnotic pull to pay a call on Sillery grew increasingly strong, disinclination—that was, of course, far too strong a word, indeed not the right word at all—scarcely lessening, so much as the Sillery magnetism itself gathering force. Pretendedly heedless enquiries revealed that, although retired for some time from all administrative duties in his own college, Sillery still retained his old rooms, receiving visitors willingly, even avidly, it was reported, with so far as possible the traditional elements of welcome.

To enter Sillery's sitting-room after twenty years was to drive a relatively deep fissure through variegated seams of Time. The faintly laundry-cupboard odour, as one came through the door, generated in turn the taste of the rock-buns dispensed at those tea-parties, their gritty indeterminate flavour once more dehydrating the palate. The props round about designed for Sillery's nightly performance remained almost entirely unaltered. Eroded loose-covers of immemorially springless armchairs still precariously endured; wide perforations frayed long since in the stretch of carpet before the door, only a trifle more hazardous to the unwary walker. As might be expected, the framed photographs of jaunty young men had appreciably increased, several of the new arrivals in uniform, one in a turban, two or three American.

In this room, against this background, Sillery's machinations, such as they were, had taken shape for half a century. Here a thousand undergraduate attitudes had been penitentially acted out. Youth, dumb with embarrassment,

5

breathless with exhibitionism, stuttering with nerves, inarticulate with conceit; the socially flamboyant, the robustly brawny, the crudely uninstructed, the palely epicene; one and all had obediently leapt through the hoop at Sillery's ringmaster behest; one and all submitted themselves to the testing flame of this burning fiery furnace of adolescent experience. Such concepts crowded in only after a few minutes spent in the room. At the moment of entry no more was to be absorbed than the fact that another guest had already arrived, to whom Sillery, with much miming and laughter, was narrating an anecdote. Any immediate responses on my own part were cut short at once, for Sillery, as if ever on his guard against possible assassination, sprang from his chair and charged forward, ready to come to grips with any assailant.

'Timothy? . . . Mike? . . . Cedric? . . .'

'Nick—'

'Carteret-Owen? . . . Jelf? . . . Kniveton? . . .'

'Jenkins—how are you, Sillers?'

'So you've come all the way from New South Wales, Nick?'

'I—'

'No—of course— you were appointed to that headmastership after all, Nick?'

'It's—'

'I can see you haven't quite recovered from that head wound . . .'

The question of identification was finally established with the help of the other caller, who turned out to be Short, a member of Sillery's college a year senior to myself. Short had been not only a great supporter of Sillery's tea-parties, but also vigorously promulgated Sillery's reputation as—Short's own phrase— a 'power in the land'. We had known each other as undergraduates, continued to keep up some sort of an acquaintance in early London

6

days, then drifted into different worlds. I had last heard his name, though never run across him, during the war when Short had been working in the Cabinet Office, with which my War Office Section had occasional dealings. He had probably transferred there temporarily from his own Ministry, because he had entered another branch of the civil service on leaving the University.

Short's demeanour, now a shade more portentous, more authoritarian, retained, like the sober suit he wore, the same consciously buttoned-up character. This mild, well-behaved air concealed a good deal of quiet obstinacy, a reasonable amalgam of malice. Always of high caste in his profession, now almost a princeling, he stemmed nevertheless from the same bureaucratic ancestry as a mere tribesman like Blackhead, prototype of all the race of *fonctionnaires*, and, anthropologically speaking, might be expected to revert to the same atavistic obstructionism if roused.

Sillery, moustache a shade more ragged and yellow, blue bow tie with its white spots, more likely than ever to fall undone, was not much changed either. Perhaps illusorily, his body and face had shrunk, physical contraction giving him a more simian look than formerly, though of no ordinary monkey; Brueghel's Antwerp apes (admired by Pennistone) rather than the Douanier's homely denizens of *Tropiques*, which Soper, the Divisional Catering Officer, had resembled. Even the real thing, Maisky, defunct pet of the Jeavonses, could not compare with Sillery's devastating monkeylike shrewdness. So strong was this impression of metempsychosis that he seemed about to bound up on to the bookcases, scattering the photographs of handsome young men, and pile of envelopes (the top one addressed to the Home Secretary) as he landed back on the table. He looked in glowing health. No one had ever pronounced with certainty on the subject of Sillery's age.

Year of birth was omitted in all books of reference. He was probably still under eighty.

'Sit down, Nick, sit down. Leonard and I were talking of an old friend—Bill Truscott. Remember Bill? I'm sure you do. Of course he was a wee bit older than you both'—Sillery had now perfectly achieved his chronological bearings—'but not very much. These differences get levelled out in the sands of time. They do indeed. Going to do great things was Bill. Next Prime Minister but three. We all thought so. No use denying it, is there, Leonard?'

Short smiled a temperate personal acquiescence that could not at the same time be interpreted for a moment as in any way committing his Department.

'Wrote some effective verse too,' said Sillery. 'Even if it was a shade derivative. Mark Members always sneered at Bill as a poet, even when he respected him as a coming man. Rupert Brooke at his most babbling, Mark used to say, Housman at his most lad-ish. Mark's always so severe. I told him so when he was here the other day addressing one of the undergraduate societies. You know Mark's hair's gone snow white. Can't think what happened to cause that, he's always taken great care of himself. Rather becoming, all the same. Gives just that air of distinction required by the passing of youth—and nobody got more out of being a professional young man than Mark when the going was good. He was talking of his old friend—*our* old friend—J. C. Quiggin. JG's abandoned the pen, I hear, perhaps wisely. A literary caesarean was all but required for that infant of long gestation *Unburnt Boats*, which I often feared might come to birth prematurely as a puling little magazine article. Now JG's going to promote literary works rather than write them himself. In brief, he's to become a publisher.'

'So I heard,' said Short. 'He's starting a new firm called Quiggin & Craggs.'

'To think I used to sit on committees with Howard Craggs discussing arms embargoes for Bolivia and Paraguay,' said Sillery. 'Sounds like an embargo on arms for the Greeks and Trojans now. Still, I read a good letter from Craggs the other day in one of the papers about the need for Socialists and Communists hammering out a common programme of European reconstruction.'

'Craggs was a temporary civil servant during the war,' said Short. 'Rationing paper, was it? Something of the sort.'

'That was when JG made himself useful as caretaker at Boggis & Stone,' said Sillery. 'I expect that explains why JG dresses like a partisan now, a man straight from the *maquis*, check shirts, leather jackets, ankle-boots. "Well, Quiggin's always been in the forefront of the Sales Resistance where clothes were concerned." That was Brightman's comment. "Even if he did live 'reservéd and austere' during hostilities—'reservéd' anyway." We all enjoy Brightman's rather cruel wit. Brightman and I are buddies now, by the way, all forgiven and forgotten. Besides, I expect JG's circumscribed by lack of clothing coupons. All right for such as me, still wearing the suit I bought for luncheon with Mr Asquith at Downing Street before the Flood, but then it was a good piece of cloth to start off with, not like those sad old reach-me-downs of JG's we're all so familiar with. No doubt they disintegrated under the stress of war conditions. Why not ankle-boots, forsooth? I'd be glad of a pair myself in winter here.'

Sillery paused. He seemed to feel he had allowed himself to rattle on rather too disconnectedly, at the same time could not remember what exactly had been the subject in hand. Like a conjuror whose patter for a specific trick has become misplaced, he had to go back to the beginning again.

'We were talking of Bill Truscott and his verse. I expect

Bill has abandoned the Muse now, though you never know. It's a hard habit to break. Would you believe it, I produced a slim volume myself when a young man? Did you know that, either of you? Suggested the influence of Coventry Patmore, so the pundits averred. I suppose most of us think of ourselves as poets at that age. No harm done. Well, that shouldn't be such a bad job at the Coal Board for Bill, if things are constituted as you prophesy, Leonard. Once Bill's been well and truly inducted there, he should be safe for a lifetime.'

Again Short allowed polite agreement to be inferred, without prejudice to official discretion, or additional evidence that might be subsequently revealed.

'But what mysterious mission brings you to our academic altars, Nick? We don't even know what you are doing these days. Back writing those novels of yours? I expect so. I used to hear something of your activities when you were a gallant soldier looking after those foreign folk. You know what an interest I take in old friends. Leonard and I were just speaking of poor Prince Theodoric, who was once going to perform all sorts of benefits for us here, endow scholarships and whatnot. Donners-Brebner was to co-operate, Sir Magnus Donners having interests in those parts. Now, alas, the good Prince is in exile, Sir Magnus gathered to his fathers. The University will never see any of those lovely scholarships. But we must march with the times. There's a new spirit abroad in Prince Thedoric's country, and, whatever people may say, there's no doubt about Marshal Stalin's sincerity in desire for a good-neighbour policy, if the West allows it. What I wrote to *The Times*. Those Tolland relations of yours, Nick? That unsatisfactory boy Hugo, how is he?'

I dealt with these personal matters as expeditiously as possible, explaining my purpose in staying at the University.

'Ah, Burton?' said Sillery. 'An interesting old gentleman, I've no doubt. Many years since I looked into the *Anatomy*.'

That was undoubtedly true. Sillery was not a great reader. He was also wholly uncurious about the byways of writing, indeed not very approving of writing at all, unless books likely to make a splash beyond mere literary consideration, of which there was no hope here. He abandoned the subject, satisfied apparently that the motive alleged was not designed to conceal some less pedestrian, more controversially viable activity, and the unexciting truth had been told. A pause in his talk, never an opportunity to be missed, offered a chance, the first one, of congratulating him on the peerage conferred in the most recent Honours List. Sillery yelled with laughter at such felicitations.

'Ain't it absurd?' he shouted. 'As you'll have guessed, my dear Nick, I didn't want the dratted thing at all. Not in the least. But it looked unmannerly to refuse. Doesn't do to look unmannerly. Literal case of *noblesse oblige*. So there it is. A Peer of the Realm. Who'd have prophesied that for crude young Sillers, that happy-go-lucky little fellow, in the days of yore? It certainly gave some people here furiously to think. Ah, the envies and inhumanities of the human heart. You wouldn't believe. I keep on telling the college servants to go easy with all that my-lording. Makes me feel as if I was acting in Shakespeare. They will have it, good chaps that they are. Fact is they seem positively to enjoy addressing their old friend in that majestic way, revel in it even. Strange but true. Genuinely glad to see old Sillers a lord. Ah, when you're my age, dear men, you'll know what an empty thing is worldly success and human ambition—but we mustn't say that to an important person like Leonard, must we, Nick? And of course I don't want to seem ungrateful to the staunch movement that ennobled me, of which I remain the most loyal of supporters. Indeed, we've just been talking of some of Labour's young lions, for Leonard has forgone his former Liberal allegiances in favour of Mr Attlee and his merry men.'

'Of course, as a civil servant, I'm strictly speaking neutral,' said Short primly. 'I was merely talking with Sillers of my present Minister's PPS, who happens to live in the same block of flats as myself—one Kenneth Widmerpool. You may have come across him.'

'I have—and saw he got in at a by-election some months ago.'

'This arose from speaking of Bill Truscott and his troubles,' said Sillery. 'I was telling Leonard how I always marvelled at the quietly dextrous way Mr Widmerpool had poor Bill sacked from Donners-Brebner, just at the moment Bill thought himself set for big things. Between you and me, I would myself have doubted whether Bill offered serious rivalry by that time, but, extinct volcano or not, Widmerpool accepted him as a rival, and got rid of him. It was done in the neatest manner imaginable. That was where the rot set in so far as Bill was concerned. Put him on the downward path. He never recovered his status as a coming man. All this arose because I happened to mention to Leonard that Mr Widmerpool had written to me about joining a society—in fact two societies, one political, one cultural—to cement friendship with the People's Republic where Theodoric's family once held sway.'

'I ran across Widmerpool when I was on loan to the Cabinet Office from my own Ministry,' said Short. 'We first met when I was staying in the country one weekend with a person of some import. I won't mention names, but say no more than that the visit was one of work rather than play. Widmerpool came down on Sunday about an official matter, bringing some highly secret papers with him. We played a game of croquet in the afternoon as a short relaxation. I always remember how Widmerpool kept his briefcase under his arm—he was in uniform, of course—throughout the game. He nearly won it, in spite of that. Our host joked with him about his high regard for security, but Widmerpool would not risk losing his papers, even when he made his stroke.'

Sillery rocked himself backwards and forwards in silent enjoyment.

'A very capable administrator,' said Short. 'Of course one can't foretell what prospects such a man can have on the floor of the House. He may not necessarily be articulate in those very special surroundings. I've heard it suggested Widmerpool is better in committee. His speeches are inclined to alienate sympathy. Nevertheless, I am disposed to predict success.'

Neither of them would listen to assurances that I had known Widmerpool for years, which had indeed no particular relevance to his election to the House of Commons some little time before this. The event had taken place while I was myself still submerged in the country, getting through my army gratuity. At the time, Widmerpool's arrival in Parliament seemed just another of the many odd things taking place roundabout, no concern of mine after reading of it in the paper. Back in London, occupied with sorting out the débris, physical and moral, with which one had to contend, Widmerpool's political fortunes—like his unexpected marriage to Pamela Flitton—had been forgotten in attempts to warm up, as it were, charred fragments left over from the pre-war larder.

'He'd probably have become a brigadier had hostilities continued,' said Short. 'I'm not at all surprised by the course he's taken. At one moment, so he told me, he had ambitions towards a colonial governorship—was interested in those particular problems—but Westminster opens wider fields. The question was getting a seat.'

Sillery dismissed such a doubt as laughable for a man of ability.

'Elderly trade unionists die, or reap the reward of years of toil by elevation to the Upper House—better merited, I add in all humility, than others I could name. The miners can spare a seat from their largesse, those hardy crofters of Scotland show a canny instinct for the right candidate.'

'Between ourselves, I was able to do a little liaison work in the early stages,' said Short. 'That was after return to my old niche. I'd been told there was room for City men who'd be sensibly co-operative, especially if of a Leftward turn to start. Widmerpool's attitude to Cheap Money made him particularly eligible.'

'Cheap Money! Cheap Money!'

The phrase seemed to ravish Sillery by its beauty. He continued to repeat it, like the pirate's parrot screeching 'Pieces of eight', while he clenched his fist in the sign of the old Popular Front.

Then suddenly Sillery's manner changed. He began to rub his hands together, a habit that usually indicated the launching of one of his anti-personnel weapons, some explosive item of information likely to be brought out with damaging effect to whoever had just put forward some given view. Short, still contemplating Widmerpool's chances, showed no awareness that danger threatened.

'I don't think he'll be a back-bencher long,' he said. 'That's my view.'

Sillery released the charge.

'What about his wife?'

After that question Sillery paused in one of his most characteristic attitudes, that of the Chinese executioner who has so expertly severed a human head from the neck that it remains still apparently attached to the victim's shoulders, while the headsman himself flicks an infinitesimal, all but invisible, speck of blood from the razor-sharp blade of his sword. Short coughed. He gave the impression of being surprised by a man of such enlightened intelligence as Sillery asking that.

'His wife, Sillers?'

Short employed a level requisitive tone, suggesting he had indeed some faint notion of what was behind the enquiry, but it was one scarcely worthy of answer. There could be little doubt that, in so treating the matter, Short was playing for time.

'You can't close your ears to gossip in this University, however much you try,' said Sillery. 'It's rampant, I regret to say. Even at High Table in this very college. Besides, it's always wise to know what's being bruited abroad, even if untrue.'

He rubbed his hands over and over again, almost doubling up with laughter.

'I haven't the pleasure of knowing Mrs Widmerpool so well as her husband,' said Short severely. 'We sometimes see each other where we both live, in the hall or in the lift. I understand the Widmerpools are to move from there soon.'

'Comely,' said Sillery. 'That's what I've been told—comely.'

He was more convulsed than ever.

'Certainly, certainly,' allowed Short. 'She is generally agreed to be good looking. I should myself describe her as a little—'

Short's power to define feminine beauty abandoned him at this point. He simply made a gesture with his hand. Unmarried himself, he spoke as if prepared to concede that good looks in a wife, anyway the wife of a public man, might reasonably be regarded as a cause for worry.

'I expect she'll make a good canvasser, an admirable canvasser.'

Sillery rocked.

'Sillers, what are you getting at?'

Short spoke quite irritably. I laughed.

'I see Nick knows what I mean,' said Sillery.

'What does Nick know?'

'I met her during the war, when she was called Pamela Flitton. She was an ATS driver.'

'What's your story, Sillers? I see you must have a story.'

Short spoke in a tone intended to put a stop to frivolous treatment of what had been until then a serious subject, Widmerpool's career. Being in the last resort rather afraid of Sillery, he was clearly not too sure of his ground. No doubt even Short had heard rumours, however muffled, of Pamela's goings-on. Sillery decided to play with him a little longer.

'My information about Mrs Widmerpool brought in a few picturesque details, Leonard. Just a few picturesque details—I say no more than that. I call her young Mrs Widmerpool because I understand she is appreciably junior to her spouse.'

'Yes, she's younger.'

'The name of a certain MP on the Opposition benches has been mentioned as a frequent escort of hers.'

'By whom?'

'I happen to have a friend who knows Mrs W quite well.'

Sillery sniggered. Short pursed his lips.

'A man?'

The question seemed just worth asking.

'No, Nick, not a man. A young lady. You didn't think an old fogey like me knew any young ladies, did you? You were quite wrong. This little friend of mine happens also to be a friend of Mrs Widmerpool—so you see I am in a strong position to hear about her doings.'

Sillery's own sexual tastes had, of course, been endlessly debated by generations of undergraduates and dons. It was generally agreed that their physical expression was never further implemented than by a fair amount of arm-pinching and hair-rumpling of the young men with whom he was brought in contact; not necessarily even the better-looking ones, if others had more substantial assets to offer in the power world. More ardent indiscretions charged against him had either no basis, or were long forgotten in the mists of the past. Certainly he was held never to have taken the smallest physical interest in a woman, although at the same time in no way setting his face against all truck with the opposite sex. Sillery's attitude might in this respect be compared with the late St John Clarke's, both equally appreciative of invitations from ladies of more or less renowned social status and usually mature age; 'hostesses', in short, now an extinct species, though destined to rise again like Venus from a sea of logistic impediment. Accordingly, Sillery was right to suppose his boast would cause surprise. The scandal-mongering female friend would probably turn out to be a young married woman, I thought, the wife of a don. Before Sillery had time further to develop his theme, from which he showed signs of deriving a lot of pleasure in the form of teasing Short, a knock sounded on the door.

'Come in, come in,' cried Sillery indulgently. 'Who is this to be? What a night for visitors. Quite like old times.'

He must have expected another version of Short or myself to enter the room. If so, he made a big mistake. A far more dramatic note was struck; dramatic, that is, for those used to the traditional company to be met in Sillery's rooms, also in the light of his words immediately before. A young woman, decidedly pretty, peeped in. Leaning on the door knob, she smiled apologetically, registering a diffidence not absolutely convincing.

'I'm sorry, Sillers. I see you're engaged. I'll come round in the morning. I'd quite thought you'd be alone.'

This was certainly striking confirmation of Sillery's boast that he had contacts with young women. However, its corroboration in this manner did not seem altogether to please him. For once, a rare thing, he appeared uncertain how best to deal with this visitor: dismiss her, retain her. He grinned, but with a sagging mouth. The intrusion posed a dilemma. Short looked embarrassed too, indeed went quite pink. Then Sillery recovered himself. 'Come in, Ada, come in. You've arrived at just the right moment. We all need the company of youth.'

Irresolution, in any case observable only to those accustomed to the absolute certainty of decision belonging to Sillery's past, had only been momentary. Now he was himself again, establishing by these words that, for all practical purposes, there was no difference between his own age and that of Short and myself, anyway so far as 'Ada' was concerned. He settled down right away to get the last ounce out of this new puppet, if puppet she were. The girl was in her twenties, fair, with a high colour, a shade on the plump side, though only enough to suggest changes in the female figure then pending.

'I didn't want to disturb you, Sillers. I didn't really, but I'm almost sure you gave me the wrong notebook yesterday. There were two years missing at least.'

Her manner, self-possessed, was also forthcoming. She smiled round at all of us, not at all displeased at finding unexpected company in Sillery's rooms. It looked as if some twist of post-war academic administration had committed Sillery to aspects of tutoring that included the women's colleges. In the old days that would have been much against all his known principles, but changed conditions, possibly in the line of post-graduate courses, might have brought about some such revolutionary situation in the University as now constituted.

'Two years missing?' said Sillery. 'That will never do,

Ada, that will never do, but I must introduce you to two old friends of mine. Mr Short, one of our most cultivated and humane of bureaucrats, and Mr Jenkins who is—you just explained to me, Nick, but I can't recall for the minute —no, no, don't tell me, I'll remember in a second—come here to do some research of a very scholarly kind, something he is planning to write—Burton, yes, Burton, melancholy and all that. This is Miss Leintwardine, my—well—my secretary. That's what you are, Ada, ain't you? Sounds rather fast. All sorts of jokes about us, I'm sure. Sit 'ee down, Ada, sit 'ee down. I'll look into your complaints forthwith.'

Miss Leintwardine took a chair. Clearly well used to Sillery's ways and diction, she accepted this presentation of herself as all part of the game. In the role of secretary she was a little more explicable, though why on earth Sillery should require a secretary was by no means apparent. Perhaps a secretary went with being made a peer. Whatever it was, he now retired to a corner of the room, where, lowering himself on to the floor, he squatted on the worn carpet, while he began to rummage about amongst a lot of stuff stored away in the bottom of a cupboard. All the time he kept up a stream of comment.

'What a way to preserve sacred memories. Isn't that just like me? Might be a lot of old boots for all the trouble I've taken. Nineteen-eight . . . nineteen-four . . . here we are, I think, here we are.'

Miss Leintwardine, who had sat down as requested, showed willingness to make herself agreeable by a laudatory reference to a novel I had written before the war. She was about to expand her views on this subject, but, whatever other modifications had taken place in Sillery's approach, tolerance of his guests' books being discussed in front of him was not among them. Sillery's enemies were inclined to imply that aversion to other people writing was the fruit of pure envy, but it was much more probable that talk about 'writing' simply bored him, unless arousing a sense of conflict. He began a loud confused monologue to put a stop to all other conversation, then suddenly found what he sought, closed the cupboard and rose without effort, holding two or three tattered exercise books. He cast these on the table.

'Here they are. I don't know what I can have been thinking about, Ada. Was it the nineteen-twelve volume I gave you? Let me have a look. Ah, no, I think I understand now. This is supplementary. Ada's helping me get my old diaries in order. Not only typing them, but giving me her valuable—I should say invaluable—advice. I'm pleading as a suppliant before the inexorable tribunal of Youth. That's what it comes to. Don't know what I'd do without her. I'd be lost, wouldn't I, Ada?'

'You certainly would, Sillers.'

'Diaries?' said Short. 'I didn't know you kept a diary, Sillers?'

Sillery, laughing heartily, lowered himself again into a vast collapsed armchair in which he lay crouched.

'Nobody did, nobody did. Strict secret. Of course it's possible nothing will appear until old Sillers is dead and gone. That's no reason why the diaries shouldn't be put in proper order. Then perhaps a few selections might be published. Who can tell until Ada has done her work—and who should help make the decision better than Ada?'

'But, Sillers, they'll be absolutely . . .'

Short was again without words. Only an ingrained professional habit of avoiding superlatives, so he implied, prevented him from giving more noisy expression to welcome a Journal kept by Sillery.

'You've met *everybody*, Sillers. They'll be read as the most notable chronicle of our time.'

Sillery made no attempt to deny that judgment. He

screwed up his eyes, laughed a great deal, blew out his moustache. Miss Leintwardine took up the exercise books from the table. She glanced through them with cold professional competence.

'That's better, Sillers. These are the ones. I'd better bear them away with me.'

She rose from the chair, smiling, friendly, about to leave. Sillery held up his right hand, as if to swear a solemn oath.

'Stay, Ada. Stay and talk with us a while. You must meet people younger than myself sometimes, eligible bachelors like Mr Short. By the way, these gentlemen are contemporaries of another friend of ours, Mark Members, whom you talked of when he was up the other day lecturing on whatever it was. He's left the Ministry of Information now.'

'*Kleist, Marx, Sartre, the Existentialist Equilibrium.*'

'Of course,' said Sillery.' One of Vernon Gainsborough's *jeux d'esprit*. I can't remember, Leonard, whether you've met our latest Fellow. He's a German—or rather was—a "good" German, of course, called Werner Guggenbühl, but Gainsborough's better, we all agree. Of patrician background, but turned early to the Left.'

'You're interested in German literature, Miss Leintwardine?' asked Short.

He must have hoped to gloss over Sillery's rather malicious reference to 'eligible bachelors', but notably failed in this attempt to guide conversation into intellectual channels.

'We were talking of old friends like Mark,' said Sillery. 'J. G. Quiggin, Bill Truscott, all names with which you are familiar from my reminiscing, Ada. Conversation led from them to that interesting couple the Widmerpools, about whom you were speaking when we last met. How goes that union? Well, I hope.'

These last sentences put an end to doubt, explaining Sillery's momentary uncertainty at Ada Leintwardine's arrival. He was well satisfied at the surprise she caused, the confirmation by her presence that he numbered 'young ladies' amongst his acquaintance, but at the same time he had been faced with the decision whether or not to reveal her as his source of Widmerpool information. It was in the Sillery tradition to brag of a great spy network, while keeping secret the names of individual agents. At the same time, with an audience like Short and myself, fullest advantage might be derived from Miss Leintwardine by admitting her as fount of that information, now she was on the spot. That at any rate was what happened. Sillery had decided the veil of mystery was not worth sustaining, especially as Miss Leintwardine herself might at any moment give the show away. However, it turned out she was well aware that contacts with the Widmerpool ménage were too profitable to be squandered in casual enquiry. She was giving nothing away that evening. This attitude was probably due also to other matters connected with her relationship with Sillery which only came to light some minutes later.

'They're both all right so far as I know, Sillers.'

'Leonard here lives in the same block of flats.'

'Oh, do you?'

She spoke politely, no more.

'You were saying Mrs W finds the place rather poky,' persisted Sillery.

Miss Leintwardine did not choose to answer that one. Instead, she addressed herself to me.

'I think you know Pam and Kenneth, Mr Jenkins. They spoke of you. Like so many people, Pam's been having rather a painful reaction now the war's over. Tired, I mean, and listless. Always ill. We've been friends since we were in the ATS together.'

'She was a driver in the ATS when I first met her.'

'Then we both went into secret shows, different ones,

and always kept in touch—but for God's sake don't let's talk about the war. Such a boring subject.'

Sillery shouted assent to that, showing distinct signs of displeasure at this interchange. What was the good of presenting Ada Leintwardine as a woman of mystery, if she shared a crowd of acquaintances in common with another guest? Besides, long experience of extracting information out of people must have warned him she was not prepared to furnish anything of great interest that evening, unless matters took an unexpected turn. Grasp of the fact was to Sillery's credit, in some degree justifying the respect paid him in such traffickings by Short and others. He rose once more from his chair, again throwing himself to the floor with surprising suppleness of movement, to scrabble further at the stuff in the cupboard.

'You're sure you've got the right notebooks now, Ada? I'm putting away the ones you brought back, ere worse befall. Don't want to lose them, do we?'

Miss Leintwardine chose this moment of Sillery's comparative detachment on the floor to announce something probably intended to take a less abrupt form. Possibly she had even paid the visit for this purpose, the diaries only an excuse. Since she had not found Sillery alone, she had to take the best opportunity available.

'Talking of J. G. Quiggin, you've heard about this new publishing firm of his?'

She spoke rather self-consciously. Sillery, swivelling round where he squatted orientally on a hole in the carpet, was attentive to this.

'Have you any piquant details, Ada? I should like to know more of JG's publishing venture.'

'I'm rather committed myself. Perhaps you heard that too, Sillers?'

Whatever this meant, clearly Sillery had not heard. He sat up sharply. Miss Leintwardine's manner of asking the question strongly suggested he had been given no opportunity to hear anything of the sort.

'How so, Ada?'

'As it happens, I'm joining the firm myself. I've been reading manuscripts for them since they started. I thought I told you.'

'No, Ada, no. You never told me.'

'I thought I had.'

This showed Sillery in the plainest terms he was not the only one to discharge bombshells. He took it pretty well, though there could be no doubt he was shaken. His eyes showed that.

'Craggs brought in the goodwill of Boggis & Stone, together with such Left-Wing steadies as survive. Of course the new firm won't be nearly so limited as Boggis & Stone. We're hoping to get the young writers. We've signed up X. Trapnel, for example.'

She spoke all this quickly, more than a little embarrassed, even upset, at having to break the news to Sillery. He did not say anything. She continued in the same hurried tone.

'I was wondering whether the possibility wasn't worth exploring for publication of your own Journal, Sillers. You haven't decided on a publisher yet, have you? There's often something to be said for new and enterprising young firms.'

Sillery did not pledge himself on that point.

'Does this mean you're going to live in London, Ada?'

'I suppose so, Sillers. I can't very well commute from here. Of course it won't make any difference to my work for you. I shall always have time for that. I do think it should be an interesting job, don't you?'

Again Sillery made no pronouncement on such expectations. His face provisionally suggested that the future for those entering publishing offices was anything but optimistic. There could be no doubt the whole matter was intensely displeasing to him. His annoyance, together with Miss

Leintwardine's now very definitely troubled manner, confirmed that in a peculiar way they must have been having some sort of flirtation, an hypothesis scarcely to be guessed by even the most seasoned Sillery experts. The girl's nervousness, now confession had been made, well illustrated that odd contradictory feminine lack of assurance so typical of the moment when victory has been won—for there could be little doubt that progression on to the staff of Quiggin & Craggs represented a kind of victory over Sillery on her part, escape from his domination. It looked as if she had half dreaded telling him, half hoped to cause him to suffer. Sillery had been made the object of a little affectionate feminine sadomasochism. That was the grotesque presumption. She jumped up.

'I must go now, Sillers. I've got an awful lot of work waiting at home. I thought I'd just bring those wrong notebooks along as they were worrying me.'

She laughed, almost as though near tears. This time Sillery made no effort to detain her.

'Goodnight, Ada.'

'Goodnight, Mr Short. Goodnight, Mr Jenkins. Goodnight, Sillers.'

However much put out by her unexpected arrival, refusal to discuss the Widmerpools, final news that she was abandoning him, Sillery's usual resilience, his unyielding capacity for making the best of things, was now displayed, though he could not conceal relief at this withdrawal. He grinned at Short and myself after the door closed, shaking his head whimsically to show he still retained a sense of satisfaction in knowing such a wench. Short, on the other hand, was anxious to forget about Miss Leintwardine as soon as possible.

'Tell us something about your diaries, Sillers. I'm more interested than I can say.'

Sillery, anyway at that moment, did not want to talk

about the diaries. Ada Leintwardine was still his chosen theme. If she had displeased him, all the more reason to get full value out of her as an attendant personality of what remained of the Sillery court.

'Local doctor's daughter. Clever girl. Keen on making a career in—what shall we say?—the world of letters. Writing a novel herself. All that sort of thing. Just the person I was looking for. Does the work splendidly. Absolutely reliable. We mustn't have pre-publication leaks, must we? That would never do. I hope she's aware of Howard Craggs's little failings. Just as bad as ever, even at the age he's reached, so I'm told. All sorts of stories. She must know. Everyone knows that.'

His manner of enunciating the remark about pre-publication leaks made one suspect Sillery meant the opposite to what he said. Pre-publication leaks were what he aimed at, Miss Leintwardine the ideal medium for titbits proffered to stimulate interest. The Diary was to be Sillery's last bid for power, imposing his personality on the public, as an alternative to the real thing. However, he had no wish to talk to Short about this. If the Journal was of interest, it was likely Sillery would have published its contents, at least a selection, before now. Even if the interest were moderate, there would be excitement in preparation and advance publicity, whetting the appetite of the public. When, in due course, Short and I left the rooms—Sillery admitted he went to bed now earlier than formerly—it was only after solemn assurances we would call again. Outside, the night was mild for the time of year.

'I'm staying in college,' said Short. 'Sillers is always talking of my becoming an Honorary Fellow, I don't know how serious he is. I'll walk with you as far as the gate. Sillers is wonderful, isn't he? What did you make of that young woman? I didn't much care for her style. Too florid. Still, Sillers must need a secretary if he has all that diary material to weld into order. Rather inconsiderate of her to give up work for him, as she seems to be doing. Interesting your knowing Widmerpool. I wouldn't have thought you'd much in common. I believe myself he's got a future. You must lunch with me one day at the Athenaeum, Nicholas. I'm rather full of work at the moment, but I'll tell my secretary to make a note.'

'Is she as pretty as Miss Leintwardine?'

Short accepted that pleasantry in good part, leaving the question in the air.

'Brightman calls Sillers the last of the Barons. Pity there'll be no heir to that ancient line, he says. Brightman's wit, as Sillers remarked, can be a shade cruel. Nice to have met in these peaceful surroundings again.'

Traversing obscure byways on the way back to my own college, I had to admit the evening had been enjoyable, although there was a kind of relief in escaping from the company of Sillery and Short, into the silent night. One had to concur, too, in judging Sillery 'wonderful'; wonderful anyway in categorical refusal to allow neither age nor anything else to deflect him from the path along which he had chosen to approach life. That was impressive, to be honoured: at least something the world honoured, capacity for sticking to your point, whatever it might be, through thick and thin.

'There have never been any real salons in England,' Moreland once said. 'Everyone here thinks a salon is a place for a free meal. A true salon is conversation—nothing to eat and less to drink.'

Sillery bore out the definition pretty well. The following day I was to knock off Burton, and go back to London. That was a cheering thought. When I reached my own college there was a telegram at the porter's lodge. It was from Isobel. Erridge, her eldest brother, had died suddenly. This was a contingency altogether unexpected, not only dispersing from the mind further speculation about Sillery and his salon, but necessitating reconsideration of all immediate plans.

Erridge, a subject for Burton if ever there was one, had often complained of his health, in this never taken very seriously by the rest of his family. Lately, little or nothing had been heard of him. He lived in complete seclusion. The inter-service organization, a secret one, which had occupied Thrubworth during the earlier years of the war had been later moved, or disbanded, the place remaining requisitioned, but converted into a camp for German prisoners-of-war. Administrative staff and stores occupied most of the rooms, except the small wing at the back of the building that Erridge, on succeeding his father, had adapted for his own use; quarters where his sister Blanche had later joined him to keep house. This suited Blanche well enough, because she preferred a quiet life. She undertook, when feasible, the many local duties unwelcome to Erridge himself whose dedication to working for the public good never mitigated an unwillingness to burden himself with humdrum obligations. This disinclination to play a part in local affairs owed something to his innate uneasiness in dealing with people, together with an aversion from personal argument and opposition, unless such contentiousness was 'on paper'. What Erridge disliked was having to wrangle with a lot of not very well-informed adversaries face to face. In these attitudes poor health may well have played a part, for even unhampered by 'pacifist' convictions, his physical state would never have allowed any very active participation in the war.

However much recognized as, anyway in his own eyes, living in a more or less chronic convalescence, Erridge was certainly not expected to die in his middle-forties. George Tolland, next brother in point of age, was another matter. George, badly wounded in the Middle East, had long been too ill to be brought home. From the first, it seemed unlikely he would survive. Back in England, he made some sort of recovery, then had a relapse, almost predictable from the manner in which Death had already cast an eye on him. The funeral had been only a few months before. George's wife Veronica, pregnant at the time, had not yet given birth. The question of the baby's sex, in the light of inheritance, added another uncertainty to the present situation.

The following morning I set out for London. The train was late. Waiting for it like myself was a man in a blue-grey mackintosh, who strolled rather furtively up and down the platform. His movements suggested hope to avoid recognition, while a not absolutely respectable undertaking was accomplished. At first the drooping moustache disguised him. It was an adjunct not at all characteristic. Then, a minute or two after, the nervous swinging walk gave this figure away. There could be no doubt. It was Books-do-furnish-a-room Bagshaw.

The cognomen dated back to the old Savoy Hill days of the BBC, though we had not known each other in that very remote period. A year or two older than myself, Bagshaw had been an occasional drinking companion of Moreland's. They shared a taste for white port. Possibly Bagshaw had even served a brief stint as music critic. The memory persisted—at our first encounter—of Bagshaw involved in an all but disastrous incident on top of a bus, when we were going home after Moreland had been conducting a performance of *Pelleas and Melisande*. If Bagshaw, at no moment in his past, had ever written music criticism, that must have been the sole form of journalism he had omitted to tackle. We had never seen much of each other, nor met for seven or eight years. Bagshaw's war turned out to have been waged in the Public Relations branch of the RAF. He had grown the moustache in India. Like a lot of acquaintances encountered at this period, his talk had become noticeably more authoritative in tone, product of the war itself and its demands, or just the ponderous onset of middle age. At the same time he had surrendered none of his old wheedling, self-deprecatory manner, which had procured him a wide variety of jobs, extracted him from equally extensive misadventures. He was in the best of spirits.

'The subcontinent has its moments, Nicholas. It was a superlative experience, in spite of the Wingco's foul temper. I had to tell that officer I was not prepared to be the Gunga Din of Royal Air Force Public Relations in India, even at the price of being universally accepted as the better man. There were a lot of rows, but never mind. There was much to amuse too.'

This clearcut vignette of relations with his Wing-Commander defined an important aspect of Bagshaw's character, one of which he was very proud.

'You're a professional rebel, Bagshaw,' some boss-figure had remarked when sacking him.

That was true in a sense, though not in such an entirely simple sense as might be supposed at first sight. All the same, Bagshaw had obtained more than one subsequent job merely on the strength of repeating that estimate of himself. The label gave potential employers an enjoyable sense of risk. Some of them lived to regret their foolhardiness.

'After all, I warned him at the start,' Bagshaw used to say.

The roots of this revolutionary spirit lay a long way back. Did he not boast that on school holidays he had plastered the public lavatories of Cologne with anti-French stickers at the time of the occupation of the Rhineland? There were all sorts of later insurgent activities, 'chalkings', marchings, making policemen's horses shy at May Day celebrations, exertions which led, logically enough, to association with Gypsy Jones. Bagshaw was even reckoned to have been engaged to Gypsy at one time. His own way of life, the fact that she herself was an avowed Party Member, made it likely he too had been 'CP' in his day, possibly up to the Spanish Civil War. At that period Quiggin used to talk a lot about him, and had probably learnt a good deal from him. Then Bagshaw was employed on some sort of eye-witness reporting assignment in Spain. Things went wrong. No one ever knew quite what happened. There had been one of Bagshaw's rows. He came back. Some people said he was lucky to get home. Politically speaking, life were never the same again. Bagshaw had lost his old enthusiasms. Afterwards, when drunk, he would attempt to expound his changed standpoint, never with great clarity, though he would go on by the hour together to friends like Moreland, who detested talking politics.

'There was a chap called Max Stirner ... You've probably none of you ever heard of *Der Einzige und sein Eigentum* ... You know, *The Ego and his Own* ... Well, I don't really know German either, but Stirner believed it would be all right if only we could get away from the tyranny of abstract ideas ... He taught in a girls' school. Probably what gave him the notion. Abstract ideas not a bit of use in a girls' school ...'

Whatever Bagshaw thought about abstract ideas when drunk—he never reached a stage when unable to argue— he was devoted to them when sober. He resembled a man long conversant with racing, familiar with the name of every horse listed in *Ruff's Guide to the Turf*, who has now ceased to lay a bet, even feel the smallest desire to visit a racecourse; yet at the same time never lost his taste for talking about racing. Bagshaw was for ever fascinated by revolutionary techniques, always prepared to explain everybody's standpoint, who was a party-member, fellow-traveller, crypto, trotskyist, anarchist, anarcho-syndicalist, every refinement of marxist theory, every subtle distinction within groups. The ebb and flow of subversive forces wafted

31

the breath of life to him, even if he no longer believed in the beneficial qualities of that tide.

Bagshaw's employment at the BBC lasted only a few years. There were plenty of other professional rebels there, not to mention Party Members, but somehow they were not his sort. All the same, the Corporation left its mark. Even after he found more congenial occupations, he always spoke with a certain nostalgia of his BBC days, never entirely losing touch. After abdicating the air, he plunged into almost every known form of exploiting the printed word, where he always hovered between the sack and a much more promising offer on the horizon. He possessed that opportune facility for turning out several thousand words on any subject whatsoever at the shortest possible notice: politics: sport: books: finance: science: art: fashion—as he himself said, 'War, Famine, Pestilence or Death on a Pale Horse'. All were equal when it came to Bagshaw's typewriter. He would take on anything, and—to be fair—what he produced, even off the cuff, was no worse than what was to be read most of the time. You never wondered how on earth the stuff had ever managed to be printed.

All this suggests Bagshaw had a brilliant journalistic career ahead of him, when, as he described it, he set out 'with the heart of a boy so whole and free'. Somehow it never came off. A long heritage of awkward incidents accounted for much of the furtiveness of Bagshaw's manner. There had been every sort of tribulation. Jobs changed; wives (two at least) came and went; once DT was near at hand; from time to time there were periods 'on the waggon'; all the while legend accumulating round this weaker side, which Bagshaw's nickname celebrated. Its origin was lost in the mists of the past, but the legend emphasized aspects of Bagshaw that could make him a liability.

There were two main elucidations. One asserted that, the worse for drink, trying to abstract a copy of *The Golden*

Treasury from a large glass-fronted bookcase in order to verify a quotation required for a radio programme, Bagshaw overturned on himself this massive piece of furniture. As volume after volume descended on him, it was asserted he made the comment: 'Books do furnish a room.'

Others had a different story. They would have it that Bagshaw, stark naked, had spoken the words conversationally as he approached the sofa on which lay, presumably in the same state, the wife of a well-known dramatic critic (on duty at the theatre that night appraising the First Night of *The Apple Cart*), a clandestine meeting having reached emotional climax in her husband's book-lined study. Bagshaw was alleged to have spoken the words, scarcely more than muttered them—a revolutionary's tribute to bourgeois values—as he rapidly advanced towards his prey: 'Books do furnish a room.'

The lady, it could have been none other, was believed later to have complained to a third party of lack of sensibility on Bagshaw's part in making such an observation at such a juncture. Whichever story were true—probably neither, the second had all the flavour of having been worked over, if not invented, by Moreland—the nickname stuck.

'There'll be a stampede of dons' wives,' said Bagshaw, as we watched the train come in 'Let's be careful. We don't want to be injured for life.'

We found a compartment, crowded enough, but no impediment to Bagshaw's flow of conversation.

'You know, Nicholas, whenever I come away from this place, I'm always rather glad I skipped a novitiate at a university. My university has been life. Many a time I've put that in an article. Tell me, have you read a novel called *Camel Ride to the Tomb*?'

'I thought it good—who is X. Trapnel? Somebody else mentioned him.'

'The best first novel since before the war,' said Bagshaw.

'Not that that's in itself particularly high praise. Trapnel was a clerk in one of our New Delhi outfits—the people who used to hand out those pamphlets about Civics and The Soviet Achievement, all that sort of thing. I was always rapt in admiration at the way the Party arranged to have its propaganda handled at an official level. As a matter of fact Trapnel himself wasn't at all interested in politics, but he was always in trouble with the authorities, and I managed to help him one way and another.'

Although not in the front rank of literary critics—there might have been difficulty in squeezing him into an already overcrowded and grimacing back row—Bagshaw had reason in proclaiming Trapnel's one of the few promising talents thrown up by the war; in contrast with the previous one, followed by no marked luxuriance in the arts.

'Then he got a poisoned foot. Trapnel was a low medical category anyway, that's why he was doing the job at his age. He got shipped back to England. By the end of the war he'd winkled himself into a film unit. He's very keen on films. Wants to get back into them, I believe, writing novels at the same time—but what about your own novels, Nicholas? Have you started up at one again?'

I told him why I was staying at the University, and how work was going to be disrupted during the following week owing to Erridge's funeral. The information about Erridge at once disturbed Bagshaw.

'Lord Warminster is no more?'

'Heard it last night.'

'This is awful.'

'I'd no idea you were a close friend.'

Bagshaw's past activities, especially at the time when he was seeing a good deal of Quiggin, might well have brought him within Erridge's orbit, though I had never connected them in my mind.

'I didn't know Warminster well. Always liked him when we met, and of course sorry to hear the sad news, but why it might be ominous for me was quite apart from personal feelings. The fact was he was putting up the money for a paper I'm supposed to be editing. I was on the point of telling you about it.'

At this period there was constant talk of 'little magazines' coming into being. Professionally speaking, their establishment was of interest as media for placing articles, reviewing books, the various pickings of literary life. Erridge had toyed with some such project for years, although the sort of paper he contemplated was not likely to be of much use to myself. It was no great surprise to hear he had finally decided to back a periodical of some sort. The choice of Bagshaw as editor was an adventurous one, but, if they knew each other already, Bagshaw's recommendation of himself as a 'professional rebel' might well have been sufficient to get a job in Erridge's gift.

'A new publishing firm, Quiggin & Craggs, is going to produce the magazine. Warminster—Erry, as you call him —was friends with both directors. You must know J. G. Quiggin. Doubt if he's ever been CP, but Craggs has been a fellow-traveller for years, and my old friend Gypsy toes the Party line as consistently as anyone could.'

'What's Gypsy got to do with it?'

'As Craggs's wife.'

'Gypsy married to Craggs?'

'Has been for a year or two. Quiggin's an interesting case. He's always had Communist leanings, but afraid to commit himself. JG doesn't like too many risks. He feels he might get into more trouble as a Party Member than outside. He hasn't got Craggs's staying power.'

'But Erry wasn't a Communist at all. In many ways he disapproved, I believe, though he never came out in the open about it.'

35

'No, but he got on all right with JG and Howard Craggs. There was even a suggestion he did more than get on well with Gypsy at one time. He was going to back the publishing firm too, though they are to be run quite separately.'

'What's the magazine to be called?'

'*Fission*. That was thought to strike the right note for the Atomic Age. Something to catch the young writers coming out of the services—Trapnel, for example. That was why I mentioned him. The firm would, of course, be of a somewhat Leftward tendency, given its personnel, but general publishing, not like Boggis & Stone. The magazine was to be Warminster's toy to do more or less what he liked with. I hope his demise is not going to wreck things. It was he who wanted me to edit it. There were one or two others after the job. Gypsy wasn't all that keen for me to get it, in spite of old ties. I know a bit too much.'

Bagshaw's lack of orthodoxy, while at the same time soaked in Left-Wing lore, was something to make immediate appeal to Erridge, once considered. Then another idea occurred to me. It was worth firing a shot at random.

'You've been seeing Miss Ada Leintwardine about all this?'

Bagshaw was not in the least taken aback. He stroked his moustache, an utterly unsuitable appendage to his smooth round somewhat priest-like face, and smiled.

'You know Ada? I thought she was my secret. Where did you run across her?'

He listened to an account of what had taken place in Sillery's rooms; then nodded, as if understanding all.

'Sillery's an interesting case too. I've heard it suggested he's been in the Party himself for years. Myself I think not, though there's no doubt he's given quite a bit of support from time to time in his day. I'd be interested to know where he really stands. So the little witch has ensnared this venerable scholar?'

'She's kept that to herself so far as you were concerned?'

'Absolutely.'

'Is she a Party Member too?'

Bagshaw laughed heartily.

'Ada's ambitions are primarily literary. Within that area she'll take any help she can get, but I doubt if she'd get much from the Party. What did you think of her?'

'All right.'

'She's got a will of her own. Quiggin & Craggs did right to sign her up. JG was much taken.'

'You produced her?'

'We met during the war—all too briefly—but have remained friends. She's to be on the publishing side, not *Fission*. I'd like you to meet Trapnel. I really do think there's promise there. I'll call you up, and we'll have a drink together. I won't be able to arrange anything next week, as I'm getting married on Tuesday—thanks very much, my dear fellow, thanks very much...yes, of course...nice of you to put it that way... I just didn't want to be a bore about a lot of personal matters...'

2

RATHER UNEXPECTEDLY, ERRIDGE WAS FOUND to have paid
quite recent attention to his will. He had replaced George
Tolland (former executor with Frederica) by their youngest,
now only surviving brother, Hugo. Accordingly, by the
time I reached London, Hugo and Frederica had already
gone down to Thrubworth. Accommodation in Erridge's
wing of the house was limited. The rest of the family, as at
George's funeral, had to make up their minds whether to
attend as a day's expedition, or stay at The Tolland Arms,
a hostelry considerably developed from former times, since
the establishment in the neighbourhood of an RAF station.
Norah, Susan and her husband Roddy Cutts, with Isobel
and myself, chose The Tolland Arms. As it happened
Dicky Umfraville had just arrived on leave from Germany,
where he was serving as lieutenant-colonel on the staff of
the Military Government (a job to which he was well
disposed), but he flatly refused to accompany Frederica.

'I never met your brother,' he said. 'Therefore it would
be an impertinence on my part to attend his funeral.
Besides—in more than one respect the converse of another
occasion—there's room at the inn, but none at the stable.
Nobody would mind one of the Thrubworth loose-boxes
less than myself, but we should be separated, my love, so
near and yet so far, something I could not bear. In addition

38

—far more important—I don't like funerals. They remind me of death, a subject I always try to avoid. You will have to represent me, Frederica, angel that you are, and return to London as soon as possible to make my leave a heaven upon earth.'

Veronica, George Tolland's widow, was not present either. She was likely to give birth any day now.

'Pray God it will be a boy,' Hugo said. 'I used to think I'd like to take it all on, but no longer—even though I'd hardly make a scruffier earl than poor old Erry.'

His general demeanour quietened by the war, Hugo's comments tended to become grimmer. He had remained throughout his service bombardier in an Anti-Aircraft battery, not leaving England, but experiencing a reasonably lively time, for example, one night the only man on the gun not knocked out. Now he had returned to selling antiques, a trade at which he became increasingly proficient, recently opening a shop of his own with a former army friend called Sam—he seemed to possess no surname— not a great talker, but good-natured, of powerful physique, and said to be quick off the mark when a good piece came up at auction.

Like Hugo—although naturally in terms of his own very different temperament and approach to life—Roddy Cutts had also quietened. There was sufficient reason for that. The wartime romance at HQ Persia/Iraq Force, with the cipherine he had at one moment planned to marry, had collapsed not long after disclosure of the situation in a letter to his wife. While on leave in Teheran the cipherine had suddenly decided to abscond with a rich Persian, abandoning Roddy to his own resources. Susan, who had behaved impeccably during this unhappy interlude, now took over. When Roddy came back to England for the 1945 election, she worked exceptionally hard. He retained his seat by a few hundred votes. As a consequence, Susan's

39

ascendancy was now complete, Roddy utterly under her control. She made him toil like a slave. That was no doubt right, what he wanted himself. All the same, these factors were calculated to reduce high spirits, even in one so generally appreciative of his own good qualities as Roddy Cutts. His handsome, rather too large features were now marked with signs of stress, everything about him a shade less strident, even the sandy hair. At the same time he retained the forceful manner, half hectoring, half subservient, common to representatives of all political parties, together with the politician's endemic hallmark of getting hold of the wrong end of the stick. He was almost pathetically thankful to be back in the House of Commons.

When George Tolland had been buried a few months before, Erridge had not been present at the funeral. He had, in fact retired to bed with an attack of gastritis—then very prevalent—but from the start this absence had been assumed almost as a matter of course by his sisters. That was not because any of them accepted too seriously Erridge's own complaint about chronic ailments, but on the general principle that for an eldest son, no matter how progressive his views, it was reasonable to avoid a ceremony where a younger brother must inevitably occupy the limelight; in this case additionally so in the eyes of those—however much Erridge himself might deplore such sentiments—who felt an end such as George's traditionally commendable; as Stringham had commented, 'awfully smart to be killed'. This last factor was likely to be emphasized by the religious service, in itself distasteful to Erridge. There was therefore more than one reason to keep him away, as of late years he had become all but incapable of doing anything he disliked. It was agreed that, even without illness, he would never have attended.

'A psychosomatic attack was a foregone conclusion,' said Norah. 'Anyway all parties go better without Erry.'

Nevertheless George's death had undoubtedly agitated his eldest brother. Blanche, in her sad, willing, never wholly comprehending way of describing things, had been insistent about that. At least Blanche always appeared uncomprehending. Possibly she really grasped a great deal more than her own relations supposed. The local doctor, Erridge's sole confidant in the neighbourhood, had not seen him for a month, a most uncharacteristic omission. Blanche repeated Dr Jodrill's words.

'The coronary thrombosis revealed by the post-mortem could owe something to emotional disturbance. I venture to suggest Lord Warminster was greatly unsettled by Colonel Tolland's death.'

Perhaps Jodrill was right. Long submerged sentiments might all at once have taken charge. Even Erridge's indisposition at the time of the funeral could have had something to do with these. Still, it was hard to contradict Norah in thinking Erridge better absent. Several army friends turned up at the church, Tom Goring, always a crony—'Rifleman notwithstanding', as George used to say—who had commanded a brigade in the sector where George was wounded. Ted Jeavons was there too, punctilious observance on the part of an uncle by marriage, whose own health was notoriously poor. For obscure reasons of his own, Jeavons made the journey by a different railway line from the rest of the family, returning the same night. The church had not been full, fog and rationed petrol keeping people away.

At George's funeral, as so often on such occasions, the sharp contrast between life and death was emphasized by one of those incongruous incidents that seem to bear on the character or habits of the deceased. So far from diminishing the nature of the ceremony, their aptness often increases its intensity, by-passing, so to speak, ingenuities of ritual and music, bridging with some peculiar fitness the gulf presented to the imagination by the fact of death. The sensibilities are brought up with a start to accept what has happened by action or scene, outwardly untimed, inwardly apposite.

George's coffin had been committed to the moss-lined earth, the mourners moving away, when a party of German prisoners-of-war from the camp, their guard equipped with a tommy-gun (carried with the greatest nonchalance), straggled across the churchyard on the way back from a local excursion. They seemed quite unaware of what had been taking place a moment before, mingling, as it were, with the mourners, at whom they sheepishly gazed. During the service there had been, in fact, no music, a minimum of anything that could be called ritual. The POWs seemed in a manner to take the place of whatever had been lacking in the way of external effects, forming a rough-and-ready, unknowing guard-of-honour; final reminder of the course of events that had brought George's remains to that quiet place.

The church, at the end of the village, was a few hundred yards from the gates of the park. On the day of Erridge's interment, though the weather was not cold for the time of year, rain was pouring down in steely diagonals across the gravestones. Within the mediaeval building, large for a country church, the temperature was lower than in the open, the interior like a wintry cave. Isobel and Norah sat on either side of me under the portrait medallion, lilac grey marble against an alabaster background, of the so-called 'Chemist-Earl', depicted in bas relief with sidewhiskers and a high collar, the accompanying inscription in gothic lettering. A scientist of some distinction and FRS, he had died unmarried in the eighteen-eighties.

'My favourite forebear,' Hugo said. 'He did important research into marsh gases, and something called alcohol-radicles. As you may imagine, there were a lot of contemporary witticisms about the latter, also jokes within the family about his work on the deodorization of sewage, which was, I believe, outstanding.'

Heraldry had evidently been considered inappropriate for the Chemist-Earl, but two or three escutcheons in the chancel displayed the Tolland gold bezants—'talents', in the punning connotation of the arms—over the similarly canting motto: *Quid oneris in praesentia tollant*. The family's memorials went back no further than the middle of the eighteenth century, when the Hugford heiress (only child of a Lord Mayor) had inhabited Thrubworth; her husband, the Lord Erridge of the period, migrating there from a property further north. On the other side of the aisle, almost level with where we sat, a tomb in white marble, ornate but elegant, was surmounted with sepulchral urns and trophies of arms.

Sacred to the Memory of
Henry Lucius 1st Earl of Warminster,
Viscount Erridge, Baron Erridge of Mirkbooths,
G.C.B., Lieutenant-General in the Army, etc.

'Be of good courage and let us behave ourselves valiantly
for our people, and for the cities of our God:
and let the Lord do that which is good in his sight.'
I. Chronicles. xix. 13.

Even if Wellington were truly reported in expressing reservations about his abilities as a commander, Henry Lucius had left some sort of a legend behind him. An astute politician, he had voted at the right moment for Reform. 'Lord Erridge made a capital speech,' wrote Creevey, 'causing the damn'dest surprise to the Tory waverers, and as I have heard he is soon to retire with an earldom, he must have decided to present his valedictions with a flourish before devoting the remaining years of his life to his *hobbies*.' Gronow's Memoirs throw light on this

43

last comment, endorsing the caution displayed by the commemorative text in fields other than military. After noting that Brummell paid Henry Lucius the compliment of asking who made his driving-coat, Captain Gronow adds: 'His Lordship was not indifferent to the charms of the fair sex, but the exquisitely beautiful Creole of sixteen, who was under his immediate protection when he breathed his last in lodgings at Brighton, was believed by many people in society to be his daughter.'

It looked as if Erridge, long shut away from everyday life, would bring together an even smaller gathering of mourners than his brother George. Two or three elderly neighbours were there as a matter of form, a couple of Alfords from his mother's side of the family, a few tenants and people from the village. Most of this congregation stole in almost guiltily, as if—like Bagshaw—they hoped to draw the least possible attention to themselves, choosing pews at the back of the church in which they sat hunched and shivering. There was a longish, rather nerve-racking wait, emphasized by much coughing and clearing of throats. Then came manifestations from the porch. At last something was happening. There was a noise, quite a commotion. It sounded as if the coffin-bearers—just enough men of required physique had been found available on the estate for that duty—were encountering difficulties. The voices outside were raised in apparent argument, if not altercation. From among these tones of dissension a female note was perceptible; perhaps the protests of more than one woman. A pause of several minutes followed before whoever was arguing in the porch entered the church. Then the steps of several persons sounded on the uncarpeted flagstones. A general turning of heads took place to ascertain whether the moment had come to stand up.

A party of six persons, four men and two women, were advancing up the aisle in diamond formation. Widmerpool was at the head. Carrying a soft black hat between his hands and in front of his chest, he was peering over it as he proceeded slowly, reverently, rather suspiciously, up the unlighted interior of the church. His appearance at this moment was wholly unexpected. George, in his City days, had done business with Donners-Brebner when Widmerpool worked there, but, so far as I knew, Widmerpool had no contacts with Erridge. There had been no sign of Widmerpool at George's funeral. At first sight, the rest of the group seemed equally unlooked for, even figments of a dream, as faces became recognizable in the gloom. A moment's thought revealed their presence as explicable enough, even if singular in present unison. To limit examination of this cluster of figures to a mere glance over the shoulder was asking too much, even to pretend any longer that the glance was only a requisite precaution for keeping abreast of the progress of the service. In fact most of the congregation settled down to a good stare.

A man in his sixties, tall, haggard, bent, bald, walked behind Widmerpool, his untidy self-satisfied air for some reason suggesting literary or journalistic affiliations. Beside him was a woman about twenty years younger, short, wiry, her head tied up in a red handkerchief, somehow calling to mind old-fashioned Soviet posters celebrating the Five Year Plan. Too stocky and irritable in appearance, in fact, to figure in pictorial propaganda, she had the right sort of aggressiveness. This was Gypsy Jones. Oddly enough, the look of King Lear on the heath attached to Mr Deacon, when, years before, I had seen him selling *War Never Pays!* with Gypsy at Hyde Park Corner, was suddenly recalled. However different his sexual tastes, Howard Craggs had developed much of the same wandering demented appearance. It was almost as if association with Gypsy—they had lived together years before the marriage reported by Bagshaw—brought about this mien.

Behind these two walked another couple unforeseen as proceeding side by side up the aisle of a church One of these was J. G. Quiggin, certainly an old friend of Erridge's, in spite of many ups and downs. It was also natural enough that he should have travelled here with Craggs, co-director of the new publishing firm. Sillery's description of Quiggin's current Partisan-style dress was borne out by the para-military overtones of khaki shirt, laced ankle boots, belted black leather overcoat. To be fair, the last dated back at least to the days when Quiggin was St John Clarke's secretary. Beside Quiggin, contrasted in a totally achieved funereal correctness, smoothing his grey moustache in unmistakable agonies of embarrassment—either at arriving at the church so late, or presenting himself on such an occasion in the company of mourners so unconformist in dress—walked the Tollands' Uncle Alfred.

However, the last figure in the cortège made the rest seem humdrum enough. At the rear of this wedge-shaped phalanx, a long way behind the others, moving at a stroll that suggested she was out by herself on a long lonely country walk, her thoughts far away in her own melancholy daydreams, walked, almost glided, Widmerpool's wife. Her eyes were fixed on the ground as she advanced slowly, with extraordinary grace, up the aisle. As centre of attention she put the rest of the procession utterly in the shade. That was not entirely due to her slim figure and pent-up sullen beauty. Another beautiful girl could have created no more than the impression that she was a beautiful girl. It was not easy to say what marked out Pamela Widmerpool as something more than that. Perhaps her absolute self-confidence, her manner of expressing without words that to be present at all was a condescension; to have allowed herself to be one of that particular party, an accepted abasement of the most degrading sort. Above all, she seemed an appropriate attendant on Death. This was not an account of her clothes. They were far from sombre. They looked—so Isobel remarked afterwards—as if bought for a cold day's racing. This closeness to Death was carried within herself. Even in his chastened state, Roddy Cutts could not withhold an audible drawing in of breath.

When they were halfway up the aisle, level with a fairly wide area of unoccupied seats, Widmerpool turned sharply, grinding his heel on the stone in a drill-like motion, a man intentionally emphasizing status as military veteran. His back to the altar, he barred the way, almost as if about to stage an anti-liturgical, even anti-clerical demonstration. However, instead of creating any such untoward disturbance, he shot out the hand of a policeman directing traffic, to indicate where each was to sit of the group apparently under his command.

This authority was by no means unquestioned. Discussion immediately arose among the others, no doubt similar in bearing to whatever disagreements had taken place in the porch. Jeavons, from where he was sitting up at the front of the church, beckoned vehemently to Alfred Tolland in an effort to show where a place could be found among the family. The two of them knew each other not only as relations, but also as fellow air-raid wardens, duties during the course of which an inarticulate friendship may have been obscurely cemented. However, Alfred Tolland was at that moment too dazed by the journey, or oppressed by other circumstances in which he found himself, to be capable of reaching a goal so far afield. He stood there patiently awaiting Widmerpool's instructions, scarcely noticing Jeavons's arms swinging up and down at semaphore angles.

These directions of Widmerpool's had not yet been fully implemented, when Pamela, pushing past the others, precipitately entered the pew her husband was allotting to Alfred Tolland. She placed herself at the far end, under the

47

marble fascicles of standards, lances and sabres that encrusted the Henry Lucius tomb. Whether or not this seating arrangement accorded with Widmerpool's intention could only be guessed; probably not, from the expression his face at once assumed. Nevertheless, now it had happened, he curtly directed Alfred Tolland to follow, without attempting to reclassify this order of precedence. There was a moment of gesturing between them, Alfred Tolland putting forward some contrary suggestion—he may just have grasped the meaning of Jeavons's signals—so that very briefly it looked as if a wrestling match were about to take place in the aisle. Then Widmerpool shoved Alfred Tolland almost bodily into the pew, where, leaving a wide gap between himself and Pamela, Tolland immediately knelt, burying his face in his hands like a man in agonies of remorse. At Widmerpool's orders, Quiggin went in next; Craggs and Gypsy into the pew behind. They were followed by Widmerpool himself.

The last time I had seen Pamela in church had been at Stringham's wedding, child bridesmaid of six or seven, an occasion when, abandoning responsibilities in holding up the bride's train, she had walked away composedly, later, so it was alleged, causing herself to be lifted in order to be sick into the font. 'That little girl's a fiend,' someone had remarked afterwards at the reception. Now she sat, so to speak, between Henry Lucius and his descendant Alfred Tolland. Would Henry Lucius, 'not indifferent to the charms of the fair sex', rise from the dead? She had closed her eyes, either in prayer, or to express the low temperature of the nave, but did not kneel. Neither did Quiggin, Craggs or Gypsy kneel, but Widmerpool leant forward for a few seconds in a noncommittally devotional attitude that did not entirely abandon a sitting posture, and might have been attributable merely to some interior discomfort.

The dead silence that had momentarily fallen was

broken by Widmerpool levering himself back on the seat. He removed his spectacles and began to wipe them. He was rather thinner, or civilian clothes gave less impression of bulk than the 'utility' uniform that enclosed him when last seen. The House of Commons had already left its indefinable, irresoluble mark. His thick features, the rotundities of his body, always amenable to caricature, now seemed more than ever simplified in outline, positively demanding treatment in political cartoon. The notion that a few months at Westminster had brought this about was far fetched. Alteration, if alteration there were, was more likely to be accountable to marriage.

Craggs too shared some of this air of a figure from newspaper caricature, a touch of the Mad Hatter mingling with that of King Lear. His shabbiness, almost griminess, was certainly designed to convey to the world that he was a person of sufficient importance to rise above bourgeois convention, whatever its form. Smiling to himself, snuffling, fidgeting, he gazed round the church in a manner to register melodramatic wonder that such places could still exist, even for the purpose that had brought him there. Such views were certainly held by Gypsy too—who had refused to attend her old friend Mr Deacon's funeral on strictly anti-religious grounds—but unmitigated anger now appeared to prevent her from knowing, or caring, where she found herself. Quiggin looked as if his mind were occupied with business problems. On the other hand, he might have been thinking of the time when Erridge had taken Mona, Quiggin's girl, to the Far East. That difference had been long made up, but circumstances could have recalled it, giving Quiggin a strained uneasy expression.

One of the least resolvable problems posed by Widmerpool's presence was his toleration of Gypsy as member of the party. Once—haunted by that dire incident in the past when he had paid for her 'operation'—he would have

49

gone to any lengths to avoid even meeting her. If, as Craggs's wife, she had to come, that would have been sufficient to keep Widmerpool away. Some overriding political consideration must explain this, such as the idea of attaching himself to a kind of unofficial deputation paying last respects to a 'Man of the Left'. In Widmerpool's case that would be a way of establishing publicly his own *bona fides*, sentiments not sufficiently recognized in himself. Acceptance of Gypsy could be regarded as a gesture of friendship to the extremities of Left-Wing thought, an olive branch appropriate (or not) to Erridge's memory.

The more one thought about it, the more relevant—to employ one of their own favourite terms—were Quiggin and Craggs, in fact the whole group, to consign Erridge to the tomb; in certain respects more so than his own relations. It was true that Erridge's abnegation of the family as a social unit was capable of exaggeration, by no means so total as he himself liked to pretend, or his cronies, many of those unsympathetic to him too, prepared to accept. The fact remained that it was with Quiggin and Craggs he had lived his life, insomuch as he had lived it with other people at all, sitting on committees, signing manifestoes, collaborating in pamphlets. (Burton—who provided instances for all occasions, it was hard not to become obsessed with him —spoke of those who 'pound out pamphlets on leaves of which a poverty-stricken monkey would not wipe'.) In fact, pondering on these latest arrivals, they might be compared with the squad of German POWs straying across the face of George Tolland's obsequies, each group a visual reminder of seamy realities—as opposed to idealistic aspirations—the former of war, the latter, politics.

The train of thought invited comparison between the two brothers, their characters and fates. Erridge, high-minded, willing to endure discomfort, ridicule, solitude, in a fervent anxiety to set the world right, had at the same time, as a comfortably situated eldest son, a taste for holding on to his money, except for intermittent doles—no doubt generous ones—to Quiggin and others who represented in his own eyes what Sillery liked to call The Good Life. Erridge was wholly uninterested in individuals; his absorption only in 'causes'.

George, on the other hand, had never shown much concern with righting the world, except that in a sense his death might be regarded as stemming from an effort at least to prevent the place from becoming worse. He had not been at all adept at making money, but never, so to speak, set the glass of port he liked after lunch—if there were any excuse—before, say, educating his step-children in a generous manner. A competent officer (Tom Goring had praised him in that sphere), his target was always the regular soldier's (one thought of Vigny) to do his duty to the fullest extent, without, at the same time seeking supererogatory burdens or looking out for trouble.

With newsprint still in short supply, Erridge's obituaries were briefer than might have been the case in normal times, but he received some little notice: polite reference to life-long Left-Wing convictions, political reorientations in that field, final pacifism; the last contrasted with having 'fought' (the months in Spain having by now taken mythical shape) in the Spanish Civil War. George was, of course, mentioned only in the ordinary death announcements inserted by the family. Musing on the brothers, it looked a bit as if, in an oblique manner, Erridge, at least by implication, had been given the credit for paying the debt that had in fact been irrefutably settled by George. The same was true, if it came to that, of Stringham, Templer, Barnby—to name a few casualties known personally to one—all equally indifferent to putting right the world.

The sound came now, unmistakable, of the opening Sentences of the burial service. Everyone rose. Coughing briefly ceased. The parson, a very old man presented to the living by Erridge's grandfather, moved slowly, rather painfully forward, intoning the words in a high quavering chant. The heavy boots of the coffin-bearers shuffled over the stones. The faces of the bearers were set, almost agonizingly concentrated, on what they were doing, that of Skerrett, the old gamekeeper, of gnarled ivory, like a skull. He was not much younger than the parson. A boy of sixteen supporting one of the back corners of the coffin was probably his grandson. The trembling prayers raised a faint echo throughout the dank air of the church, on which the congregation's breath floated out like steam. Such moments never lose their intensity. A cross-reference had uncovered Herbert's lines a few days before.

> The brags of life are but a nine-days wonder:
>   And after death the fumes that spring
> From private bodies, make as big a thunder
>   As those which rise from a huge king.

One thought of Father Zossima in *The Brothers Karamazov*. Reference to bodily corruption was a natural reaction from 'Whom none should advise, thou hast persuaded'. Ralegh might be grandiloquent, he was also authoritative, even hypnotic, no less resigned than Herbert, as well. I thought about death. It seemed most unlikely Burton had really hanged himself, as rumoured, to corroborate the accuracy of the final hour he had drawn in his own horoscope. The fact was he was only mildly interested in astrology.

By this time the bearers were showing decided strain from the weight of the coffin. They had reached a stage about halfway up the aisle, and were going fairly slowly. Suddenly a commotion began to take place in one of the pews opposite this point. Pamela was attempting to make her way out. Her naturally pale face was the colour of

chalk. She had already thrust past Alfred Tolland and
Quiggin, but Widmerpool, an absolutely outraged expression on his face, stepped quickly from the pew behind to
delay her.

'I'm feeling faint, you fool. I've got to get out of here.'

She spoke in quite a loud voice. Widmerpool seemed to
make a momentary inner effort to decide for himself the
degree of his wife's indisposition, whether she were to be
humoured or not, but she pushed him aside so violently that
he nearly fell. As she hurried into the aisle he recovered
himself, for a second made as if to follow her, then decided
against any such action. Had he seriously contemplated
pursuit, there had been in any case too great delay. Although Pamela herself managed to skirt the procession
advancing with the coffin, it was doubtful whether anyone of more considerable bulk could have freely negotiated
the available space in the same manner, especially after
the disruption caused. She had brushed past the vicar so
abruptly that he gasped and lost the thread of his words.
A second later the bearers, recovering themselves, were
level with Widmerpool, blocking his own egress from the
pew. Pamela's heels clattered away down the flags. When
she reached the door, there was difficulty in managing the
latch. It gave out discordant rattles; then a creak and loud
slam.

'My God,' said Norah.

She spoke the words softly. They recalled her own
troubles with Pamela. The service continued. I tried to
recompose the mind by returning to Ralegh and Herbert.
'Whom none should advise, thou hast persuaded.' Was
that true of everyone who died? Of Erridge, eminently
true: true too, in its way, of Stringham and Templer: to
some extent of Barnby: not at all true of George Tolland:
yet, after all, was it true of him too? I thought of the
portraits of Ralegh, stylized in ruff, short cloak, pointed

beard, fierce look. 'All the pride, cruelty and ambition of men.' Ralegh knew the form. Still, Herbert was good too. I wondered what Herbert had looked like. In the end one got back to Burton's 'vile rock of melancholy, a disease so frequent, as few there are that feel not the smart of it'. Melancholy was so often the explanation, anyway melancholy in Burton's terms. The bearers took up the coffin once more. The recession was slow, though this time uninterrupted.

'I hope old Skerrett will be all right,' whispered Isobel. 'He looked white as a sheet when he passed.'

'Whiter than Mrs Widmerpool?'

'Much whiter.'

Outside, the haze had thickened. The air struck almost warm after the church. Rain still fell in small penetrating drops. The far corner of the churchyard was occupied with an area of Tolland graves: simple headstones: solid oblong blocks of stone with iron railings: crosses, two unaccountably Celtic in design: one obelisk. Norah, who had never got on at all well with her eldest brother, was in convulsions of tears, the other sisters dabbing with their handkerchiefs. There was no sign of Pamela in the porch. The mourners processed to the newly dug grave. The old parson, his damp surplice clinging like a shroud, refused to be hurried by the elements. He took what he was doing at a thoroughly leisurely pace. There seemed no reason why the funeral should ever end. Then, all at once, everything was over. The mourners began to move slowly, rather uncomfortably away.

'I'll just have a word with Skerrett,' said Isobel. 'He's looking better now. Meet you at the gate.'

Before I reached the lychgate, a tall, rather distinguished-looking woman separated herself from other shapes lurking among the tombstones, and came towards me. She must have sat at the back of the church, because I had not seen

her until that moment. She was fortyish, a formal maga-
zine-cover prettiness organized to make her seem not only
younger than that, but at the same time a girl not exactly
of the present, rather of some years back. Her voice too
struck a note at that moment equally out of fashion.

'I thought I *must* say hullo, Nick, though it's *years* since
we met—you remember me, Mona, I used to be married to
Peter Templer—what ages. Yes, poor Peter, wasn't it sad?
So brave of him at his age too. Jeff says you're *never* the
same in war after you're thirty. We're weaving about fairly
close here, and I've got to *scamper* home this minute, because Jeff's quite *insane* about punctuality. We're living in
a *horrible* house over by Gibbet Down, so I thought I
ought to make a pilgrimage for Alf. It's poor Alf now too,
as well as poor Peter, isn't it? Alf didn't have much of a
time, did he, though he *was* kindhearted in his way,
even if he *abominated* spending a farthing on drink—one's
throat got absolutely *arid* travelling with him. I shall
never forget Hong Kong. JG used to get so *angry* in the
old days if I complained about the *drought* when we
dined at Thrubworth with Alf, which wasn't all that
often. Lack of drink was even worse when I was alone
with him, I can assure you. Fancy JG turning up today too.
So unexpected when he does the right thing for once. I
hear he lived for a time with someone called *Lady Anne
Stepney*, and then she went off with one of the Free
French. That did make me laugh—and Gypsy here too.
Do you think she *did* have a walk out with Alf? He
used to talk about seeing her at those *awful* political con-
ferences he loved going to. I sometimes wondered. Well,
we'll never know now. I just *waved* to JG and Gypsy. I
thought that would be *quite enough*.'

Isobel reappeared.

'Your *wife*? How sad it must be to lose a brother, I
never had one, but I'm sure it is. And not at all old either,

55

except we're all *centuries* old now, I feel a *million*, but, of course—well, I don't know—anyway, I just thought it was my *duty* to come, even in *daunting* weather. I'll have to proceed back now with all possible speed, or Jeff will be having *kittens*. Jeff's an Air Vice-Marshal now. Isn't that grand? *Burdened* with gongs. He was rather worried about my using the car for a funeral, but I said I was going to a POW camp, and if an Air Vice-Marshal's lady can't inspect a POW camp, what in hell can she do? Well, it's been nice seeing you, Nick, *and* your wife, not to mention having a word about those poor dears who are no more. That erk will have to drive like *stink* if I'm not to be late. We've got some personnel coming to *tea* of all things—drink quite impossible to get for love or money these days, anyway to dish out to all and sundry, as well you must know, so I'll just say bye-bye for now . . .'

While talking, she had fallen more than once into what Mr Deacon used to call a 'vigorous pose'. Now, as she walked away, the controlled movement of her long swift strides recalled the artists' model she once had been. In the road stood a large car, a uniformed aircraftman at the wheel. She turned and waved, then disappeared within.

'Who on earth?'

'That's Mona.'

'Not the girl Erry took to China?'

'Of course.'

'Why didn't you indicate that? I could have had a closer look. What a pity the poor old boy didn't hang on. She might have kept him going.'

As the RAF car drove away, the outlines of Alfred Tolland, picking his way between the graves, came into view. He had been waiting for Mona to move on before he approached. It now struck me that he must have met Widmerpool at the Old Boy dinners of Le Bas's house, because Alfred Tolland retained sentiments about his schooldays that age had in no way diminished. Except for Le Bas himself, he had always—in the days long past when I myself attended them—been the eldest present by at least twenty years.

'Uncle Alfred's a sad case in that respect,' Hugo had remarked. 'Personally I applaud that great enemy of the Old School Tie, the Emperor Septimius Severus, who had a man scourged merely for drawing attention to the fact that they had been at school together.'

However, Le Bas dinners could explain why Widmerpool and Alfred Tolland had travelled down together after seeing each other at the station. Widmerpool was, in fact, now revealed as standing close behind, as if he expected Alfred Tolland to make some statement that concerned himself or his party, the rest of whom were no longer to be seen. They could be concealed by mist, or have left in a body after the committal. To make sure his own presence as a mourner was not overlooked by Erridge's family would be characteristic of Widmerpool, even though the reason for his attendance remained at present unproclaimed. He was looking even more worried than in the church. If he had merely desired to register attendance and go away, he would certainly have pushed in front of Alfred Tolland, whose hesitant, deferential comportment always caused delays, particularly at a time like this. Neat, sad, geared perfectly in outward appearance to the sombre nature of the occasion, Tolland stood, head slightly bent, gazing at the damp grass beneath his feet. He had once admitted to having travelled as far as Singapore. One wondered how he had ever managed to get there and back again. Unlikely he had taken with him a girl like Mona, though one could never tell. Barnby always used to insist it was misplaced to speak categorically about other people's sexual experiences, whoever they were.

'Uncle Alfred?'

'My dear Isobel, this is very . . .'

He was all but incapable of finishing a sentence, a form of diffidence implying unworthiness to force a personal opinion on others. Even when Alfred Tolland spoke his own views, they were hedged round with every sort of qualification. Erridge's passing, the company in which he found himself on the way down, stirred within him concepts far too unmanageable to be accommodated in a single phrase. Isobel helped him out.

'A very sad occasion, Uncle Alfred. Poor Erry. It was so unexpected.'

'Yes—quite unexpected. These things are unexpected sometimes. Absolutely unexpected, in fact. Of course Erridge always did . . .'

What did Erridge always do? The question was capable of many answers. The wrong thing? Know he was a sick man? Fear the winter? Hope the end would be sudden? Want Alfred Tolland to reveal some special secret after his own demise? Perhaps just 'do the unexpected'. On the whole that termination was the most probable. Alfred Tolland, this time unassisted by Isobel, may have feared that any too direct statement about what Erridge 'did' might sound callous, if spoken straight out. Instead of completing, he altogether abandoned the comment, this time bringing out in its entirety another concept, quite different in range.

'I'm feeling rather ashamed.'

'Ashamed, Uncle Alfred?'

'Never got down here for George's . . . In bed, as a matter of fact.'

'Nothing bad, I hope, Uncle Alfred.'

'Had a bit of—chest. Felt ashamed, all the same. Not absolutely right now, but can get about. Can't be helped. Didn't want to stay away when it came to the head of the family.'

He spoke as if he would have risen from the dead to

reach the funeral of the head of the family. Perhaps he had. The idea was not to be too lightly dismissed. There was something not wholly of this world about him. Time, for example, seemed to mean nothing. One hoped he would come soon to the point of what he had to say. Although the worst of the rain had stopped, a pervasive damp struck up from the ground and into the bones. Obviously something was on his mind. In the background Widmerpool shifted about, stamping his feet and kicking them together.

'We'll give you a lift back to the house, Uncle Alfred, if you want one. That's if any of the cars will start. Some of them are rather ancient. It may be rather a squeeze.'

'Quite forgot, quite forgot . . . These good people I travelled down with . . . shared a taxi from the station . . . Mr—met him at those dinners Nicholas and I . . . and his wife . . . very good looking . . . another couple too, Sir Somebody and Lady Something . . . also another old friend of Erridge's . . . nice people . . . something they wanted to ask . . .'

Alfred Tolland turned towards Widmerpool, in search of help, to give words to a matter not at all easy to summarize in a few broken phrases. At least he himself found that hard, which was usual enough, even if the situation were not as ticklish as this one appeared. Widmerpool, not happy himself, was prepared at the same time to accept his cue. He began to speak in his least aggressive manner.

'Two things, Nicholas—though I don't expect you're really the person to ask, sure as I am, as an old friend, you'll be prepared to act for us as—well, as what?—intermediary, shall we say? You know already, I think, the other members of the party I came down with. J. G. Quiggin, of course—must know him as a literary bloke like yourself—and as for Sir Howard and Lady Craggs, of course you remember them.'

One had to admit that 'Sir Howard and Lady Craggs'

conjured up a rather different picture from Mr Deacon's birthday party, Gypsy lolling on Craggs's knee, struggling to divert a too exploratory hand back to a wide area of pink thigh. If it came to that, one had one's own reminiscences of Lady Craggs in an easy-going mood.

'We all wanted, of course, to pay last respects to your late brother-in-law, Lord Warminster—much to my regret I never managed to meet him—but there was also something else. This seemed a golden opportunity to have a preliminary word, if possible, with the appropriate member, or members, of the family, now collected together, as to the best means of approaching certain matters arisen in consequence of Lord Warminster's death.'

Widmerpool paused. He was relieved to have made a start on whatever he wanted to say, for clearly this was by no means the end.

'The late Lord Warminster left certain instructions in connexion with the publishing house Sir Howard Craggs —well, we can talk about all that later. As I say, this seemed a good moment to have a tentative word with the— in short with the executors, as I understand, Mr Hugo Tolland and Lady Frederica Umfraville.'

Whatever complications now threatened were beyond conjecture. Within the family it had been generally agreed that for Erridge to leave the world without arranging some testing problem to be settled by his heirs and successors, was altogether unthinkable. The form such a problem, or problems, might take was naturally not to be anticipated. That Widmerpool should be involved in any such matters was unlooked for. His relief at having made the statement about Erridge's dispositions, whatever they were, turned out to be due to anxiety to proceed to a far more troublesome enquiry from his own point of view.

'Another matter, Nicholas. My wife—you know her, of course, I'd forgotten—Pamela, as I say, was overcome with faintness during the service. In fact had to leave the church. I hope no one noticed. She did so as quietly as possible. These attacks come on her at times. Largely nerves, in my opinion. It was arranged between us she should await me in the porch. She no doubt found the stone seat there too cold in her distressed state. I thought she might have taken refuge in our taxi, but the driver said, on the contrary, he saw her walking up the drive in the direction of the house.'

Widmerpool stopped speaking. His efforts to present in terms satisfactory to himself two quite separate problems, so that they merged into coherent shape, seemed to have broken down. The first question was what Craggs and Quiggin wanted from the executors, no doubt something to do with the matters of which Bagshaw had spoken; the second, which Widmerpool, judging by past experience, regarded as more important, the disappearance of his wife.

Frederica and Blanche, saying goodbye to the Alford relations to whom they had been talking, came over to have a word with their uncle. Alfred Tolland, still considerably discomposed by all that was happening round him, managed to effect a mumbled introduction of Widmerpool, who seized his opportunity, settling on Frederica. He began at once to put forward the advantages of having a preliminary talk, 'quite informal', about straightening out Erridge's affairs. Frederica had hardly time to agree this would be a good idea, before he returned to the question of Pamela, certainly worrying him a lot. Frederica, a very competent person when it came to making arrangements, took these problems in her stride. Like Erridge, she was not greatly interested in individuals as such, so that Widmerpool's desire to talk business, coupled with anxiety about his wife, were elements to be accepted at their face value. Neither aroused Frederica's curiosity.

'Where are these friends of yours now, Mr Widmerpool?'

'In the church porch. They wanted to get out of the rain. They're waiting—in fact waiting for me to obtain your permission, Lady Frederica, to come up to the house as I suggest. I really think the house is probably where my wife is too.'

This then was the crux of the matter. They all wanted to come up to the house. While that was arranged, Widmerpool had judged it best to confine them to the porch. Possibly there had been signs of mutiny. Judged as a group, they must have been just what Frederica would expect as representative friends of her brother, even though she could not guess, had no wish to examine, subtleties of their party's composition. In her eyes Widmerpool's conventional clothes, authoritative manner, made him a natural enough delegate of an otherwise fairly unpresentable cluster of Erridge hangers-on, a perfectly acceptable representative. Frederica and Erridge had been next to each other in age. Although living their lives in such different spheres, they were by no means without mutual understanding. The whim to leave complicated instructions after death was one with which Frederica could sympathize. Sorting out her brother's benefactions gratified her taste for tidying up.

An uncertain quantity was whether or not she remembered anything of Widmerpool's wife. There could be little doubt that at one time or another Dicky Umfraville had made some reference to Pamela's gladiatorial sex life during the war. It would have been very unlike him to have let that pass without comment. On the other hand, Frederica not only disapproved of such goings-on, she took little or no interest in them, was capable of shutting her eyes to misbehaviour altogether. Unaccompanied by Umfraville, whose banter kept her always on guard against being ragged about what Molly Jeavons used to call her own 'correctness', Frederica, on such an exceptional family occasion, may have reverted to type; closing her eyes by an act of will to the fact, even if she knew that, for example, her sister Norah had been one of Pamela's victims. In short, for one reason or another, she did not in the least at that moment concern herself with the identity of Widmerpool's wife. While she was talking to him, Blanche and Isobel made arrangements about getting old Skerrett home. Alfred Tolland drew me aside.

'Thought it would be all right—best—not to wear a silk hat. See you haven't either, nor the rest of the men. Quite right. Not in keeping with the way we live nowadays. What Erridge would have preferred too, I expect. I always like to do that. Behave as—well—the deceased would have done himself. Doubt if Erridge owned a silk hat latterly. Anthony Eden hats they call this sort I'm wearing now, don't quite know why. Mustn't lose count of time and miss my train, because when I get back I've got to . . .'

Again one wondered what on earth he had 'got to' do when he returned to London. It was not the season for reunion dinners. Molly Jeavons no longer alive, he could not drop in there to be teased about family matters. To picture him at any other sort of engagement than these was difficult. It was doubtful whether amicable relations with Jeavons included visits to the house now Molly was gone. One returned to the earlier surmise that he had risen from the dead, had to report back to another graveyard by a stated time.

'I haven't seen Frederica's husband.'

He spoke tentatively, like many of his own age-group, prepared always for the worst when it came to news about the marriages of the next generation.

'Dicky couldn't come. He's with the Control Commission.'

There seemed no point in emphasizing Umfraville's flat refusal to turn up. The fact of his absence seemed to bring relief to Alfred Tolland.

63

'Remember I once told you Umfraville was my fag at school? Not a word of truth in it. My fag was an older man. Not older than Umfraville is now, of course, he was younger than me, and naturally still is, if he's alive, but older than Frederica's husband would have been at that age. Made a mistake. Found there were two Umfravilles. Been on my conscience ever since telling you that. Hope it never got passed on. Didn't want to meet him, and seem to be claiming acquaintance . . .'

'Probably a relation. It's an uncommon name.'

'Never safe to assume people are relations. That's what I've found.'

'Isobel's beckoning us to a car.'

The dilapidated Morris Eight to which we steered him was driven by Blanche and already contained Norah. Accommodation was cramped. As we drove away, Widmerpool was to be seen marshalling his own party outside the porch. They were lost to sight moving in Indian file between the tombstones, making for a large black car, the taxi in which they had all arrived, far more antiquated than our own vehicle.

'Of course, I knew—Mr—Mr Whatever-his-name-is, knew his face when I saw him at the train,' said Alfred Tolland. 'As soon as he spoke I remembered the excellent speech he made that night—what's the man's name?— took over the house from Cordery—your man—Le Bas— that's the one. The night Le Bas had a stroke or something. Always remember that speech. Full of excellent stuff. Good idea to get away from all that—what is it, *Eheu fugaces*, something of the sort, never any good at Latin. All that sentimental stuff, I mean, and talk about business affairs for a change. Sound man. Great admirer of Erridge, he told me—takes rather a different view of him to most—I don't say *most*—anyway some of the family, who were always a bit what you might call lacking in understanding of Erridge—not exactly disapproving but . . . Widmerpool, that's the fellow's name. He's an MP now. Labour, of course. Thinks very highly of Mr Attlee. Sure he's right . . . I was a bit worried about Mrs Widmerpool. So quiet. Very shy, I expect. Rare these days for a young woman to be as quiet as that. Thought she might be upset about something. Daresay funerals upset her. They do some people. Beautiful young woman too. I couldn't help looking at her. She must have thought me quite rude. Hope somebody's seeing to her properly after she had to leave the service . . .'

This was the longest dissertation I had ever heard Alfred Tolland attempt. That he should allow himself such conversational licence showed how much the day had agitated him. He might also be trying to keep his mind from the discomfort suffered where we sat at the back of the small car. A long silence followed, as if he regretted having given voice to so many private opinions.

'True Thrubworth weather,' said Norah.

She had recovered from her tears. Rain was pouring down again. Mist hid the woods on the high ground behind the house, the timber preserved from felling by St John Clarke's fortuitous legacy to Erridge. The camp was visible enough. On either side of the drive Nissen huts were enclosed by barbed wire. The dismal climate kept the POWs indoors. A few drenched guards were the only form of life to be seen. Blanche made a circuit round the back of the house, the car passed under an arch, into the cobbled yard through which Erridge's wing was approached. She stopped in front of a low door studded with large brass nails.

'I'll put the car away. Go on up to the flat.'

The door turned out to be firmly shut.

'Probably no one at home,' said Norah. 'They've all been to the funeral. I hope Blanchie's got the key. It would be just like her to leave the house without bringing the key with her.'

She knocked loudly. We waited in the rain. After a minute the door was opened. I expected an elderly retainer of some sort, if the knocking were answered at all. Instead of that, a squat, broad-shouldered young man, with fair curly hair and a ruddy face, stood on the threshold. He wore a grey woollen sweater and chocolate-coloured trousers patched in many places. I thought he must be some new protégé of Erridge's about whom one had not been warned. He seemed wholly prepared for us.

'Come in, please, come in.'

Blanche appeared at that moment.

'They'll all be along soon, Siegfried. Will you put the kettle on? I'll come and help in a second. I thought we left the door on the latch.'

'Miss must have closed it.'

'Mrs Skerrett did? Well, leave it unlatched now, so the others can get in without bringing you down to open it.'

'Make her tea.'

'You've made tea already, Siegfried?'

'Of course.'

Grinning delightedly about something, apparently his own ingenuity, he bustled off.

'Who the hell?' asked Norah.

'Siegfried? He's one of the German prisoners working on the land. He loves doing jobs about the house so much, there seemed no point in trying to prevent him. It's a great help, as there's too much for Mrs Skerrett singlehanded, especially on a day like this.'

We passed along the passages leading to Erridge's flat, the several rooms of which were situated up a flight of stairs some little way from the door opening on the court-yard. In the dozen years or so since I had last been at Thrubworth more lumber than ever had collected in these back parts of the house, much of it no doubt brought there after requisitioning. There was an overwhelming accumulation: furniture: pictures: rolled-up carpets: packing cases. Erridge's father, an indefatigable wanderer over the face of the earth, had been responsible for much of this hoard, buying everything that took his fancy. There were 'heads' of big game: a suit of Japanese armour: two huge vases standing on plinths: an idol that looked Mexican or South American. Alfred Tolland identified some of these odds and ends as we made our way through them.

'That oil painting on its side's the First Jubilee. Very old-fashioned in style. Nobody paints like that now. Those big pots are supposed to be eighteenth-century Chinese. Walter Huntercombe came to shoot here once, and insisted they were nothing of the sort. Nineteenth-century copies, he said, and my brother had been swindled. Of course Warminster didn't like that at all. Told Walter Huntercombe he was a conceited young ass. Goodness knows where the tricycle came from.'

Erridge's flat, at the top of a flight of narrow stairs at the end of the corridor, in most respects a severely unadorned apartment, with the air of a temple consecrated to the beliefs of a fanatically austere sect, included a few pieces of furniture that suggested quite another sort of life. His disregard for luxury, anything like fastidious selection of objects, allowed shabby chairs and tables that had seen better days in other parts of the house. In the sitting-room someone—probably Frederica—had removed from the wall the pedigree-like chart, on which what appeared to be descending branches of an ancient lineage, had turned out an illustration of the principles of world economic distribution; now, in any case, hopelessly outdated in consequence of the war.

The books on the shelves, most of them published twelve or fifteen years before, gave the impression of having been bought during the same period of eighteen months or two years: *Russia's Productive System* . . . *The Indian Crisis* . . .

Anthology of Soviet Literature ... Towards the Understanding of Karl Marx ... From Peasant to Collective Farmer. There was also a complete set of Dickens in calf, a few standard poets, and—Erridge's vice, furtive, if not absolutely secret—the bound volumes of *Chums* and the *Boy's Own Paper*, the pages of which he would turn unsmiling for hours at times of worry or irritation. Erridge's Russian enthusiasms had died down by the late thirties, but he always retained a muted affection for the Soviet system, even when disapproving. This fascination for an old love was quite different from Bagshaw's. Bagshaw delighted in examining every inconsistency in the Party Line: who was liquidated: who in the ascendant: which heresies persecuted: which new orthodoxies imposed. Such mutations were painful to Erridge. He preferred not to be brought face to face with them. He was like a man who hoped to avoid the distress of hearing of the depravities into which an adored mistress has fallen.

In this room Erridge had written his letters, eaten his meals, transacted political business with Craggs and Quiggin, read, lounged, moped, probably seduced Mona, or *vice versa*; the same, or alternate, process possibly applying also to Gypsy Jones—or rather Lady Craggs. He used rarely to digress into other parts of the house. The 'state apartments' were kept covered in dust sheets. Once in a way he might have need to consult a book in the library, to which few volumes had been added since the days of the Chemist-Earl, who had brought together what was then regarded as an unexampled collection of works on his own subject. Once in a way a guest—latterly these had become increasingly rare—likely to be a new political contact of one kind or another, for example, an unusually persistent refugee, might be shown round. Erridge had never entirely conquered a taste for exhibiting his own belongings, even though rather ashamed of the practice, and of the belongings themselves.

The once wide assortment of journals on a large table set aside for this purpose had been severely reduced—probably by Frederica again—to a couple of daily newspapers, neither of a flavour her brother would have approved. Beyond this table stood a smaller one at which Erridge and his guests, if any, used to eat. The most comfortable piece of furniture in the room was a big sofa facing the fireplace, its back to the door. The room appeared to be empty when entered, the position of this sofa concealing at first the fact that someone was reclining at full length upon it. Walking across the room to gain a view of the park from the window, I saw the recumbent figure was Pamela's. Propped against cushions, a cup of tea beside her on the floor, by the teacup an open book, its pages downward on the carpet, she was looking straight ahead of her, apparently once more lost in thought. I asked if she were feeling better. She turned her large pale eyes on me.

'Why should I be feeling better?'

'I don't know. I just enquired as a formality. Don't feel bound to answer.'

For once she laughed.

'I mean obviously you weren't well in church.'

'Worse than the bloody corpse.'

'Flu?'

'God knows.'

'A virus?'

'It doesn't much matter does it?'

'Diagnosis might suggest a cure.'

'Are Kenneth and those other sods on their way here?'

'So I understand.'

'The kraut got me some tea.'

'That showed enterprise.'

'He's got enterprise all right. Why's he at large?'

'He's working on the land apparently.'

'His activities don't seem particularly agricultural.'

'He winkled himself into the house somehow.'

'He knows his way about all right. He was bloody fresh. Who's that awful woman we travelled down with called Lady Craggs?'

The sudden appearance beside us of Alfred Tolland spared complicated exposition of Gypsy's origins. In any case the question had expressed an opinion rather than request for information. Alfred Tolland gazed down at Pamela. He seemed to be absolutely fascinated by her beauty.

'Do hope you're . . .'

'I'm what?'

'Better.'

He brought the word out sharply. Probably he ought always to be treated in an equally brusque manner, told to get on with it, make a move, show a leg, instead of being allowed to maunder on indefinitely trying to formulate in words his own obscurities of thought; licence that his relations had fallen too long into the habit of granting without check. Siegfried appeared again, this time carrying a tray loaded with cups and saucers. His personality lay somewhere between that of Odo Stevens and Mrs Andriadis's one-time boy-friend, Guggenbühl, now Gainsborough. He made firmly towards Alfred Tolland, who stood between him and the table where he planned to lay the tea things.

'Sir, excuse, you are in the way, please.'

Called to order only a second before by Pamela, Alfred Tolland again reacted more quickly than usual. He almost jumped aside. Siegfried pushed adroitly past him, set the tray on a table, then returned to retrieve Pamela's cup from the floor.

'More of tea, Miss, please?'

'No.'

'Not good?'

'Not particularly.'

'Why not so?'

'God knows.'

'Another cup then, please. There is enough. China tea for the ration more easy.'

'I said I don't want any more.'

'No?'

She did not answer this time, merely closed her eyes. Siegfried, not in the least put out, showed no sign of going away. He and Alfred Tolland stood side by side staring at Pamela, expressing in their individual and contrasted ways boundless silent admiration. Her contempt for both of them was absolute. It seemed only to stimulate more fervent worship. After remaining thus entranced for some little time, Siegfried must have decided that after all work came first, because he suddenly hurried away, no less complacent and apparently finding the situation irresistibly funny. He had certainly conceived a more down-to-earth estimate of Pamela's character and possibilities than Alfred Tolland, who was in any case taken over at that moment by Blanche. He allowed himself to be led away, showing signs of being even a little relieved at salvage in this manner. Pamela opened her eyes again, though only to look straight in front of her. When I spoke of a meeting with Ada Leintwardine, she showed a little interest.

'I warned her that old fool Craggs, whose firm she's joining, is as randy as a stoat. I threw a glass of Algerian wine over him once when he was trying to rape me. Christ, his wife's a bore. I thought I'd strangle her on the way here. Look at her now.'

Gypsy, followed by Craggs, Quiggin and Widmerpool, had just arrived, ushered in by Siegfried, to whom Widmerpool was talking loudly in German. Whatever he had been saying must have impressed Siegfried, who stuck out his elbows and clicked his heels before once more leaving the room. Widmerpool missed this mark of respect, because he had already begun to look anxiously round for his wife. Frederica went forward to receive him, and the others, but Widmerpool scarcely took any notice of her, almost at once marking down Pamela's location and hurrying towards her. To run her to earth was obviously an enormous relief. He was quite breathless when he spoke.

'Are you all right?'

'Why should I be all right?'

'I meant no longer feeling faint. How did you find your way here? It was sensible to come and lie down.'

'I didn't fancy dying of exposure, which was the alternative.'

'Is it one of your nervous attacks?'

'I told you I'd feel like bloody hell if I came on this ghastly party—you insisted.'

'I know I did, dear, I didn't want to leave you alone. We'll be back soon.'

'Back where?'

'Home.'

'After another lovely journey with your friends.'

Widmerpool was not at all dismayed by this discouraging reception. What he wanted to know was Pamela's whereabouts. Having settled that, all was well. The physical state she might or might not be in was in his eyes a secondary matter. In any case he was probably pretty used to rough treatment by now, would not otherwise have been able to survive as a husband. Barnby used to describe the similar recurrent anxieties of the husband of some woman with whom he had been once involved, the man's disregard for everything except ignorance on his own part of his wife's localization. Having her under his eye, no matter how ill-humoured or badly-behaved, was all that mattered. Widmerpool seemed to have reached much the same stage in married life. Anything was preferable to lack of information as to what Pamela might be doing. His tone now altered to one of great relief.

'You'd better lie still. Rest while you can. I must go and talk business.'

'Do you ever talk anything else?'

Disregarding the question, he turned to me.

'Why is that Tory MP Cutts here?'

'He's another brother-in-law.'

'Of course, I'd forgotten. Retained his seat very marginally. I must have a word with him. That's Hugo Tolland he's talking to, I believe?'

'I haven't had an opportunity yet to congratulate you on winning your own seat.'

Widmerpool grasped my arm in the chumminess appropriate to a public man to whom all other men are blood brothers.

'Thanks, thanks. It showed the way things are going. A colleague in the House rather amusingly phrased it to me. We are the masters now, he said. The fight itself was a heartening experience. I used to meet Cutts when I was younger, but we have not yet made contact at Westminster. He had a sister called Mercy, I remember from the old days. Rather a plain girl. There are some things I'd like to discuss with him.'

He left the area of the sofa. Now the war was over one constantly found oneself congratulating people. In a mysterious manner almost everyone who had survived seemed also to have had a leg up. For example, books written by myself, long out of print, appeared better known after nearly seven years of literary silence. This was a more acceptable side of growing older. Even Quiggin, Craggs and Bagshaw had the air of added stature. Craggs was talking to Norah. Either to get away from him, or because she had decided that contact with Pamela was unavoidable, better to be faced coolly, she made some excuse, and came towards us. She may also have felt the need to restore her own reputation for disregarding commonplaces of sentiment in relation to such things as love and death. A brisk talk to Pamela offered opportunity to cover both elements with lightness of touch.

'Hullo, Pam.'

Norah's manner was jaunty.

'Hullo.'

'I never expected to see you here today.'

'You wouldn't have done, if I'd had my way.'

'Unlike you not to have your way, Pam.'

'That's good from you. You were always wanting me to do things I hated.'

'But didn't succeed.'

'It didn't look like that to me.'

'How have you been, Pam?'

'Like hell.'

After saying that Pamela picked up the book from the floor—revealed as Hugo's copy of *Camel Ride to the Tomb*, which he had brought down with him—smoothed out the crumpled pages, and began to turn them absently. Conceiving Norah well qualified by past experience to contend with manoeuvring of this particular kind, in which emotional undercurrents were veiled by unpromising mannerisms, I moved away. Their current relationship would be better hammered out unimpeded by male surveillance. Craggs, left on his own by Norah, had joined Quiggin and Frederica, who were talking together. In his elaborately refined vocables, reminiscent of a stage clergyman in spite of his anti-clericalism, he began to speak of Erridge.

'Such satisfying recollections of your brother were brought home to us—JG and myself, I mean—by the letter you are discussing. It revealed the man, the humanity under a perplexed, one might almost say headstrong exterior.'

Quiggin nodded judiciously. He may have felt a follow-up by Craggs would be helpful after whatever he had himself been saying, because he led me away from the other two. He had been looking rather fiercely round the room while engaged with Frederica. Now his manner became jocular.

'Only through me you infiltrated this house.'

Notwithstanding fairly powerful efforts on his own part to prevent any such ingress, that was broadly speaking true. Obstructive tactics at such a distant date could be overlooked in the light of subsequent events. In any case Quiggin seemed to have forgotten this obverse side of his own benevolence. I supposed he was going to explain whatever dispositions Erridge had left which affected the new publishing firm, but something else was on his mind.

'You saw Mona?' he asked.

'I had quite a talk with her.'

'She was looking very prosperous.'

'She's married to an Air Vice-Marshal.'

'Good God.'

'She appears to like it.'

'Rather an intellectual comedown.'

'You never can tell.'

'Did she ask about me?'

'Said she'd sighted you outside the church and waved.'

'Not particularly good taste her coming, I thought. But listen—I understand you met Bagshaw, and he talked about *Fission*?'

'Not in detail. He said Erry had an interest—that to some extent the magazine would propagate his ideas.'

'Unfortunately that will be possible only in retrospect, but the fact Alf is no longer with us does not mean the paper will not be launched. In fact it will be carried forward much as he would have wished, subject to certain modifications. Kenneth Widmerpool is interested in it now. He wants an organ for his own views. There is another potential backer keen on the more literary, less political side. We have no objection to that. We think the magazine should be open to all opinion to be looked upon as progressive, a rather broader basis than Alf envisaged might be advantageous.'

'Why not?'

'Bagshaw was in Alf's eyes editor-designate. He has had a good deal of experience, even if not of actually running a magazine. I think he should make a tolerable job of it. Howard does not altogether approve of his attitude in certain political directions, but then Howard and Alf did not always see eye to eye.'

I could not quite understand why I was being told all this. Quiggin's tone suggested he was leading up to some overture.

'There will be too much for Bagshaw to keep an eye on with books coming in for review. We'd have liked Bernard Shernmaker to do that, but everyone's after him. Then we tried L. O. Salvidge. He'd been snapped up too. Bagshaw suggested you might like to take the job on.'

The current financial situation was not such as to justify turning down out of hand an offer of this sort. Researches at the University would be at an end in a week or two. I made enquiries about hours of work and emoluments. Quiggin mentioned a sum not startling in its generosity, none the less acceptable, bearing in mind that one might ask for a rise later. The duties he outlined could be fitted into existing routines.

'It would be an advantage having you about the place as a means of keeping in touch with Alf's family. Also you've known Kenneth Widmerpool a long time, he tells me. He's going to advise the firm on the business side. The magazine and the publishing house are to be kept quite separate. He will contribute to *Fission* on political and economic subjects.'

'Do Widmerpool's political views resemble Erry's?'

'They have a certain amount in common. What's more important is that Widmerpool is not only an MP, therefore a man who can to some extent convert ideas into action—but also an MP untarnished by years of back-benching, with all the intellectual weariness that is apt to bring—I say, look what that girl's doing now.'

On the other side of the room Widmerpool had been talking for some little time to Roddy Cutts. The two had gravitated together in response to that law of nature which rules that the whole confraternity of politicians prefers to operate within the closed circle of its own initiates, rather than waste time with outsiders; differences of party or opinion having little or no bearing on this preference. Paired off from the rest of the mourners, speaking rather louder than the hushed tones to some extent renewed in the house after seeming befitted to the neighbourhood of the church, they were animatedly arguing the question of interest rates in relation to hire-purchase; a subject, if only in a roundabout way, certainly reconcilable to Erridge's memory. Widmerpool was apparently giving some sort of an outline of the Government's policy. In this he was interrupted by Pamela. For reasons of her own she must have decided to break up this tête-à-tête. Throwing down her book, which, having freed herself from Norah, she had been latterly reading undisturbed, she advanced from behind towards her husband and Roddy Cutts.

'People refer to the suppressed inflationary potential of our present economic situation,' Widmerpool was saying. 'I have, as it happens, my own private panacea for—'

He did not finish the sentence because Pamela, placing herself between them, slipped an arm round the waists of the two men. She did this without at all modifying the fairly unamiable expression on her face. This was the action to which Quiggin now drew attention. Its effect was

77

electric; electric, that is, in the sense of switching on currents of considerable emotional force all round the room. Widmerpool's face turned almost brick red, presumably in unexpected satisfaction that his wife's earlier ill-humour had changed to manifested affection, even if affection shared with Roddy Cutts. Roddy Cutts himself—who, so far as I know, had never set eyes on Pamela before that afternoon—showed, reasonably enough, every sign of being flattered by this unselfconscious demonstration of attention. Almost at once he slyly twisted his own left arm behind him, no doubt the better to secure Pamela's hold.

This was the first time I had seen her, so to speak, in attack. Hitherto she had always exhibited herself, resisting, at best tolerating, sorties of greater or lesser violence against her own disdain. Now she was to be observed in assault, making the going, preparing the ground for further devastations. The sudden coming into being of this baroque sculptural group, which was what the trio resembled, caused a second's pause in conversation, in any case rather halting and forced in measure, the reverential atmosphere that to some extent had prevailed now utterly subverted. Susan, glancing across at her husband clasped lightly round the middle by Pamela, turned a little pink. Quiggin may have noticed that and judged it a good moment for reintroduction—when they first met he had shown signs of fancying Susan—because he brought our conversation to a close before moving over to speak to her.

'I'll have a further word with Bagshaw,' he said. 'Then he or I will get in touch with you.'

Siegfried entered with a large teapot. He set it on one of the tables, made a sign to Frederica, and, without waiting for further instructions, began to organize those present into some sort of a queue. Frederica, now given opportunity to form a more coherent impression of Widmerpool's wife and her temperament, addressed herself with cold firmness to the three of them.

'Won't you have some tea?'

That broke it up. Siegfried remarshalled the party. Hugo took on Pamela. Widmerpool and Roddy Cutts, left once more together, returned to the principles of hire-purchase. Alfred Tolland, wandering about in the background, seemed unhappy again. I handed him a cup of tea. He embarked once more on one of his new unwonted bursts of talkativeness.

'I'm glad about Mrs Widmerpool . . . glad she found her way . . . the foreign manservant here . . . whoever he is, I mean to say . . . they're lucky to have a . . . footman . . . these days . . . hall-boy, perhaps . . . anyhow he looked after Mrs Widmerpool properly, I was relieved to find . . . Confess I like that quiet sort of girl. Do hope she's better. I'm a bit worried about the train though. We'll have to be pushing off soon.'

'You'll have time for a cup of tea.'

'Please, this way,' said Siegfried.' Please, this way now.'

He managed to break up most of the existing conversations.

'Just like Erry to find that goon,' said Hugo. 'He's worse than Smith, the butler who drank so much, and raised such hell at Aunt Molly's.'

In Siegfried's reorganization of the company, Gypsy was placed next to me, the first opportunity to speak with her. All things considered, she might have been more friendly in manner, though her old directness remained.

'Is this the first time you've been here?'

'No.'

That was at any rate evidence of a sort that she had visited Erridge on his home ground at least once; whether with or without Craggs, or similar escort, was not revealed.

'Who's that Mrs Widmerpool?'

To describe Pamela to Gypsy was no lesser problem than the definition of Gypsy to Pamela. Again no answer was required, Gypsy supplying that herself.

'A first-class little bitch,' she said.

Craggs joined his wife.

'JG and I have completed what arrangements can be made at present. We may as well be going, unless you want another cup of tea, Gypsy?'

The way he spoke was respectful, almost timorous.

'The sooner I get out, the better I'll be pleased.'

'Ought to thank for the cupper, I suppose.'

Craggs looked round the room. Frederica, as it turned out, had gone to fetch some testamentary document for Widmerpool's inspection. While they had been speaking Roddy Cutts took the opportunity of slipping away and standing by Pamela, who was listening to a story Hugo was telling about his antique shop. She ignored Roddy, who, seeing his wife's eye on him, drifted away again. Widmerpool drummed his fingers against the window frame while he waited. Until Roddy's arrival in her neighbourhood, Pamela had given the appearance of being fairly amenable to Hugo's line of talk. Now she put her hand to her forehead and turned away from him. She went quickly over to Widmerpool and spoke. The words, like his answer, were not audible, but she raised her voice angrily at whatever he had said.

'I tell you I'm feeling faint again.'

'All right. We'll go the minute I get this paper—what is that, my dear Tolland?—yes, of course we're taking you in the taxi. I was just saying to my wife that we're leaving the moment I've taken charge of a document Lady Frederica's finding for me.'

He spoke absently, his mind evidently on business matters. Pamela made further protests. Widmerpool turned to Siegfried, who was arranging the cups, most of them odd ones, in order of size at the back of the table.

'Fritz, mein Mann, sagen Sie bitte der Frau Gräfin, dass Wir jetzt abfahren.'

'Sofort, Herr Oberst.'

Pamela was prepared to submit to no such delays. 'I'm going at once—I must. I'm feeling ghastly again.'

'All right, dearest. You go on. I'll follow—the rest of us will. I can't leave without obtaining that paper.'

Widmerpool looked about him desperately. Marriage had greatly reduced his self-assurance. Then a plan suggested itself.

'Nick, do very kindly escort Pam to the door. She's not feeling quite herself, a slight recurrence of what she went through earlier. Those passages are rather complicated, as I remember from arriving. Your sister-in-law's looking for a document I need. I must stay for that, and to thank her for her hospitality.'

Pamela had certainly gone very white again. She looked as if she might be going to faint. Her withdrawal from church, in the light of previous behaviour likely to be prompted by sheer perversity, now took on a more excusable aspect. That she was genuinely feeling ill was confirmed by the way she agreed without argument to the suggested compromise. We at once set off down the stairs together, Pamela bidding no one goodbye.

'Is the taxi outside?'

'Parked in the yard.'

'Your coat?'

'Lying on some of that junk by the door.'

We hurried along. About halfway to the goal of the outside door, amongst the thickest of the bric-à-brac that littered the passage, she stopped.

'I'm feeling sick.'

This was a crisis indeed. If we returned to Erridge's

quarters, again negotiating the stairs and passing through the sitting-room, resources existed—in the Erridge manner, unelaborate enough—for accommodating sudden indisposition of this sort, but the sanctuary, such as it was, could not be called near. I lightly sketched in the facilities available, their means of approach. She looked at me without answering. She was a greenish colour by now.

'Shall we go back?'

'Back where?'

'To the bathroom—'

Pamela seemed to consider the suggestion for a second. She glanced round about, her eyes coming to rest on the two tall oriental vessels, which Lord Huntercombe had disparaged as nineteenth-century copies. Standing about five foot high, patterned in blue, boats sailed across their surface on calm sheets of water, out of which rose houses on stilts, in the distance a range of jagged mountain peaks. It was a peaceful scene, very different from the emergency in the passage. Pamela came to a decision. Moving rapidly forward, she stepped lightly on one of the plinths where a huge jar rested, in doing so showing a grace I could not help admiring in spite of the circumstances. She turned away and leant forward. All was over in a matter of seconds. On such occasions there is no way in which an onlooker can help. Inasmuch as it were possible to do what Pamela had done with a minimum of fuss or disagreeable concomitant, she achieved that difficult feat. The way she brought it off was remarkable, almost sublime. She stepped down from the plinth with an air of utter unconcern. Colour, never high in her cheeks, slightly returned. I made some altogether inadequate gestures of assistance, which she unsmilingly brushed aside. Now she was totally herself again.

'Give me your handkerchief.'

She put it in her bag, and shook her hair.

'Come on.'

'You wouldn't like to go back just for a moment?'

'Of course not.'

Her firmness was granite. Just as we were proceeding on towards the outside door, the rest of the party, Widmerpool, Alfred Tolland, Quiggin, Craggs, Gypsy, appeared at the far end of the corridor. Hugo was seeing them out. Widmerpool was at the head, explaining some apparently complicated matter to Hugo, so that he did not notice Pamela and myself until a yard or two away.

'Ah, there you are, dear. I thought you'd have reached the car by now. I expect you are better, and Nicholas has been pointing out the *objets d'art* to you. It's the kind of thing he knows about. Rather fine some of the pieces look to me.'

He paused and pointed.

'What are those great vases, for example? Chinese? Japanese? I am woefully ignorant of such matters. I intend to visit Japan when opportunity occurs, see what sort of a job the Americans are doing there. I doubted the wisdom of retaining the Emperor. Feudalism must go whenever and wherever it survives. We must also keep an eye on Uncle Sam's mailed fist—but I am running away with myself. Pam, you must go carefully on the journey home. Rest is what you need.'

She did not utter a word but, turning from them, walked quickly towards the door. Morally speaking, some sort of warning seemed required that all had not been well, yet any such announcement was hard to phrase. Before anything could be said—if, indeed, there were anything apposite to say—Hugo had gently encouraged the group to move on.

'I think a revised seating arrangement might be advisable on the way back to the station,' said Widmerpool.

'I'm going in front,' said Pamela.

The rest were contained somehow at the back. Alfred Tolland looked like a man being put to the torture for conscience sake, but determined to bear the torment with fortitude. Pamela lay back beside the driver with closed eyes. The taxi moved away slowly towards the arch, hooted, disappeared from sight. No one waved or looked back. Hugo and I re-entered the house. I told him what had happened in the passage.

'In one of the big Chinese pots?'

'Yes.'

'You don't mean literally?'

'Quite literally.'

'Couldn't you stop her?'

'Where was there better?'

'You mean otherwise it would have been the floor?'

'I suppose so.'

'Does that mean she's going to have a baby?'

'I hadn't thought of that.'

'It's the only excuse.'

'I think it was just rage.'

'Nothing whatever was said?'

'Not a word.'

'You just looked on?'

'What was there to say? It wasn't my business, if she didn't want the others to sympathize with her.'

Hugo laughed. He thought for a moment.

'I believe if I were given to falling for women, I'd fall for her.'

'Meanwhile, how is the immediate problem to be dealt with?'

'We'll consult Blanche.'

The news of Pamela's conduct was received at the beginning with incredulity, the first reaction, that Hugo and I were projecting a bad-taste joke. When the crude truth was grasped, Roddy Cutts was shocked, Frederica furious,

Norah sent into fits of hysterical laughter. Jeavons only shook his head.

'Knew she was a wrong 'un from the start,' he said. 'Look at the way she behaved to that poor devil Templer. You know I often think of that chap. I liked having him in the house, and listening to all those stories about girls. Kept your mind off the blitz. Turned out we'd met before in that night-club of Umfraville's, though I couldn't remember a word about it.'

Complications worse than at first envisaged were contingent on what had happened. The Chinese vase had to be sluiced out. Blanche, although totally accepting responsibility for putting right this misadventure, like the burden of every other disagreeable responsibility where keeping house was concerned, voiced these problems first.

'I don't think we can very well ask Mrs Skerrett to clean things up.'

'Quite out of the question,' said Frederica.

There was unanimous agreement that it was no job for Mrs Skerrett in the circumstances.

'Why not tell that Jerry to empty it,' said Roddy Cutts. 'He's doubtless done worse things in his time. His whole demeanour suggests the Extermination Squad.'

'Oh, God, no,' said Hugo. 'Can you imagine explaining to Siegfried what has happened? He would either think it funny in that awful gross German way, or priggishly disapprove in an equally German manner. I don't know which would be worse. One would die of embarrassment.'

'No, you couldn't possibly ask a German to do the cleaning up,' said Norah. 'That would be going a bit far—and a POW at that.'

'I can't see why not,' said Roddy Cutts. 'Rather good for him, to my way of thinking. Besides, the Germans are always desperately keen on vomiting. In their cafés or

85

restaurants they have special places in the Gents for doing so after drinking a lot of beer.'

'It's not him,' said Norah. 'It's us.'

'Norah's quite right,' said Frederica.

For Frederica to support a proposition of Norah's was sufficiently rare to tip the scale.

'Well, who's going to do it?' asked Blanche. 'The jar's too big for me to manage alone.'

In the end, Jeavons, Hugo and I, with shrewd advice from Roddy Cutts, bore the enormous vessel up the stairs to Erridge's bathroom. It passed through the door with comparative ease, but, once inside, every kind of difficulty was encountered. Apart from size and weight, the opening at the top of the pot was not designed for the use to which it had been put; not, in short, adapted for cleansing processes. The job took quite a long time. More than once the vase was nearly broken. We returned to the sitting-room with a good deal of relief that the business was at an end.

'It's Erry's shade haunting the place,' said Norah. 'His obsession with ill-health. All the same, we all supposed him a *malade imaginaire*. Now the joke's with him.'

'I was thinking the other day that hypochondria's a step-brother to masochism,' said Hugo.

This sort of conversation grated on Frederica.

'Do you know how Erry occupied his last week?' she asked. 'Writing letters about the memorial window.'

'The old original memorial window?'

'Yes.'

'But Erry was always utterly against it,' said Norah. 'At least refused ever to make a move. It was George who used to say the window had been planned at the time and ought to be put up, no matter what.'

'Erry appears to have started corresponding about stained-glass windows almost immediately after George's funeral. Blanche found the letters, didn't you?'

Blanche smiled vaguely. Norah threw her cigarette into the fireplace in a manner to express despair at all human behaviour, her own family's in particular.

'Apart from going into complete reverse as to his own values, fancy imagining you could get a stained-glass window put up to your grandfather when you can't find a bloody builder to repair the roof of your bloody bombed-out flat. That was Erry all over.'

'Perhaps he meant it as a kind of tribute to George.'

'I don't object to George wanting to stick the window up. That was George's line. It's Erry. It was just like darling George to be nice about that sort of thing—just as he went when he did, and didn't hang about a few months after Erry to make double death duties. George was always the best behaved of the family.'

Frederica did not comment on that opinion. It looked as if a row, no uncommon occurrence when Frederica and Norah were under the same roof, might be about to break out. Hugo, familiar with his sisters' wars and alliances, changed the subject.

'There's always something rather consoling about death,' he said. 'I don't mean Erry, because of course one's very sorry about the old boy and all that. What you must admit is there's a curious pleasure in hearing about someone's death as a rule, even if you've quite liked them.'

'Not George's,' said Susan. 'I cried for days.'

'So did I,' said Norah. 'Weeks.'

She was never to be outdone by Susan.

'That's quite different again,' said Hugo. 'I quite agree I was cut up by George too. Felt awful about him in an odd way—I mean not the obvious way, but treating it objectively. It seemed such bloody bad luck What I'm talking about is that sense of relief about hearing a given death has taken place. One can't explain it to oneself.'

'I think you're all absolutely awful,' said Roddy Cutts.

'I don't like hearing about death or people dying in the least. It upsets me even if I don't know them—some film star you've hardly seen or foreign statesman or scientist you've only read about in the paper. It thoroughly depresses me. I agree with Dicky about that. Let's change the subject.'

I asked whether he had settled with Widmerpool the rights and wrongs of hire-purchase.

'I don't much care for the man. In the margins where we might be reasonably in agreement, he always takes what strikes me as an unnecessarily aggressive line.'

'What's Cheap Money?'

'The idea is to avoid a superfluity of the circulating medium concentrated on an insufficiency of what you swop it for. When Widmerpool and his like have put the poor old *rentier* on the spot they may find he wasn't performing too useless a rôle.'

'But Widmerpool's surely a *rentier* himself?'

'He's a bill-broker, and the bill-brokers are the only companies getting any sympathy from the Government these days. He's in the happy position of being wooed by both sides, the Labour Party—that is to say his own party—and the City, who hope to get concessions.'

'I find politics far more lowering a subject than death,' said Norah. 'Especially if they have to include discussing that man. I can't think how Pam can stand him for five minutes. I'm not surprised she's ill all the time.'

'I was told that one moment she was going to marry John Mountfichet,' said Susan. 'He was prepared to leave his wife for her. Then he was killed. She made this marriage on the rebound. Decided to marry the first man who asked her.'

'Don't you believe it,' said Jeavons. 'That sort of story always gets put round. Who was Mountfichet's wife—the Huntercombes' girl Venetia, wasn't she? I bet they suited each other a treat in their own way. Married couples usually do.'

'What's that got to do with whether he was going off with Pamela Flitton?' asked Norah. 'Or whether she married Widmerpool on the rebound?'

'People get divorced just because they don't know they suit each other,' said Jeavons.

He did not enlarge further on this rebuttal of the theory that people married 'on the rebound', or that the first choice was founded on an instinctive rightness of judgment. Instead, he turned to the question of how he himself was to get back to London. Wandering about the room chain-smoking, he looked more than ever like a plain-clothes man.

'Wish the train didn't arrive back so late. They must be getting familiar with my face on that line. Probably think I'm working the three-card trick. Anything I can do to help sort things out while I'm here? Cleaning up that mess in the jar's whetted my appetite for work. I'd have offered to be a bearer, if I'd thought I could hold up the coffin for more than a minute and a half, but that lump of gunmetal in my guts has been giving trouble again. Never seems to settle down. Sure the army vets left a fuse there, probably a whole shellcap. Can't digest a thing. Becomes a bore after a time. Never know what you may do when you're in that state. Didn't want to be halfway up the aisle, and drop my end of the coffin. Still, that couldn't have disrupted things, or made more row, than that girl did going out. Wish Molly was alive. Nothing Molly didn't know about funerals.'

Frederica, who had just come in, looked not altogether approving of all this. She was never in any case really sure that she liked Jeavons, certainly not when in moods like his present one. That had been Jeavons's standing with her even before she married Umfraville, for whom Jeavons himself had no great affection. Umfraville, on the other hand, liked Jeavons. He used to give rather subtle imitations of him.

'What you could do, Uncle Ted, is to make a list of the wreaths,' said Frederica. 'Would you really do that? It would be a great help.'

'Keep me quiet, I suppose,' said Jeavons.

He often showed an unexpected awareness that he was gettting on the nerves of people round him.

'I'll duly render a return of wreaths,' he said. 'Show the state (a) as to people who ought to have sent them and haven't, (b) those who've properly observed regulations as to the drill on such occasions.'

Never finding it easy to set his mind to things, the process, if Jeavons decided to do so, was immensely thorough. When he married, he had, for example, taken upon himself to memorize the names of all his wife's relations, an enormous horde of persons. Jeavons familiarized himself with these ramifications of kindred as he would have studied the component parts of a piece of machinery or mechanical weapon. He 'made a drill of it', as he himself expressed his method, in the army sense of the phrase, inventing a routine of some sort that enabled him to retain the name of each individual in his mind, together with one small fact, probably quite immaterial, about each one of them. As a consequence, his knowledge in that field was encyclopaedic. No one was better placed to list the wreaths. Hugo stretched himself out on the sofa.

'Mortality breeds odd jobs,' he said.

'And the men to do them,' said Jeavons.

Later, as he worked away, he could be heard singing in his mellow, unexpectedly attractive voice, some music-hall refrain from his younger days:

'When Father went down to Southend,
To spend a happy day,

He didn't see much of the water,
But he put some beer away.
When he landed home,
Mother went out of her mind,
When he told her he'd lost the seaweed,
And left the cockles behind.'

A footnote to the events of Erridge's funeral was supplied by Dicky Umfraville after our return to London. It was to be believed or not, according to taste. Umfraville produced the imputation, if that were what it was to be called, when we were alone together. Pamela Widmerpool's name had cropped up again. Umfraville, assuming the manner he employed when about to give an imitation, moved closer. Latterly, Umfraville's character-acting had become largely an impersonation of himself, Dr Jekyll, even without the use of the transforming drug, slipping into the skin of the larger-than-life burlesque figure of Mr Hyde. In these metamorphoses, Umfraville's normal conversation would suddenly take grotesque shape, the bright bloodshot eyes, neat moustache, perfectly brushed hair— the formalized army officer of caricature—suddenly twisted into some alarming or grotesque shape as vehicle for improvisation.

'Remember my confessing in my outspoken way I'd been pretty close to Flavia Stringham in the old days of the Happy Valley?'

'You put it more bluntly than that, Dicky—you said you'd taken her virginity.'

'What a cad I am—well, one sometimes wonders.'

'Whether you're a cad, Dicky, or whether you were the first?'

'Our little romance was scarcely over before she married Cosmo Flitton. Now the only reason a woman like Flavia could want to marry Cosmo was because she needed a husband in a hurry, and at any price. Unfortunately my own circumstances forbade me aspiring to her hand.'

'Dicky, this is pure fantasy.'

Umfraville looked sad. Even at his most boisterous, there was a touch of melancholy about him. He was a pure Burton type, when one came to think of it. Melancholy as expressed by giving imitations would have made another interesting sub-section in the *Anatomy*.

'All right, old boy, all right. Keep your whip up. Cosmo dropped a hint once in his cups.'

'Not a positive one?'

'There was nothing positive about Cosmo Flitton—barring, of course, his Wassermann Test. Mind you, it could be argued Flavia found an equally God-awful heel in Harrison F. Wisebite, but Harrison came on to the scene too late to have fathered the beautiful Pamela.'

'I'm not prepared to accept this, Dicky. You've just thought it up.'

Umfraville's habit of taking liberties with dates, if a story could thereby be improved, was notorious.

'You can never tell,' he repeated. 'My God, Cosmo was a swine. A real swine. Harrison I liked in his way. He mixed a refreshing cocktail of his own invention called Death Comes for the Archbishop.'

3

IN THE COURSE OF PRELIMINARY conclaves with Bagshaw on the subject of *Fission*'s first number, mention was again made of an additional personage, a woman, who was backing the magazine. Bagshaw, adept at setting forth the niceties of political views, if these happened to attach to the doctrinaire Left, was less good at delineating individuals, putting over no more than that she was a widow who had always wanted some hand in running a paper. As it turned out, excuse existed for this lack of precision in grasping her name, in due course revealed in quite unforeseen circumstances. Bagshaw thought she would cause little or no trouble editorially. That was less true of Widmerpool, who certainly harboured doubts as to Bagshaw's competence as editor. Quiggin and Craggs were another matter. They were old acquaintances who differed on all sorts of points, but they were familiar with Bagshaw's habits. Widmerpool had no experience of these. He might take exception to some of them. Bagshaw himself was much too devious to express all this in plain terms, nor would it have been discreet to do so openly. His disquiet showed itself in repeated attempts to pinpoint Widmerpool himself politically.

'From time to time I detect signs of fellow-travelling. Then I think I'm on the wrong tack entirely, he's positively Right Wing Labour. Again, you find him stringing along with the far, but anti-Communist, Left. You can't help admiring the way he conceals his hand. My guess is he's playing ball with the Comrades on the quiet for whatever he can get out of it, but trying to avoid the appearance of doing so. He doesn't want to prejudice his chances of a good job in the Government when the moment comes.'

'Was that the game Hamlet was playing when he said:

> The undiscovered country from whose bourn
> No fellow-traveller returns, puzzles the will?'

'There was something fishy about Hamlet's politics, I agree,' said Bagshaw. 'But the only fellow-travellers we can be certain about were Rosencrantz and Guildenstern.'

Meanwhile I worked away at Burton, and various other jobs. The three months spent in the country after demobilization had endorsed the severance with old army associates, the foreign military attachés with whom I had been employed 'in liaison'. One returned to a different world. Once in a way the commemorative gesture might be made by one or other of them of inviting a former colleague, now relegated to civilian life; once in a way an unrevised list of names might bring one incongruously to the surface again. On the whole, attendance at such gatherings became very infrequent.

When we were asked to drinks by Colonel and Madame Flores, the invitation derived from neither of these two sources. It was sent simply because the hostess wanted to take another look at a former lover who dated back to days long before she had become the wife of a Latin American army officer; or—the latter far more probable, when one came to think of it—was curious, as ladies who have had an inclination for a man so often are, regarding the appearance and demeanour of his wife; with whom, as it happened, the necessity had never arisen to emphasize that particular conjunction of the past.

The Flores's drawing-room presented a contrast with the generally austere appearance almost prescriptive to apartments given over to official entertaining; not least on account of the profusion of flowers set about, appropriate to the host's surname, but at that period formidably expensive. This rare display, together with the abundance and variety of drinks on offer—as Mona had remarked, still hard to obtain—suggested that Colonel Flores was fairly rich himself, or his Government determined to make a splash. It struck me all at once, confronted with this luxuriance, that, although never behaving as if that were so, money was after all what Jean really liked. In fact Duport, even apart from his other failings, had not really been rich enough. It looked as if that problem were now resolved, Jean married to a rich man.

Almost every country which had not been at war with us was represented among the guests round about, 'Allies' and 'Neutrals' alike. The 'Iron Curtain' states (a new phrase), from time to time irascible about hospitality offered or accepted, had on this occasion turned up in force. Looking round the room, one noted an increase in darker skins. Aiguillettes were more abundant, their gold lace thicker. Here was gathered together again an order of men with whom I should always feel an odd sense of fellowship, though now, among this crowd of uniformed figures, chattering, laughing, downing their drinks, not one of their forerunners remained with whom I had formerly transacted military business. Only two or three of those present were even familiar by sight.

Jean, rather superb in what was called 'The New Look' (another recent phrase), was dressed in a manner to which hardly any woman in this country, unless she possessed unusually powerful tentacles, could at that time aspire. She greeted us at the door. That she had become so fashionable had to be attributed, one supposed, to her husband. In the old days much of her charm—so it had seemed—had been to look like a well-turned-out schoolgirl, rather than an enchantress on the cover of a fashion magazine. The slight, inexpressibly slight, foreign intonation she had now acquired, or affected, went well with the splendours of *haute couture*.

'How *very* kind of you both to come.'

Colonel Flores had his CBE ribbon up, a decoration complimenting his country rather than rewarding any very tangible achievement of his own since taking up his appointment in London; indeed presented to him on arrival like a gift at a children's party to animate a cosy atmosphere. There was no doubt—as his predecessor and less triumphant husband, Bob Duport, had remarked—Flores did possess a distinct look of Rudolph Valentino. I thought how that comparison dated Duport and myself. Handsome, spruce, genial, the Colonel's English was almost more fluent than his wife's, at least in the sense that his language had that faintly old-world tinge that one associated with someone like Alfred Tolland—though naturally far more coherent in delivery—or multilingual royalties of Prince Theodoric's stamp.

'My dear fellow—don't mind if I call you Nick, just as Jean does when she speaks of you—how marvellous it must be to have left the army behind. I am always meaning to send in my papers, as you call it, get to hell out of it. Then I give the old show another chance—but you must have a drink. Pink gin? My tipple too. Contigo me entierren. But the army? How should I occupy myself if there was no one to order me about? That's what I ask. Jean always tells me also that I should be getting into trouble if I had too little to do. Our wives, our wives, what slaves they make of us. She thinks I should turn to politics. Well, I might one day, but how much I envy you to be free. My time will come at last. I shall then at least be able to look after my horses properly

'. . . Ah, my dear General . . . but of course . . . pernod, bourbon—I must tell you I have even got a bottle of tequila hidden away . . . Hasta mañana, su Excelencia . . . à bientôt, cher Colonel . . .'

I wondered whether Jean trompé'd him with the gauchos, or whatever was of the most tempting to ladies in that country. Probably she did; her husband, having plenty of interests of his own, quite indifferent. The fact was Flores showed signs of being a great man. That had to be admitted. They were quite right to give him a CBE as soon as he arrived. His manner of handling his party suggested he well deserved it.

I circulated among the 'Allies', polite majors, affable colonels, the occasional urbane general, all the people who had once made up so much of daily life. Now, for some reason, there seemed little or nothing to talk about. It was no use broaching to these officers the subject of the newly founded publishing house of Quiggin & Craggs, the magazine *Fission* that was to embody the latest literary approach. At the same time the most superficial military topics once mutually exchanged seemed to have altered utterly overnight, everything revised, reorganized, reassembled; while —an awkward point—to approach, as a civilian, even the exterior trimmings of the military machine, when making conversation with the professional who controlled some part of it, was to risk, if not a snub, conveying an impression of curiosity either impertinent, or stemming from personal connexion with the Secret Service. While I wrestled with this problem, Jean reappeared.

'Your wife has so kindly asked us to dine with you. It's very hospitable, because I know how absolutely impossible it is to give dinner parties these days, not only rationing, but all sorts of other things. They are difficult enough even if you have official supplies and staff to draw on like ourselves. Carlos and I would so much have loved to come, but there has been a surprise. We have just received news from our Defence Ministry that we must go home.'

'Already?'

'We have to leave London almost at once. There has been a change of Government and a big reorganization.'

'Promotion, I hope?'

'Carlos has been given a military area in the Northern Province. It is quite unexpected and might lead to big things. There are, well, political implications. It is not just the same as being in the army here. So we have to make immediate arrangements to pack up, you see.'

She smiled.

'I should offer congratulations as well as regrets?'

'Of course Carlos is delighted, though he pretends not to be. He is quite ambitious. He makes very good speeches. We are both pleased really. It shows the new Government is being sensible. To tell the truth we were sent here partly to get Carlos out of the country. Now all that is changed—but the move must be done in such a hurry.'

'How foolish of them not to have wanted such a nice man about the place.'

She laughed at that.

'I was hoping to take Polly round a little in London. However, she is going to stay in England for a time in any case. She has ambitions to go on the stage.'

'I haven't seen her at your party?'

'She's with her father at the moment—I think you've met my first husband, Bob Duport?'

'Several times—during the war among others. He'd been ill in the Middle East, and we ran across each other in Brussels.'

'Gyppy tummy and other things left poor Bob rather a wreck. He ought to marry somebody who'd look after him properly, keep him in order too, which I never managed to do. He's rather a weak man in some ways.'

'Yes, poor Bob. No good being weak.'

She laughed again at this endorsement of her own estimate of Duport's character, but at the same time without giving anything away, or to the smallest degree abandoning the determined formality of her manner. That particular laugh, the way she had of showing she entirely grasped the point of what one had said, once carried with it powerful intoxications; now—a relief to ascertain even after so long—not a split second of emotional tremor.

'What's he doing now?'

'Bob? Oil. Something new for him—produced by an old friend of his called Jimmy Brent. You may have met him with my brother Peter. How I miss Peter, although we never saw much of each other.'

'I came across Jimmy Brent in the war too.'

'Jimmy's a little bit awful really. He's got very fat, and is to marry a widow with two grown-up sons. Still, he's fixed up Bob, which is the great thing.'

To make some comment that showed I knew she had slept with Brent—by his own account, been in love with him—was tempting, but restraint prevailed. Nevertheless, recollecting that sudden hug watching a film, her whisper, 'You make me feel so randy,' I saw no reason why she should go scot free, escape entirely unteased.

'How well you speak English, Madame Flores.'

'People are always asking if I was brought up in this country.'

She laughed again in that formerly intoxicating manner. A small dark woman, wearing an enormous spray of diamonds set in the shape of rose petals trembling on a stalk, came through the crowd.

'Rosie, how lovely to see you again. Do you know each other? Of course you do. I see Carlos is making signs that I must attend to the Moroccan colonel.'

Jean left us together. Rosie Manasch took a handful of stuffed olives from a plate, and offered one.

'I saw you once at a meeting about Polish military hospitals. You were much occupied at the other end of the room, and I had to move on to the Titian halfway through. Besides, I didn't know whether you'd remember me.'

The Red Cross, Allied charities, wartime activities of that sort, explained why she was at this party. It was unlikely that she had known Jean before the war, when Rosie had been married to her first husband, Jock Udall, heir apparent to the newspaper proprietor of that name, archenemy of Sir Magnus Donners. Rosie Manasch's parents, inveterate givers of musical parties and buyers of modern pictures, had been patrons of both Moreland and Barnby in the past. Mark Members had made a bid to involve them in literature too, but without much success, enjoying a certain amount of their hospitality, but never bringing off anything spectacular in the way of plunder. It had been rumoured in those days that Barnby had attempted to start up some sort of a love affair with Rosie. If so, the chances were that nothing came of it. Possessing that agreeable gift of making men feel pleased with themselves by the way she talked, she was in general held to own a less sensual temperament than her appearance suggested. Quite how she accomplished this investiture of male self-satisfaction was hard to analyse, perhaps simply because, unlike some women, she preferred men that way.

Udall was shot by the SS, on recapture, after a mass escape from a prisoner-of-war camp in Germany. The marriage—in the estimation of those always prepared to appraise explicitly other people's intimate relationships—was judged to have been only moderately happy. There were no children. There was also, even the most inquisitorial conceded, no gossip about infidelities on either side, although Udall was always reported to be 'difficult'. Quite soon after her husband's death, Rosie married a Pole called Andreszlwsiski, a second-lieutenant, though not at all young. I never came across him at the Titian during my period of liaison duty, but his appointment there, Polish GHQ in London, sounded fairly inconsiderable even within terms of the rank. Andreszlwsiski, as it turned out, was suffering from an incurable disease. He died only a few months after the wedding. Rosie resumed her maiden name.

'I've just been talking to your wife. We'd never met before, though I knew her sister Susan Tolland before she married. I hear you didn't guess that I was the mysterious lady in the background of *Fission*.'

'Was this arranged by Widmerpool?'

'The Frog Footman? Yes, indirectly. He used to do business when he was at Donners-Brebner with my cousin James Klein. Talking of Donners-Brebner, did you go to the Donners picture sale? I can't think why Lady Donners did not keep more of them herself. There must be quite a lot of money left in spite of death duties—though one never knows how a man like Sir Magnus Donners may have left everything.'

'If I'd been Matilda, I'd have kept the Toulouse-Lautrec.'

'Of course you must have known Matilda Donners when she was married to Hugh Moreland. Matilda and I don't much like each other, though we pretend to. Do you realize that a relation of mine—Isadore Manasch—was painted by Lautrec? Isn't that smart? A café scene, in the gallery at Albi. Isadore's slumped on a chair in the background. The Lautrec picture's the only thing that keeps his slim volume of Symbolist verse from complete oblivion. Isadore's branch of the family are still embarrassed if you talk about him. He was very disreputable.'

To emphasize the awful depths of Isadore's habits, Rosie stood on tiptoe, clasping together plump little hands that seemed subtly moulded out of pink icing sugar, then tightly caught in by invisible bands at the wrist. At forty or so, she herself was not unthinkable in terms of Lautrec's brush, more alluring certainly than the ladies awaiting custom on the banquettes of the Rue de Moulins, though with something of their resignation A hint of the seraglio, and its secrets, that attached to her suggested oriental costume in one of the masked ball scenes.

'Do you ever see Hugh Moreland now? Matilda told me he's still living with that strange woman called Maclintick. They've never married. Matilda says Mrs Maclintick makes him work hard.'

'I don't even know his address.'

That was one of the many disruptions caused by the war. Rosie returned to *Fission*.

'What do you think of the Frog Footman's beautiful wife? Did you hear what she said to that horrid girl Peggy Klein—who's a sort of connexion, as she was once married to Charles Stringham? James had adored Peggy for years when he married her—I'll tell you some other time. There's the Frog Footman himself making towards us.'

Widmerpool gave Rosie a slight bow, his manner suggesting the connexion with *Fission* put her in a category of business colleagues to be treated circumspectly.

'I've been having an interesting talk with the military attaché of one of the new Governments in Eastern Europe,' he said. 'He's just arrived in London. As a matter of fact I myself have rather a special relationship with his country, as a member—indeed a founder member—of no less than two societies to cement British relations with the new régime. You remember that ineffective princeling Theodoric, I daresay.'

'I thought him rather attractive years ago,' said Rosie. 'It was at Sir Magnus Donners' castle of all places. Was the military attaché equally nice?'

'A sturdy little fellow. Not much to say for himself, but made a good impression. I told him of my close connexions with his country. These representatives of single-party government are inclined to form a very natural distrust for the West. I flatter myself I got through to him successfully. I expect you've been talking about *Fission*. I hear you have been having sessions with our editor Bagshaw, Nicholas?'

'He's going to produce for me a writer called X. Trapnel, of whom he has great hopes.'

'*Camel Ride to the Tomb*?' said Rosie. 'I thought it so good.'

'I shall have to read it,' said Widmerpool. 'I shall indeed. I must be leaving now to attend to the affairs of the nation.'

Somebody came up at that moment to claim Rosie's attention, so I never heard the story of what Pamela had said to Peggy Klein.

The promised meeting with X. Trapnel came about the following week. Like almost all persons whose life is largely spun out in saloon bars, Bagshaw acknowledged strong ritualistic responses to given pubs. Each drinking house possessed its special, almost magical endowment to give meaning to whatever was said or done within its individual premises. Indeed Bagshaw himself was so wholeheartedly committed to the mystique of The Pub that no night of his life was complete without a final pint of beer in one of them. Accordingly, withdrawal of Bagshaw's company—whether or not that were to be regarded as auspicious —could always be relied upon, wherever he might be, however convivial the gathering, ten minutes before closing time. If—an unlikely contingency—the 'local' were not already known to him, Bagshaw, when invited to dinner, always took the trouble to ascertain its exact situation for the enaction of this last rite. He must have carried in his head the names and addresses of at least two hundred London pubs—heaven knows how many provincial ones—each measured off in delicate gradations in relation to the others, strictly assessed for every movement in Bagshaw's tactical game. The licensed premises he chose for the production of Trapnel were in Great Portland Street, dingy, obscure, altogether lacking in outer 'character', possibly a haunt familiar for years for stealthy BBC negotiations, after Bagshaw himself had, in principle, abandoned the broadcasting world.

'I'm sure you'll like Trapnel,' he said. 'I feel none of the reservations about presenting him sometimes experienced during the war. I don't mean brother officers in the RAF—who could be extraordinarily obtuse in recognizing the good points of a man who happens to be a bit out of the general run—but Trapnel managed to get on the wrong side of several supposedly intelligent people.'

'Where does he fit into your political panorama?'

Bagshaw laughed.

'That's a good question. He has no place there. Doesn't know what politics are about. I'd define him as a Leftish Social-Democrat, if I had to. Born a Roman Catholic, but doesn't practise—a lapsed Catholic, rather as I'm a lapsed Marxist. As a matter of fact I came across him in the first instance through a small ILP group in India, but Trapnel didn't know whether it was arse-holes or Tuesday, so far as all that was concerned. As I say, he's rather odd-man-out.'

Even without Bagshaw's note of caution, I had come prepared for Trapnel to turn out a bore. Pleasure in a book carries little or no guarantee where the author is concerned, and *Camel Ride to the Tomb*, whatever its qualities as a novel, had all the marks of having been written by a man who found difficulty in getting on with the rest of the world. That might well be in his favour; on the other hand, it might equally be a source of anyway local and temporary discomfort, even while one hoped for the best.

'Trapnel's incredibly keen to write well,' said Bagshaw. 'In fact determined. Won't compromise an inch. I admire that, so far as it goes, but writers of that sort can add to an editor's work. Our public may have to be educated up to some of the stuff we're going to offer—I'm thinking of the political articles Kenneth Widmerpool is planning—so Trapnel's good, light, lively pieces, if we can get them out of him, are likely to assist the other end of the mag.'

Trapnel's arrival at that point did not immediately set at rest Bagshaw's rather ominous typification of him. Indeed, Bagshaw himself seemed to lose his nerve slightly when Trapnel entered the bar, though only for a second, and quickly recovered.

'Ah, Trappy, here you are. Take a seat. What's it to be? How are things?'

He introduced us. Trapnel, in a voice both deep and harsh, requested half a pint of bitter, somehow an un-expectedly temperate choice in the light of his appearance and gruffness of manner. He looked about thirty, tall, dark, with a beard. Beards, rarer in those days than they became later, at that period hinted of submarine duty, rather than the arts, social protest or a subsequent fashion simply for much more hair. At the same time, even if the beard, assessed with the clothes and stick he carried, marked him out as an exhibitionist in a reasonably high category, the singularity was more on account of elements within him-self than from outward appearance.

Although the spring weather was still decidedly chilly, he was dressed in a pale ochre-coloured tropical suit, almost transparent in texture, on top of which he wore an over-coat, black and belted like Quiggin's Partisan number, but of cloth, for some reason familiarly official in cut. This heavy garment, rather too short for Trapnel's height of well over six feet, was at the same time too full, in view of his spare, almost emaciated body. Its weight emphasized the flimsiness of the tussore trousers below. The greatcoat turned out, much later, to have belonged to Bagshaw during his RAF service, disposed of on terms unspecified, possibly donated, to Trapnel, who had caused it to be dyed black. The pride Trapnel obviously took in the coat was certainly not untainted by an implied, though unjustified, aspiration to ex-officer status.

The walking stick struck a completely different note. Its wood unremarkable, but the knob, ivory, more likely bone, crudely carved in the shape of a skull, was rather like old Skerrett's head at Erridge's funeral. This stick clearly bulked large in Trapnel equipment. It set the tone far more than the RAF greatcoat or tropical suit. For the rest, he was hatless, wore a dark blue sports shirt frayed at the collar, an emerald green tie patterned with naked women, was shod in grey suede brothel-creepers. These last, then relatively new, were destined to survive a long time, indeed until their rubber soles, worn to the thinness of paper, had become all but detached from fibreless uppers, sounding a kind of dismal applause as they flapped rhythmically against the weary pavement trodden beneath.

The general effect, chiefly caused by the stick, was of the Eighteen-Nineties, the *décadence*; putting things at their least eclectic, a contemptuous rejection of currently popular male modes in grey flannel demob suits with pork-pie hats, bowler-crowned British Warms, hooded duffels, or even those varied outfits like Quiggin's, to be seen here and there, that suggested recent service in the *maquis*. All such were rejected. One could not help speculating whether an eyeglass would not be produced—Trapnel was reported to have sported one for a brief period, until broken in a pub brawl—insomuch that the figure he recalled, familiar from some advertisement advocating a brand of chocolates or cigarettes, similarly equipped with beard and cane, wore an eye-glass on a broad ribbon, though additionally rigged out in full evening dress, an order round his neck, opera cloak over his shoulder. In Trapnel's case, the final effect had that touch of surrealism which redeems from complete absurdity, though such redemption was a near thing, only narrowly achieved.

Perhaps this description, factually accurate—as so often when facts are accurately reported—is at the same time morally unfair. 'Facts'—as Trapnel himself, talking about writing, was later to point out—are after all only on the surface, inevitably selective, prejudiced by subjective presentation. What is below, hidden, much more likely to be important, is easily omitted. The effect Trapnel made might indeed be a little absurd; it was not for that reason unimpressive. In spite of much that was all but ludicrous, a kind of inner dignity still somehow clung to him.

Nevertheless, the impression made on myself was in principle an unfavourable one when he first entered the pub. A personal superstructure on human beings that seems exaggerated and disorganized threatens behaviour to match. That was the immediate response. Almost at once this turned out an incorrect as well as priggish judgment. There were no frills about Trapnel's conversation. When he began to talk, beard, clothes, stick, all took shape as necessary parts of him, barely esoteric, as soon as you were brought into relatively close touch with the personality. That personality, it was at once to be grasped, was quite tough. The fact that his demeanour stopped just short of being aggressive was no doubt in the main a form of self-protection, because a look of uncertainty, almost of fear, intermittently showed in his eyes, which were dark brown to black. They gave the clue to Trapnel having been through a hard time at some stage of his life, even when one was still unaware how dangerously—anyway how uncomfortably—he was inclined to live. His way of talking, not at all affected or artificial, had a deliberate roughness, its rasp no doubt regulated for pub interchanges at all levels, to avoid any suggestion of intellectual or social pretension.

'Smart cane, Trappy,' said Bagshaw. 'Who's the type on the knob? Dr Goebbels? Yagoda? There's a look of both of them.'

'I'd like to think it's Boris Karloff in a horror rôle,' said Trapnel. 'As you know, I'm a great Karloff fan. I found it yesterday in a shop off the Portobello Road, and took charge on the strength of the Quiggin & Craggs advance on the short stories. Not exactly cheap, but I had to possess it. My last stick, Shakespeare's head, was pinched. It wasn't in any case as good as this one—look.'

He twisted the knob, which turned out to be the pommel of a sword-stick, the blade released by a spring at the back of the skull. Bagshaw restrained him from drawing it further, seizing Trapnel's arm in feigned terror.

'Don't fix bayonets, I beseech you, Trappy, or we'll be asked to leave this joint. Keep your steel bright for the Social Revolution.'

Trapnel laughed. He clicked the sword back into the shaft of the stick.

'You never know when you may have trouble,' he said. 'I wouldn't have minded using it on my last publisher. Quiggin & Craggs are going to take over his stock of the *Camel*. They'll do a reprint, if they can get the paper.'

I told him I had enjoyed the book. That was well received. The novel's title referred to an incident in Trapnel's childhood there described; one, so he insisted, that had prefigured to him what life—anyway his own life—was to be. In the narrative this episode had taken place in some warm foreign land, the name forgotten, but a good deal of sand, the faint impression of a pyramid, offering a strong presumption that the locale was Egyptian. The words that made such an impression on the young Trapnel —in many subsequent reminiscences always disposed to represent himself as an impressionable little boy—were intoned by an old man whose beard, turban, nightshirt, all the same shade of off-white, manifested the outer habiliments of a prophet; just as the stony ground from which he delivered his tidings to the Trapnel family party seemed the right sort of platform from which to prophesy.

'Camel ride to the Tomb . . . Camel ride to the Tomb . . . Camel ride to the Tomb . . . Camel ride to the Tomb . . .'

Trapnel, according to himself, immediately recognized these words, monotonously repeated over and over again, as a revelation.

'I grasped at once that's what life was. How could the description be bettered? Juddering through the wilderness, on an uncomfortable conveyance you can't properly control, along a rocky, unpremeditated, but indefeasible track, towards the destination crudely, yet truly, stated.'

If Trapnel were really so young as represented by himself at the time of the incident, the story was not entirely credible, though none the worse for that. None the worse, I mean, insomuch as the words had undoubtedly haunted his mind at some stage, even if a later one. The greybeard's unremitting recommendation of his beast as means of local archaeological transport had probably become embedded in the memory as such phrases will, only later earmarked for advantageous literary use: *post hoc, propter hoc,* to invoke a tag hard worked by Sir Gavin Walpole-Wilson in post-retirement letters to *The Times.*

The earlier Trapnel myth, as propagated in the *Camel,* was located in an area roughly speaking between Beirut and Port Said, with occasional forays further afield from that axis. His family, for some professional reason, seemed to have roamed that part of the world nomadically. This fact—if it were a fact—to some extent attested the compatibility of a pleasure trip taken in Egypt, a holiday resort, in the light of other details given in the book, otherwise implying an unwarrantably prosperous interlude in a background of many apparent ups and downs, not to say disasters. Egypt cropped up more than once, perhaps—like the RAF officer's greatcoat—adding a potentially restorative tone. The occupation of Trapnel's father was never precisely defined; obscure, even faintly shady, commercial undertakings hinted. His social life appeared marginally official in style, if not of a very exalted order; possibly tenuous connexions with consular duties, not necessarily our own. One speculated about the Secret Service. Once—much later than this first meeting—a reference slipped out to relations in Smyrna. Trapnel's physical appearance did not exclude the possibility of a grandmother, even a mother, indigenous to Asia Minor. He was, it appeared, an only child.

'I always wondered what your initial stood for?'

Trapnel was pleased by the question.

'I was christened Francis Xavier. Watching an old western starring Francis X. Bushman in a cowboy part, it struck me we'd both been called after the same saint, and, if he could suppress the second name, I could the first.'

'You might do a novel about being a lapsed Catholic,' said Bagshaw. 'It's worth considering. I know JG would like you to tackle something more *engagé* next time. When I think of the things I'd write about if I had your talent. I did write a novel once. Nobody would publish it. They said it was libellous.'

'People like JG are always giving good advice about one's books,' said Trapnel. 'In fact I hardly know anyone who doesn't. "If only I could write like you, etc. etc." They usually outline some utterly banal human situation, or moral issue, ventilated every other day on the Woman's Page.'

'Don't breathe a word against the Woman's Page, Trappy. Many a time I've proffered advice on it myself under a female pseudonym.'

'Still, there's a difference between a novel and a newspaper article. At least there ought to be. A novelist writes what he is. That's equally true of mediaeval romances or journeys to the moon. If he put down on paper the considerations usually suggested, he wouldn't be a novelist— or rather he'd be one of the fifty-thousand tenth-rate ones who crawl the literary scene.'

Trapnel had suddenly become quite excited. This business of being a 'writer'—that is, the status, moral and actual, of a writer—was a matter on which he was inordinately keen. This was one of the facets of Trapnel to emerge later. His outburst gave an early premonition.

'Reviewers like political or moral problems,' said Bagshaw. 'Something they can get their teeth into. You can't blame them. Being committed's all the go now. I was myself until a few years ago, and still enjoy reading about it.'

Trapnel was not at all appeased. In fact he became more heated than ever, striking his stick on the floor.

'How one envies the rich quality of a reviewer's life. All the things to which those Fleet Street Jesuses feel superior. Their universal knowledge, exquisite taste, idyllic loves, happy married life, optimism, scholarship, knowledge of the true meaning of life, freedom from sexual temptation, simplicity of heart, sympathy with the masses, compassion for the unfortunate, generosity—particularly the last, in welcoming with open arms every phoney who appears on the horizon. It's not surprising that in the eyes of most reviewers a mere writer's experiences seem so often trivial, sordid, lacking in meaning.'

Trapnel was thoroughly worked up. It was an odd spectacle. Bagshaw spoke soothingly.

'I know some of the critics are pretty awful, Trappy,

but Nicholas wanted to talk to you about reviewing an occasional book yourself for *Fission*. If you agree to do so, you'll at least have the opportunity of showing how it ought to be done.'

Trapnel saw that he had been caught on the wrong foot, and took this very well, laughing loudly. He may in any case have decided some apology was required for all this vehemence. All the earlier tension disappeared at once.

'For Christ's sake don't let's discuss reviews and reviewers. They're the most boring subject on earth. I expect I'll be writing just the same sort of crap myself after a week or two. It's only they get me down sometimes. Look, I brought a short story with me. Could you let me know about it tomorrow, if I call you up, or send somebody along?'

Trapnel's personality began to take clearer shape after another round of drinks. He was a talker of quite unusual persistence. Bagshaw, notoriously able to hold his own in that field, failed miserably when once or twice he attempted to shout Trapnel down. Even so, the absolutely unstemmable quality of the Trapnel monologue, the impossibility of persuading him, as night wore on, to stop talking and go home, was a menace still to be learnt. He gave a few rather cursory imitations of his favourite film stars, was delighted to hear I had only a few days before met a man who resembled Valentino. Trapnel's mimicry was quite different from Dicky Umfraville's—he belonged, of course, to a younger generation—but showed the same tendency towards stylization of delivery. It turned out in due course that Trapnel impersonations of Boris Karloff were to be taken as a signal that a late evening must be brought remorselessly to a close.

A favourite myth of Trapnel's, worth recording at this early stage because it illustrated his basic view of himself, was how a down-at-heel appearance had at one time or another excited disdain in an outer office, restaurant or bar, this attitude changing to respect when he turned out to be a 'writer'. It might well be thought that most people, if they considered a man unreasonably dirty or otherwise objectionable, would regard the culpability aggravated rather than absolved by the fact that he had published a book, but possibly some such incident had really taken place in Trapnel's experience, simply because private fantasies so often seem to come into being at their owner's behest. This particular notion—that respect should be accorded to a man of letters—again suggested foreign rather than home affiliations.

When I left the pub, where it looked as if Bagshaw contemplated spending the evening, Trapnel stood up rather formally and extended his hand. I asked if he had a telephone number. He at once brushed aside any question of the onus of getting in touch again being allowed to rest with myself, explaining why that should be so.

'People can't very well reach me. I'm always moving about. I hate staying in the same place for long. It has a damaging effect on work. I'll ring you up or send a note. I rather enjoy the old-fashioned method of missive by hand of bearer.'

That sounded another piece of pure fantasy, but increased familiarity with Trapnel, and the way he conducted his life, modified this view. He really did send notes; the habit by no means one of his oddest. That became clear during the next few months, when we met quite often, while preparations went forward for the publication of the first number of *Fission*, which was due at the end of the summer or beginning of autumn. Usually we had a drink together in one of his favourite pubs—as with Bagshaw, these were elaborately graded—and once he dined with us at home, staying till three in the morning, talking about himself, his girls and his writing. That was the first occasion when the Boris Karloff imitation went on record as indication that the best of the evening was over, the curtain should fall.

A passionate interest in writing, or merely his taste for discussing it, set Trapnel aside from many if not most authors, on the whole unwilling to risk disclosure of trade secrets, or regarding such talk as desecration of sacred mysteries. Trapnel's attitude was nearer that of a businessman or scientist, never tired of discussing his job from a professional angle. That inevitably included difficulties with editors and publishers. Many writers find such relationships delicate, even aggravating. Trapnel was particularly prone to discord in that field. He had, for example, managed to get himself caught up in a legal tangle with the publication of a *conte*, before the appearance of the *Camel*. This long short story, to be published on its own by some small press, had not yet seen light owing to a contractual row. The story was left, as it were, in baulk; unproductive, unproduced, unread. There had apparently been trouble enough for Quiggin & Craggs to take over the rights of the *Camel*.

'The next thing's the volume of short stories,' said Trapnel. 'Then the novel I'm already working on. That's really where my hopes are based. It's going to be bigger stuff than the *Camel*. The question is whether Quiggin & Craggs have the sales organization to handle it properly.'

The question was more substantially how well Quiggin & Craggs would handle Trapnel himself. That looked like a tricky problem. Their premises were in Bloomsbury according to Bagshaw, reduced in price on account of bomb damage. An architecturally undistinguished exterior bore out that possibility. The building, reconditioned sufficiently for business to be carried on there, though not on a lavish scale, had housed small publishers for years, changing hands as successive firms went bankrupt or were absorbed by larger ones. There was no waiting room. Once through the door, you were confronted with the bare statement of the sales counter; beyond it the packing department, a grim den looking out on to a narrow yard. On the far side of this yard a kind of outhouse enclosed *Fission*'s editorial staff, that is to say Bagshaw and his secretary. Ada Leintwardine would sometimes cross the yard to lend a hand when the secretary, constantly replaced in the course of time, became too harassed by Bagshaw's frequent absences from the office to carry on unaided. Apart from that, an effort was made to keep the affairs of *Fission* separate so far as possible from the publishing side, although Craggs and Quiggin sat on both boards.

'Ada's the king-pin of the whole organization,' said Bagshaw. 'Maybe I should say queen bee. She provides an oasis of much needed good looks in the office, and a few contacts with writers not sunk in middle age.'

Ada had made herself at home in London. In fact she was soon on the way to becoming an established figure in the 'literary world', such as it was, battered and reduced, but taking some shape again, over and above the heterogeneous elements that had kept a few embers smouldering throughout the war. London suited Ada. She dealt with her directors, especially Quiggin, with all the skill formerly shown in managing Sillery. She had begun to refer to 'Poor old Sillers.' I had not seen Sillery himself again, as it happened, before the period of research at the University came to an end, calling once at his college, but being told he had gone to London for several days to attend the House of Lords.

When he was not present, Bagshaw was also designated by Ada 'Poor old Books'. That did not prevent them from getting on pretty well with each other. Her emotional life had become a subject people argued about. Malcolm Crowding, the poet, not much older than herself, alleged that the novelist Evadne Clapham (niece of the publisher of that name, and by no means bigoted in a taste for her own sex) had boasted of a 'success' with Ada. On the other hand, Nathaniel Sheldon, always on the look out, though advancing in years, spoke of encouragement offered him by Ada, when he was waiting to see Craggs. No doubt she made herself reasonably agreeable to anyone—even Nathaniel Sheldon, as a reviewer—likely to be useful to the firm. The fact that no one could speak definitely of lovers demonstrated an ability to be discreet. Ada herself was reported to be writing a novel, as Sillery had alleged.

In the humdrum surroundings of everyday business life, when, for example, one met them on the doorstep of the office, both Quiggin and Craggs showed themselves more changed than they had in the hurried, unaccustomed circumstances of Erridge's funeral. For instance, it was now clear Quiggin had settled down to be a publisher, intended to be a successful one, make money. He no longer spoke of himself producing a masterpiece. *Unburnt Boats*, his 'documentary', had been well received, whatever Sillery might say, when the book appeared not long before the war, but there Quiggin's literary career was allowed to rest. He had lost interest in 'writing'. Instead, he now identified himself, body and soul, with his own firm's publications, increasingly convinced—like not a few publishers—that he had written them all himself.

Quiggin also considered that he had a right, even duty, to make such alterations in the books published by the firm as he saw fit; anyway in the case of authors prepared to be so oppressed. Certainly Trapnel would never have allowed anything of the sort. There were others who rebelled. These differences of opinion might have played a part in causing Quiggin—again like many publishers—to develop a detestation of authors as a tribe. On the contrary, nothing of the sort took place. As long as they were his own firm's authors, Quiggin would allow no breath of criticism, either of themselves or their books, to be uttered in his presence, collectively or individually. His old rebellious irritability, which used formerly to break out so violently in literary or political argument, now took the form of rage—at best, extreme sourness—directed against anyone, professional critic or too blunt layman, who wrote an unfavourable notice, dropped an unfriendly remark, calculated to discourage Quiggin & Craggs sales.

Craggs's attitude towards publishing was altogether different. Craggs had been practising the art in one form or another for a long time. That made a difference. He did not care in the smallest degree about rude remarks made on the subject of 'his' authors, or 'his' books. In some respects, so far as the former were concerned, the more people abused them, the better Craggs was pleased. Certainly he had no great affection for authors as men— for that matter, unless easily seducible, as women—but, unlike Quiggin, his policy in this respect was not subjective; at least not entirely so. It cloaked a certain commercial shrewdness. Craggs, off his guard one day with Bagshaw, expressed the view that there were more ways of advertising a book than dwelling on the intellectual and moral qualifications of its author.

'What matters is getting authors talked about,' Craggs said. 'Let people know what they're really like. It whets the appetite. Look at Alaric Kydd's odd tastes, for instance. I drop an occasional hint.'

Craggs was being unusually communicative when he let that out, because in general nowadays he affected the manner of a man distinguished in his own sphere, but vague almost to the point of senility. Such had been his conversation at Thrubworth, though more defensive than real, to be dropped immediately if swift action were required. There was evidence that he was making good use of his wartime contacts in the civil service. Widmerpool, for his part, seemed to be pulling his weight too in a trade that was new to him.

'He's laid hands on some extra paper,' said Bagshaw. 'Found it hidden away and forgotten in some warehouse in his constituency.'

Walking through Bloomsbury one day on the way to the *Fission* office, I ran into Moreland. When I first caught sight of him coming towards me, he was laughing to himself. A shade more purple in the face than formerly, he looked otherwise much the same. We talked about what we had both been doing since we last met at the time of the outbreak of war. Moreland had always been fond of *The Anatomy of Melancholy*. I told him how I was now occupied with its author.

'Gone for a Burton, in fact?'

'Books-do-furnish-a-room Bagshaw's already made that joke.'

'How extraordinary you should mention Bagshaw. He got in touch with me recently about a magazine he's editing.'

'I'm on my way there now to sort out the review copies.'

'He wanted an article on Existential Music. The last time I saw Bagshaw was coming home from a party soon after he returned from Spain. He was crawling very slowly on his hands and knees up the emergency exit stairs of a tube station—Russell Square, could it have been?'

'He must have reached the top just in time for the war, because he was in the RAF, and now has a moustache.'

'A fighter-pilot?'

'PR in India.'

'Jane Harrigan's an' Number Nine, The Reddick an' Grant Road? I should think there was a good deal of that. I refused to contribute, although I suspect I've been an existentialist for years without knowing it. Like suffering from an undiagnosed disease. The fact is I now go my own way. I've turned my back on contemporary life—but what brings you to this forsaken garden? You can't know anybody who lives in Bloomsbury these days. Personally, I've been getting a picture framed, and am now trying to outstrip the ghosts that haunt the place and tried to commune with me. Comme le souvenir est voisin du remords.'

'Burton thought that too.'

'I've been reading Ben Jonson lately. He's a sympathetic writer, who reminds one that human life always remains the same. I remember Maclintick being very strong on that when mugging up Renaissance composers. Allowing for murder being then slightly easier, Maclintick believed a musician's life remains all but unchanged. How bored one gets with the assumption that people now are organically different from people in the past—the Lost Generation, the New Poets, the Atomic Age, the last reflected in the name of your new magazine.

> Fart upon Euclid, he is stale and antick.
> Gi'e me the moderns.

It's the Moderns on whom I'm much more inclined to break wind.'

'If not too late, restrain yourself. As you've just pointed out, the Moderns no longer live round here.'

'Forgive my sneering at Youth, but what a lost opportunity within living memory. Every house stuffed with Moderns from cellar to garret. High-pitched voices adumbrating absolute values, rational states of mind, intellectual integrity, civilized personal relationships, significant form . . . the Fitzroy Street Barbera is uncorked. Le Sacre du Printemps turned on, a hand slides up a leg . . . All are at one now, values and lovers. Talking of that sort of thing, you never see Lady Donners these days, I suppose?'

'I read about her doings in the paper sometimes.'

'Like myself. Ah, well. Bagshaw's request made me wonder whether I would not give up music, and take to the pen as a profession. What about *The Popular Song from Lilliburllero to Lili Marlene?* Of course one might extricate oneself from the whole musical turmoil, cut free of it altogether. Turn to autobiography. *A Hundred Disagreeable Sexual Experiences* by the author of *Seated One Day at an Organ*—but I must be moving on. I'm keeping you from earning a living.'

I suggested another meeting, but he made excuses, murmuring something about a series of tiresome sessions with his doctor. Seen closer, he looked in less good health than suggested by the first impression.

'I've sacked Brandreth. My latest physician takes not the slightest interest in music, thank God, nor for that matter in any of the arts. He also has quite different ideas from Brandreth when it comes to assessing what's wrong with me. Life becomes more and more like an examination where you have to guess the questions as well as the answers. I'd long decided there were no answers. I'm beginning to suspect there aren't really any questions either, none at least of any consequence, even the old perennial, whether or not to stay alive.'

'Beyond Good and Evil, in fact?'

'Exactly—one touch of Nietzsche makes the whole world kin.'

On that note (recalling Pennistone) we parted. Moreland went on his way. I continued towards Quiggin & Craggs, through sad streets and squares, classical façades of grimy brick, faded stucco mansions long since converted to flats. Bagshaw had a piece of news that pleased him.

'Rosie Manasch is going to pay for a party to celebrate the First Number. That's scheduled for the last week in September. None of us have had a party for a long time.'

In the end, owing to the usual impediments, *Fission* did

not come to birth before the second week in October. The comparative headway made by then in establishment of the firm's position was reflected in the fact that, when I arrived at the Quiggin & Craggs office, where the party mentioned by Bagshaw was taking place, a member of the Cabinet was making his way up the steps. As he disappeared through the door, a taxi drove up, and someone called my name. Trapnel got out. The fare must have been already in his hand, because he passed the money to the driver with a flourish, turned immediately, and waved his stick in greeting. He was wearing sun spectacles—in which for everyday life he was something of an optical pioneer— and looked rather flustered.

'I thought I'd never get here. I'm temporarily living rather far out. Taxis are hard to find round there. I was lucky to pick up this one.'

The fact of his arriving by taxi at all did not at the time strike me as either remarkable or inevitable. I was still learning only slowly how near the knuckle Trapnel lived. The first few months of his acquaintance had been a period of comparative prosperity. They were not altogether representative. That did not prevent taxis playing a major rôle in his life. Trapnel used them when to the smallest degree in funds, always prepared to spend his last few shillings on this mode of transport, rather than descend to bus or tube. Later, when we were on sufficiently familiar terms to touch on so delicate a subject, he admitted that taxis also provided a security, denied to the man on foot, against bailiffs serving writs for debt. At the same time this undoubtedly represented as well an important factor in the practical expression of the doctrine of 'panache', which played a major part in Trapnel's method of facing the world. I did not yet fully appreciate that. We mounted the steps together.

'I don't think I'll risk leaving my stick down here,' he

said. 'It might be pinched by some detective-story writer hoping to experiment with the perfect crime.'

No one was about by the trade counter. Guests already arrived had left coats and other belongings at the back, among the stacks of cardboard boxes and brown-paper parcels of the equally deserted packing department. A narrow staircase led to the floor above, where several small rooms communicated with each other. The doors were now all open, furniture pushed back against the wall, typewriters in rubber covers standing on steel cabinets, a table covered with stacks of the first number of *Fission*. Apart from these, and a bookcase containing 'file' copies of a few books already published by the firm, other evidences of the publishing trade had been hidden away.

In the furthest room stood another table on which glasses, but no bottles, were to be seen. Ada Leintwardine was pouring drink from a jug. She had just filled a glass for the member of the Government who preceded us up the stairs. This personage, probably unused to parties given by small publishers, tasted what he had been given and smiled grimly. Craggs and Quiggin, one on either side, simultaneously engaged him in conversation. Bagshaw, not absolutely sober, waved. His editorial, perfectly competent, had spoken of the post-war world and its anomalies, making at least one tolerable joke. Trapnel's short story had the place of honour next to the editorial. We moved towards the drinks.

Bagshaw, like the Cabinet Minister, was taking on two at a time, in Bagshaw's case Bernard Shernmaker and Nathaniel Sheldon. This immediately suggested an uncomfortable situation, as these two critics had played on different sides in a recent crop of letters about homosexuality in one of the weeklies. In any case they were likely to be antipathetic to each other as representing opposite ends of their calling. Sheldon, an all-purposes journalist with a professional background comparable with Bagshaw's (Sheldon older and more successful) had probably never read a book for pleasure in his life. This did not at all handicap his laying down the law in a reasonably lively manner, and with brutal topicality, in the literary column of a daily paper. He would have been equally happy—possibly happier, if the epithet could be used of him at all—in almost any other journalistic activity. Chips Lovell, to whom Sheldon had promised a job before the war, then owing to some move in his own game withdrawn support, used often to talk about him.

Shernmaker represented literary criticism in a more eminent form. Indeed one of his goals was to establish finally that the Critic, not the Author, was paramount. He tended to offer guarded encouragement, tempered with veiled threats, to young writers; Trapnel, for example, when the *Camel* had first appeared. There was a piece by him in *Fission* contrasting Rilke with Mayakovsky, two long reviews dovetailed together into a fresh article. Shernmaker's reviews, unlike Sheldon's, would one day be collected together and published in a volume itself to be reviewed—though not by Sheldon. That was quite certain. Yet was it certain? Their present differences could become so polemical that Sheldon might think it worth while lampooning Shernmaker in his column. If Sheldon did decide to attack him, Shernmaker would have no way of getting his own back, however rude Sheldon might be. However, even offensive admission into Sheldon's column was recognition that Shernmaker was worth abusing in the presence of a mass audience. That would to some extent spoil the pleasure for Sheldon, for Shernmaker allay the pain.

Publishers, especially Quiggin, endlessly argued the question whether Sheldon or Shernmaker 'sold' any of the books they discussed. The majority view was that no sales could take place in consequence of Sheldon's notices, because none of his readers read books. Shernmaker's readers, on the other hand, read books, but his scraps of praise were so niggardly to the writers he scrutinized that he was held by some to be an equally ineffective medium. It was almost inconceivable for a writer to bring off the double-event of being mentioned, far less praised, by both of them.

The dangerous juxtaposition of Sheldon and Shernmaker was worrying Quiggin. He continually glanced in their direction, and, when Gypsy joined his group with Craggs and the Cabinet Minister, he allowed husband and wife to guide the statesman to a corner for a more private conversation, while he himself moved across the room. He paused briefly with Trapnel and myself.

'Where's your wife?'

He spoke accusingly, as if he considered a covert effort had been made to undermine the importance of the *Fission* first number, also his own prestige as a director of the magazine.

'Our child's in bed with a cold. She sent many regrets at missing the party.'

Quiggin looked suspicious, but pursued the matter no further, as the Sheldon and Shernmaker situation had become more ominous. Bagshaw was reasonably well equipped to hold the balance between a couple like this, operating expertly on two fronts, provided the other parties did not too far overstep the bounds each felt the other allowed by convention, given the fact they were on bad terms. This rule appeared to have been observed so far, but Sheldon now began to embark on a detailed account of a recent visit to the Nuremberg trials, his report on which had already appeared in print. At this new development Shernmaker's features had taken on the agonized, fractious contours of a baby about to let out a piercing cry. Quiggin stepped quickly forward.

'Bernard, I'm going to take the liberty of sending you a proof copy of Alaric Kydd's new novel *Sweetskin*. It will interest you.'

Shernmaker showed he had heard this statement by swivelling his head almost imperceptibly in Quiggin's direction, at the same time signifying by an unaltered expression that nothing was less likely than that a work of Kydd's would hold his attention for a second. However, he took the opportunity of moving out of the immediate range of Sheldon's trumpeting narrative, giving Quiggin a look to denote rebuke for ever having allowed such an infliction to be visited on a sensitive critic's nerves. Quiggin seemed to expect nothing more welcoming than this reception.

'There may be trouble about certain passages in Kydd's book—two especially. If it has to be toned down through fear of prosecution, I'd like you to have read what the author originally wrote.'

Shernmaker continued his stern silence. If he allowed his face to relax at all, it was only to register deeper suspicion of publishers and all their works. Quiggin was by no means to be put off by such severity. He smiled encouragingly. Although not by nature ingratiating, he could be industrious at the process if worth while.

'Don't tell me you've washed your hands of Kydd's work, Bernard—like Pilate?'

Shernmaker did not return the smile. He thought for a time. Quiggin, unlike Pilate for his part, awaited an answer. Shernmaker brought his own out at last.

'Pilate washed his hands—did he wash his feet?'

It was now Quiggin's turn to withhold a smile. He was as practised a punch-line killer and saboteur of other people's witticisms as Shernmaker himself. This disrespect for one of the firm's new authors must also have annoyed him. A lot was expected from Kydd. Before further exchanges could take place, Quiggin's old friend Mark Members arrived. With him was a young man whose khaki shirt, corduroy trousers, generally buccaneering aspect, suggested guerrilla warfare in the Quiggin manner, though far more effectively. This was appropriate enough in Odo Stevens, an unlikely figure to turn up at a publisher's party, though apparently an already accepted acquaintance of Members. As Sillery had remarked, white locks suited Members. He allowed them to grow fairly long, which gave him the rather dramatic air of a nineteenth-century literary man who had loved and suffered, the mane of hair weighing down his slight, spare body. Stevens made a face expressing recognition, but, before we could speak, was at once buttonholed by Quiggin, with whom he also appeared on the best of terms. Members now introduced Stevens to Shernmaker.

'I don't know whether you've met Odo Stevens, Bernard? You probably read his piece the other day about life with the Army of Occupation. Odo and I have just been discussing the most suitable European centre for cultural congress—you know my organization is trying to get one on foot. Do you hold any views? Your own co-operation would, of course, be valuable.'

Shernmaker was still giving nothing away. Frowning, moving a little closer, he watched Members's face as if trying to detect potential insincerities; allowing at the same time a rapid glance at the door to make sure no one of importance was arriving while his attention was thus occupied. Shernmaker's party personality varied a good deal according to circumstance; this evening a man of iron, on guard against attempts to disturb his own profundities of thought by petty everyday concerns. His duty, this manner implied, was with a wider world than any offered by Quiggin & Craggs and their like; if a trifle sullen, he must be forgiven. He had already shown that, once committed to such inanities, the best defence was epigram. Members, who had known Shernmaker for years—almost as long as he had known Quiggin—evidently wanted to get something out of him, because he showed himself quite prepared to put up, anyway within reason, with the Shernmaker personality as then exercised.

'You'll agree, Bernard, that effective discussion of the Writer's Position in Society is impractical in unsympathetic surroundings. Artists are vulnerable to circumstance, never more so than when compulsorily confined to their native shores.'

Still Shernmaker did not answer. Members became more blunt in exposition.

'We're none of us ever going to get out of England again, except as emissaries of culture. That's painfully clear. We're caught in a trap. Unless something is done, we'll none of us ever see the Mediterranean again.'

Evadne Clapham, L. O. Salvidge and Malcolm Crowding, the last of whom had a poem in *Fission*, had joined the group. All agreed with this deduction. Evadne Clapham went further. She clasped her hands together, and quoted:

> 'A Robin Redbreast in a Cage
> Puts all Heaven in a Rage.'

The lines suddenly brought Shernmaker to life. He stared at Evadne Clapham as if outraged. She smiled invitingly back at him.

'Rubbish.'

'You think Blake rubbish, Mr Shernmaker?'

'I disagree with him in this particular case.'

'How so?'

> 'A robin redbreast in a rage
> Puts all heaven in a cage.'

Evadne Clapham now unclasped her hands, and brought them together several times in silent applause.

'Very good, very good. You are quite right, Mr Shern-maker. I often notice what aggressive birds they are when I'm gardening. Your conclusion is, of course, that writers must not be held in check. Don't you agree, Mark? We must make ourselves heard. Do tell me about the young man you came in with. Isn't it true he's had a very glamorous war career, and is terribly naughty?'

This question was answered by Quiggin introducing Odo Stevens all round as the man who was writing a war book to make all other war books seem thin stuff. It was to be about Partisans in the Balkans. Quiggin was a little put out to find that Stevens and I had already met, but we were again prevented from talking by an incident taking place that was in a small way dramatic. Pamela Widmerpool, followed by her husband, had come into the room. Quiggin turned to greet them. Stevens was obviously as surprised to see Pamela at this party as I had been myself to find him there. As they came past he spoke to her.

'Why, hullo, Pam.'

She looked straight at, and through, him. It was not so much that she ignored what Stevens had said, as that she behaved as if he had never spoken, was not even there. She seemed to be looking at someone or something beyond him, unable to see Stevens himself at all. Stevens, by nature as sure of himself as a man could well be, was not in the least embarrassed, but certainly taken aback. When he grasped what had happened, he turned towards me and grinned. We were not near enough for comment.

'There's someone I'd like you to meet, dear heart,' said Widmerpool. 'We'll talk business later, JG. There are two misprints in my own article, but on the whole Bagshaw must be agreed to have made a creditable job of the first number.'

Apart from her treatment of Stevens—or signalizing it

by that—Pamela gave the impression of being on her best behaviour. She allowed herself to be piloted across to the Cabinet Minister. Cutting Stevens might be explained by the fact that, when last seen with him, she had slapped his face. It was quite possible that night, the first of the flying-bombs, had been also the last she had seen of him. To start again as total strangers was one way of handling such matters. The most recent news of her had been from Hugo Tolland. Pamela had appeared at his antique shop in the company of an unidentified man, who had paid cash for an Empire *bidet*, later delivered to the Widmerpool flat in Victoria Street; a highly decorative piece of furniture, according to Hugo. Inevitably her sickness at Thrubworth had developed into a legend of pregnancy, cut short artificially and not occasioned by her husband, but that was probably myth.

Widmerpool's demeanour gave no impression of having emerged from a trying domestic experience, though it could be argued the truth had been kept from him. Not long before, a speech of his in a parliamentary debate on the reduction of interest rates had been the subject of satirical comment in a *Daily Telegraph* leader, but, at the stage of public life he had reached, no doubt any mention in print was better than none. Certainly he appeared well satisfied with himself, clapping Craggs on the back, and giving an amicable greeting to Gypsy, with whom he must have established some sort of satisfactory adjustment. The article he had written for *Fission* had been called *Affirmative Action and Negative Values*. Stevens came over to talk.

'Did you notice Pam's lack of recognition? Her all over. What the hell's she doing here?'

He laughed heartily.

'Her husband's part of the Quiggin & Craggs set-up. Why did you hit on them for your book?'

'My agent thought they'd be the right sort of firm, as I was operating with the Commies most of the time I was in the Balkans. The publishers have only seen a bit of it. It's not finished yet. Will be soon. I'm spreading culture with Mark Members at the moment, but I hope to get out of an office—if the book sells, and it will.'

'All about being "dropped"?'

'A murder or two. Some rather spicy political revelations. One of the former incidents mucked up my affairs rather—lost me a DSO.'

'What did you haul in finally?'

'MC and bar, also one of the local gongs from the new régime. Don't know yet whether I'll be permitted to put it up. I shall anyway.'

'When did you get out of the army?'

'It was rather premature. I was never much of a hand at regimental life, even though I wasn't sure at one moment I wouldn't take up soldiering as a trade. So many temptations in Germany. The Colonel didn't behave too badly, but in the end he said I'd have to go. I agreed, so far as it went. I scrounged round for a bit selling space and little articles, then got myself fixed up in this culture-toting outfit. At the moment I'm in liaison with Mark Members and his conference project. I hear you're doing the books on this mag. What about some reviewing for Odo?'

'Why not, Odo? Why should you be the only man in England who's not going to review for *Fission*?'

'Who's the small dark lady talking to Sir Howard Craggs?'

'Rosie Manasch. She too has an interest in the mag.'

'Rather attractive. I think I'll meet her.'

The war had washed ashore all sorts of wrack of sea, on all sorts of coasts. In due course, as the waves receded, much of this flotsam was to be refloated, a process to continue for several years, while the winds abated. Among the many individual bodies sprawled at intervals on the shingle, quite a lot resisted the receding tide. Some just carried on life where they were on the shore; others—the more determined—crawled inland. Stevens belonged to the latter category. He knew where his future lay.

'Any books you can spare. Army matters, travel, jewellery —as you know, I'm interested in verse too. HQ, my cultural boys, always finds me.'

He strolled away. Widmerpool appeared.

'I've been having a lot to do with your relations lately. It turned out your late brother-in-law was on bad terms with the family solicitor. I've managed to arrange that some of the work should be transferred to Turnbull, Welford & Puckering—my old firm, you remember I started the struggle for existence in Lincoln's Inn—has the advantage of my being able to keep a weather eye on things from time to time. The Quiggin & Craggs interests will need a certain amount of attention. Hugo Tolland tells me he did not at all mind Mrs George Tolland giving birth to a son—one Jeremy, I understand—told me he was far from anxious to inherit responsibilities, myriad these days, of becoming head of the family. Titles are a survival one must deplore, but they can be a worry, as Howard Craggs was remarking last week. I see Hugo Tolland's point. He is a sensible young man, in spite of what at first appears a foolish manner. I understand that, as mother of the little earl, Mrs George Tolland—who has two children of her own by an earlier marriage—is going to live in the wing of Thrubworth Park formerly occupied by the late Lord Warminster. Modest premises in themselves, and a good idea. Lady Blanche Tolland is to remain there as before. An excellent arrangement for one of her retiring nature. I talked to her, and greatly approved what she had to say for herself.'

Abandoning for a moment the intense pleasure people

find in explaining in detail to someone the characteristics and doings of their own relations, he paused and glanced round the room. This could have been a routine survey to be taken wisely at regular intervals with the object of keeping check on his wife's doings. She was at that particular moment revealed as listening to some sort of a harangue being given by a dark bespectacled personage in his thirties, whom I recognized as Werner Guggenbühl, now Vernon Gainsborough. There could be no doubt there was a look of Siegfried. Widmerpool marked them down.

'I see Pam's got caught up with Gainsborough. I don't know whether you've come across him? He's a German—a "good" German—a close friend of Lady Craggs, as a matter of fact. They go about a lot together. I'm giving away no secret. Craggs, very sensibly, takes an understanding view. He is a man of the world, though you might never guess that to look at him. Gainsborough is not a bad fellow. A little pedantic.'

'He used to be a Trotskyist.'

'No longer, I think. In any case I disapprove of witch-hunting. He stands, of course, considerably to the left of centre. I am not sure he is quite the sort of person Pam likes—she is easily bored—so perhaps it would be wise to come to her rescue.'

He gave the impression that Gainsborough's relationship with Gypsy, however little Craggs might resent it, and however 'good' a German he might be, was not one to recommend sustained conversation with a wife like his own. Widmerpool was about to move off and break up the tête-à-tête. However, Trapnel came up at that moment. Rather to my surprise, he addressed himself to Widmerpool with a formal cordiality not at all like his usual manner. It looked as if he were playing one of his rôles, a habit now becoming familiar.

'It's Mr Widmerpool, isn't it? Do forgive my introducing myself. My name's X. Trapnel. I'm a writer. JG was talking about you the other day. He said you were one of the few MPs who are trying to make the Government get a move on. I do hope you'll do something about the laws defining certain kinds of writing as obscene, when it's nothing of the sort. They really ought to be looked into. As a writer I can speak. You won't have heard of me, but I'm published by Quiggin & Craggs. I've a short story in this opening number of *Fission*.'

'Of course, of course.'

It was not possible to judge how far Widmerpool had taken in Trapnel's identity. I was at a loss to understand the meaning of this move. Trapnel continued to speak his piece.

'I don't want to bother you, just to say this. It looks as if there might be a danger of their bringing a case against Alaric Kydd's *Sweetskin*. I haven't read it, of course, because it isn't out yet—but we don't want JG put inside just because some liverish judge happens to take a dislike to Kydd's work.'

Widmerpool, if rather taken aback at being appealed to in this manner, was at the same time not unflattered to be regarded as the natural protector of publishers, now that he was in a sense a publisher himself. The manoeuvre was quite uncharacteristic of Trapnel. Like most writers in favour of abolishing current restrictions, such as they were, he was not so far as I knew specially interested in the question of 'censorship'. Trapnel's writing was not of the sort to be greatly affected by prohibitions of language or subject matter. He was competent to express whatever he wanted in an oblique manner. At the same time, he might well feel that, if obliquity in the context were less concordant than bluntness, it was absurd for bluntness to be forbidden by law. Language was a matter of taste. It looked as if the theme of censorship had been evoked on the spur of the moment as a medium convenient for making himself known to Widmerpool. Although Trapnel's appearance was of a kind to which he was unused, Widmerpool showed himself equal to the challenge.

'I'm happy you mention the matter. It is one that has always been at the back of my mind as of prime importance. As with so many questions of a similar sort, there are two sides. We must consider all the evidence carefully, especially that of those best fitted to judge in such matters. Amongst them I don't doubt you are one, Mr Trapnel, an author yourself and man of experience, well versed in the subject. My own feeling is that we want to do away with the interference of old-fashioned busybodies to the furthest possible extent, while at the same time taking care not to offend the susceptibilities of simple people with a simple point of view, and their livings to earn, people who haven't time to concern themselves too closely with what may easily have the appearance of contradictory arguments put forward by the pundits of the so-called intellectual world, men whom you and I perhaps respect less than they respect themselves. The prejudices of such people may seem unnecessarily complicated to the man in the street, who has been brought up with what could sometimes be justly regarded as a lot of out-of-date notions, but notions that are nevertheless dear to him, if only because they have been dear in the past to someone whose opinion he knew and revered—I mean of course to his mother.'

Widmerpool, who had dropped his voice at the last sentence, paused and smiled. The reply was one with which no politician could have found fault. Surprisingly enough, it seemed equally satisfactory to Trapnel. His acceptance of such an answer was as inexplicable as his reason for asking the question.

'Admirably expressed, Mr Widmerpool. What I envy about an MP like yourself is not the power he wields, it's his constituency. Going round and seeing how all sorts of different people live, what their homes are like, some friendly, some hostile. It must be a fascinating experience—what background stuff for a novelist.'

This was getting so near utter nonsense that I wondered whether Trapnel had managed to get drunk in a comparatively short time on the watery cocktail available, and, for reasons still obscure, wanted to pick a quarrel with Widmerpool; was, in fact, building up to deliver some public insult. Widmerpool himself totally accepted Trapnel's words at their face value.

'It is indeed a privilege to see ordinary folk in their own homes, though I never thought of the professional advantage you put forward. Well, housing conditions need a lot of attention, and I can tell you I am giving them of my best.'

'You should come and try to pull the plug where I am living myself,' said Trapnel. 'I won't enlarge.'

Widmerpool looked rather uneasy at that. Trapnel, seeing he risked prejudicing the good impression he intended to convey, laughed and shook his head, dismissing the matter of plumbing.

'I just wanted to mention the matter. Nice of you to have listened to it—nice also to have met.'

'Just let me make a note of your bad housing, my friend,' said Widmerpool. 'Exact information is always useful.'

Trapnel had spoken his last words in farewell, but Widmerpool led him aside and took out a notebook. At the same moment Pamela abandoned Gainsborough, whose attractions her husband must have overrated. She came towards us. Widmerpool turned to her. She disregarded him, and addressed herself to me in her slow, hypnotic voice.

'Have you been attending any more funerals?'

'No—have you?'

'Just awaiting my own.'

'Not imminent, I hope?'

'I rather hope it is.'

'How are you enjoying political life?'

'Like any other form of life—sheer hell.'

She said that in a relatively friendly tone. Craggs intervened and led Widmerpool away. Trapnel returned. I introduced him to Pamela. It was not a success. In fact it was a disaster. From being in quite a good humour, she switched immediately to an exceedingly bad one. As he came up, her face at once assumed an expression of instant dislike. Trapnel himself could not fail to notice this change in her features. He winced slightly, but did not allow himself to be discouraged sufficiently to abandon all hope of making headway. Obviously he was struck by Pamela's appearance. For a moment I wondered whether that had been the real reason for making such a point of introducing himself to Widmerpool. Any such guess turned out wide of the mark. On the contrary, he had not seen them come into the room together, nor taken in who she was. His head appeared still full of whatever he had been talking about to Widmerpool, because he did not listen when I told him her name. It turned out later that he was determined in his own mind that Pamela was a writer of some sort. Having decided that point, he wanted to find out what sort of a writer she might be. This was on general grounds of her looks, rather than any very special attraction he himself found for them.

'Are you doing something for *Fission*?'

Pamela stared at him as if he had gone off his head.

'Me?'

'Yes.'

'Why should I?'

'I just thought you might.'

'Do I look the sort of person who'd write for *Fission*?'

'It struck me you did rather.'

She gave him a stare of contempt, but did not answer. Trapnel, seeing he was to be treated with deliberate offensiveness, made no further effort in Pamela's direction. Instead, he began talking of the set-to on the subject of modern poetry that had just taken place between Shernmaker and Malcolm Crowding. Pamela walked away in the direction of Ada Leintwardine. Trapnel looked after her and laughed.

'Who is she?'

'I told you—Mrs Widmerpool.'

'Wife of the MP I was chatting with?'

'She's rather famous.'

'I didn't get the name. I thought you were saying something about Widmerpool. So that's who she is? I'd never have thought he'd have a wife like that. Bagshaw was talking about him, so I thought I'd like to make contact. I can't say I was much taken with Mrs Widmerpool. Is that how she always behaves?'

'Quite often.'

'Girls like that are not in my line. I don't care how smashing they look. I need a decent standard of manners.'

At this stage of our acquaintance I did not know much about Trapnel's girls, beyond his own talk about them, which indicated a fair amount of experience. Some 'big' love affair of his had gone wrong not long before our first meeting. Ada came round with the drink jug. Trapnel filled up and moved away.

'Not much danger of intoxication from this brew,' she said.

'The Editor doesn't seem to have done too badly.'

'Books had an early go at the actual bottle—before this potion was mixed.'

Bagshaw, rather red in the face, was in fact little if at all drunker than he had been at the beginning of the party, reaching a saturation point beyond which he never over-flowed. He was clutching Evadne Clapham affectionately round the waist, while he explained to her—with some supposed reference to her short story in *Fission*—where Marx differed from Feuerbach in aiming not to interpret the world but to change it; and what was the real significance of Lenin's April Theses.

'Evadne Clapham's coiffure always reminds me of that line of Arthur Symons, "And is it seaweed in your hair?"' said Ada. 'There's been some hot negotiation with poor old Sillers, but we've come across with quite a big advance in the end. I hope the book will justify that when it appears.'

'What's Odo Stevens's work to be called?'

'*Sad Majors*, an adaption of—

> Let's have one other gaudy night: call to me
> All my sad captains . . .

JG doesn't care for the title. We're trying to get Stevens to change it.'

'Why? He must agree it's a gloomy rank.'

'God—Nathaniel Sheldon's helping himself. He must think he's not being appreciated.'

It was true. Sheldon was routing about under the drink table. Ada hurried off. It was time to go home. I sought out Quiggin to say goodbye. He was talking with Shern-maker, whose temper seemed to have improved, because he was teasing Quiggin.

'Gauguin abandoned business for art, JG—you're like Rimbaud, who abandoned art for business.'

'Resemblances undoubtedly exist between publishing and the slave trade,' said Quiggin. 'But it's not only authors who get sold, Bernard.'

Downstairs in the packing department Widmerpool was wandering about looking for something. He no longer retained his earlier geniality, was now despondent.

'I've lost my briefcase. Hid it away somewhere down here. I say, that friend of yours, Trapnel, is an odd fellow, isn't he?'

'In appearance?'

'Among other things.'

'He's a good writer.'

'So I'm told.'

'I mean should be useful on *Fission*.'

'Ah, there's the briefcase—no, I've just been talking to Trapnel, and his behaviour rather surprised me. As a matter of fact he asked me to lend him some money.'

'Following, no doubt, on your recommendations in the House that interest rates should be reduced.'

'Your joke is no doubt very amusing. At the same time you will agree Trapnel's request was unusual on the part of a man whom I had never set eyes on before tonight, when he introduced himself to me?'

'You know what literary life is like.'

'I'm beginning to learn.'

'Did you come across?'

'I handed over a pound. The man assured me he was completely penniless. However, let us speak no more of that. I merely put it on record. I consider the party for *Fission* was a success. It will get off to a good start, even though I do not feel so much confidence in Bagshaw as I could wish.'

'He knows his stuff.'

'So everyone says. He appeared to me rather drunk by the end of the evening, but I must not stay gossiping. I have to get back to Westminster. Pam had to leave early. She had a dinner engagement.'

We went outside. Trapnel was standing on the pavement. He had just hailed a cab. He must have been waiting there for one to pass for some minutes; in fact since he had taken the pound off Widmerpool.

'Dearth of taxis round this neighbourhood's almost as bad as where I'm living. Can I give anyone a lift? I'm heading north.'

We both declined the offer.

4 ·

IN THE NEW YEAR, WITHOUT further compromise, Dickensian winter set in. Snow fell, east winds blew, pipes froze, the water main (located next door in a house bombed out and long deserted) passed beyond insulation or control. The public supply of electricity broke down. Baths became a fabled luxury of the past. Humps and cavities of frozen snow, superimposed on the pavement, formed an almost impassable barrier of sooty heaps at the gutters of every crossing, in the network of arctic trails. Bagshaw sat in his overcoat, the collar turned up round a woollen muffler, from which a small red nose appeared above a gelid moustache. Ada's protuberant layers of clothing travestied pregnancy. Only Trapnel, in his tropical suit and dyed greatcoat, seemed unaware of the cold. He complained about other things: lack of ideas: emotional setbacks: financial worries. Climate did not affect him. The weather showed no sign of changing. It encouraged staying indoors. I worked away at Burton.

On the whole Bagshaw's tortuous, bantering strategy, which had seen him through so many tussles with employers and wives (the latest one kept rigorously in the background), was designed to conceal hard-and-fast lines of opinion—assuming Bagshaw still held anything of the sort—so that, in case of sudden showdown, he could without prejudice give support wherever most convenient to himself. Even so, he allowed certain assessments to let fall touching on the fierce internal polemics that raged under the surface at Quiggin & Craggs; by association, at *Fission* too. Such domestic conflict, common enough in all businesses, took a peculiarly virulent form in this orbit, according to Bagshaw, on account of political undercurrents concerned.

'There are daily rows about what books are taken on. JG's not keen on frank propaganda, especially in translation. The current trouble's about a novel called *The Pistons of Our Locomotives Sing the Songs of Our Workers*. JG thinks the title too long, and that it won't sell anyway. No doubt the party will see there's no serious deficit, but JG fears that sort of book clogs the wheels—the pistons in this case—of the non-political side of the list. He's nervous in certain other respects too. He doesn't mind inconspicuous fraternal writings inculcating the message in quiet ways. He rather likes that. What he doesn't want is for the firm to get a name for peddling the Party Line.'

'Craggs takes another view?'

'Howard's an old fellow-traveller of long standing. He hardly notices the books are propaganda. It all gives him a nostalgic feeling that he's young again, running the Vox Populi Press, having the girls from the 1917 Club. All the same, he probably wouldn't argue with JG so much if he wasn't being prodded all the time by Gypsy.'

'And Widmerpool?'

'All I'm certain about is he wants to winkle me out of the editorship. As I've said, he behaves at times like a crypto, but I suspect he's still waiting to see which way the cat will jump—and of course he doesn't want to get too far the wrong side of his Labour bosses in the House.'

'You were uncertain at first.'

'He's been repeating pure Communist arguments about

the Civil War in Greece. He may simply believe them. I'm never quite sure Gypsy hasn't a hold on him of some sort. There was a story about them in the old days. That was long before I came on the scene so far as Gypsy was concerned.'

'How does Rosie Manasch take all this?'

'She's only interested in writers and art, all that sort of thing. She doesn't cause any trouble. She holds those mildly progressive views of the sort that are not at all bothered by the Party Line. Incidentally, she seems to have taken rather a fancy to young Odo Stevens. Trappy's becoming rather a worry. We're always shelling out to him. He writes an article or a short story, gets paid on the nail, is back on the doorstep the next afternoon, or one of his stooges is, and he wants some more. I can handle him all right, but I'm not sure they're doing so well on the other side of the yard.'

Trapnel's financial embarrassments had become unambiguous enough during the months that transformed him from a mere acquaintance of Bagshaw's, and professional adjunct of *Fission*, into a recognized figure in one's own life. His personality, built up with thought, deserves a word or two on account of certain elements not restricted to himself. He was a fine specimen of a general type, to which he had added flourishes of his own, making him—it was hardly going too far to say—unique in the field. The essential point was that Trapnel always acted a part; not necessarily the same part, but a part of some kind. Insomuch as most people cling to a rôle in which they particularly fancy themselves, he was no great exception so far as that went. Where he differed from the crowd was in so doggedly sticking to the rôle—or rôles—he had chosen to assume.

Habitual rôle-sustainers fall, on the whole, into two main groups: those who have gauged to a nicety what shows them off to best advantage: others, more romantic if less fortunate in their fate, who hope to reproduce in themselves arbitrary personalities that have won their respect, met in life, read about in papers and books, or seen in films. These self-appointed players of a part often have little or no aptitude, are even notably ill equipped by appearance or demeanour, to wear the costume or speak the lines of the prototype. Indeed, the very unsuitability of the rôle is what fascinates. Even in the cases of individuals showing off a genuine pre-eminence—statesmen, millionaires, poets, to name a few types—the artificial personality can become confused with the passage of time, life itself being a confused and confusing process, but, when the choice of part has been extravagantly incongruous, there are no limits to the craziness of the performance staged. Adopted almost certainly for romantic reasons, the rôle, once put into practice, is subject to all sorts of unavoidable and unforeseen restraints and distortions; not least, in the first place, on account of the essentially rough-and-ready nature of all romantic concepts. Even assuming relative clarity at the outset, the initial principles of the rôle-sustainer can finally reach a climax in which it is all but impossible to guess what on earth the rôle itself was originally intended to denote.

So it was with Trapnel. Aiming at many rôles, he was always playing one or other of them for all he was worth. To do justice to their number requires—in the manner of Burton—an interminable catalogue of types. No brief definition is adequate. Trapnel wanted, among other things, to be a writer, a dandy, a lover, a comrade, an eccentric, a sage, a virtuoso, a good chap, a man of honour, a hard case, a spendthrift, an opportunist, a *raisonneur*; to be very rich, to be very poor, to possess a thousand mistresses, to win the heart of one love to whom he was ever faithful, to be on the best of terms with all men, to avenge savagely the lightest affront, to live to a hundred full of years and honour, to die young and unknown but recognized the following day as the most neglected genius of the age. Each of these ambitions had something to recommend it from one angle or another, with the possible exception of being poor—the only aim Trapnel achieved with unqualified mastery—and even being poor, as Trapnel himself asserted, gave the right to speak categorically when poverty was discussed by people like Evadne Clapham.

'I do so agree with Gissing,' she said. 'When he used to ask of a writer—has he starved?'

The tribute was disinterested, as Evadne Clapham did not in the least look as if she had ever starved herself. The remark ruffled Trapnel.

'Gissing was more of an authority on starvation than on writing.'

'You don't think hunger teaches things?'

'I know as much about starvation as Gissing, probably more.'

'Then you prove his point—though after all it's dedication that counts in the end.'

'Dedication's often the hallmark of inferior performance.'

Trapnel was in a severe mood on that occasion. He was annoyed at Evadne Clapham being brought to his favourite pub The Hero of Acre. The conversation was reproduced in due course, somewhat more elaborately phrased, with the heroine getting the whip-hand, when Evadne Clapham's next novel appeared. However, that is by the way. To return to Trapnel's ambitions, they were—poverty apart—not only hard to achieve individually, but, even in rotation, impossible to combine. That was over and above Trapnel's particular temperament, no great help. Infeasibility did not prevent him from behaving, where ambitions were concerned, like an alpinist who tackles the sheerest, least accessible rock face of the peak he has sworn to ascend.

The rôle of 'writer' was on the whole the one least

damaged when the strain became too severe, a heavy weight of mortal cargo jettisoned. There were times when even that rôle suffered violent stress. All writing demands a fair amount of self-organization, some of the 'worst' writers being among the most highly organized. To be a 'good' writer needs organization too, even if those most capable of organizing their books may be among the least competent at projecting the same skill into their lives. These common-places, trite enough in themselves, are restated only be-cause they have bearing on the complexity of Trapnel's existence. There was a growing body of opinion, including, as time went on, Craggs, Quiggin, even Bagshaw himself —though unwillingly—which took the view that Trapnel's shiftlessness was in danger of threatening his status as a 'serious' writer. His books might be what the critics called 'well put together'—Trapnel was rather a master of tech-nical problems—his life most certainly was the reverse. Nevertheless, people have to do things their own way, and the troubles that beset Trapnel were for the most part in what Pennistone used to call 'a higher unity'. So far as cop-ing with down-to-earth emergencies, often seemingly un-answerable ones, Trapnel could show surprising agility.

One point should be cleared up right away. If comparison of his own life with a camel ride to the tomb makes Trap-nel sound addicted to self-pity, a wrong impression has been created. Self-pity was a trait from which, for a writer —let alone a novelist—he was unusually free. On the other hand, it would be mistaken to conclude from that fact that he had a keen grasp of objectivity where his own goings-on were concerned. That judgment would be equally wide of the mark. This lack of objectivity made him enemies; that of self-pity limited sales. Whatever Trapnel's essence, the fire that generated him had to see him through diffi-cult days. At the same time he managed to retain in a reasonably flourishing state—flourishing, that is, in his own eyes—what General Conyers would have called his 'personal myth', that imaginary state of being already touched on in Trapnel's case. The General, speaking one felt with authority, always insisted that, if you bring off adequate preservation of your personal myth, nothing much else in life matters. It is not what happens to people that is significant, but what they think happens to them.

Although ultimate anti-climaxes, anyway in their most disastrous form, were still kept at bay at this period, portents were already threatening in the eyes of those—L. O. Salvidge, for example, one of the first to praise the *Camel* —who took a gloomy view. Others—Evadne Clapham led this school of thought—dismissed such brooding with execrations against priggishness, assurances that Trapnel would 'grow up'. When Evadne Clapham expressed the latter presumption, Mark Members observed that he could think of no instance of an individual who, having missed that desirable attainment at the normal stage of human development, successfully achieved it in later life. It was hard to disagree. The fact is that a certain kind of gifted irresponsibility, combined with physical stamina and a fair degree of luck—in some respects Trapnel was incredibly lucky—always holds out an attractive hope that its possessor will prove immune to the ordinary vengeances of life; that at least one human being, in this case X. Trapnel, will beat the book, romp home a winner at a million to one.

Trapnel said he preferred women to have tolerable manners. The taste was borne out by the behaviour of such girls as he produced in public. When things were going reasonably well, he would be living with a rather unusually pretty one, who was also to all appearances bright, good tempered and unambitious. At least that was the impression they gave when on view at The Hero of Acre, or another of Trapnel's chosen haunts. The fairly rapid turnover suggested they might be less amenable when alone with Trapnel, not on their best behaviour; but that, after all, was just as much potential criticism of Trapnel as of the girl. She usually kept herself by typing or secretarial work (employed in concerns other than those coming under the heading of publishing and journalism), her financial contribution tiding over the ménage more or less—on the whole less rather than more—during lean stretches of their life together.

The pair of them, when Trapnel allowed his whereabouts to be known, were likely to be camped out in a bleak hotel in Bloomsbury or Paddington, enduring intermittent persecution from the management for delayed action in payment of the bill. The Ufford, as it used to be in Uncle Giles's day, would have struck too luxurious, too bourgeois a note, but, after wartime accommodation of a semi-secret branch of the Polish army in exile, the Ufford, come down in the world like many such Bayswater or Notting Hill establishments, might well have housed Trapnel and his mistress of the moment; their laundry impounded from time to time, until satisfactory settlement of the weekly account.

Alternatively, during brief periods of relative affluence, Trapnel and his girl might shelter for a few weeks in a 'furnished flat'. This was likely to be a stark unswept apartment in the back streets of Holland Park or Camden Town. The flat might belong to an acquaintance from The Hero of Acre, for example, possibly borrowed, while a holiday was taken, custodians needed to look after the place; if Trapnel and his girl could be so regarded.

When, on the other hand, things were going badly, the girl would have walked out—this happened sooner or later with fair regularity—and, if the season were summer, the situation might not exclude a night or two spent on the Embankment. The Embankment would, of course, represent a very low ebb indeed, though certainly experienced during an unprosperous interlude immediately preceding the outbreak of war. After such disasters Trapnel always somehow righted himself, in a sense seeming to justify the optimism of Evadne Clapham and those of her opinion. Work would once more be established on a passable footing, a new short story produced, contacts revived. The eventual replacement of the previous girl invariably kept up the traditionally high standard of looks.

Like many men rather 'successful' with women, Trapnel always gave the impression of being glad to get away from them from time to time. Not at all a Don Juan—using the label in a technical sense—he was quite happy to remain with a given mistress, once established, until the next up-heaval. The question of pursuing every woman he met did not arise. Unlike, say, Odo Stevens, Trapnel was content to be in a room with three or four women without necessarily suffering the obligation to impose his personality on each one of them in turn.

All the same, if they could feel safe with him in that sphere, Trapnel's girls, even apart from shortage of money, had to put up with what was in many respects a hard life, one regulated by social routines often untempting to feminine taste. A gruelling example was duty at The Hero of Acre. They would be expected to sit there for hours while Trapnel held forth on *Portrait of the Artist*, or *The Birth of a Nation*. Incidentally, The Hero of Acre was to be avoided if absolute freedom from parasites was to be assured, even though Trapnel could drastically rebuff them, if they inter-vened when a more important assignation was in progress. Dismissal might take a minute or two, should they be drunk, and in any case their mere presence in the saloon bar could be inhibiting.

However, this body of auxiliaries was a vital aspect of the Trapnel way of life. When things were bad, they would

come into play, collect books for review, deliver 'copy'—
Trapnel in any case distrusted the post—telephone in his
name about arrangements or disputes, tactfully propound
his case if required, detail his future plans if known, try—
when such action was feasible, sometimes when not—to
raise the bid in his favour. They were to be seen lingering
patiently in waiting rooms or halls of the journal concerned—at Quiggin & Craggs in the packing room, if cold
and wet, the yard, if sunny and dry—usually the end in
view to acquire ready cash for the Trapnel piece they had
handed to the editor a short time before. Where Trapnel
recruited these auxiliaries, how he disciplined them, was
always a mystery.

This need to receive payment on the nail was never
popular with the publishers and editors. Even Bagshaw
used to grouse about it. The money in his hand, Trapnel
could rarely hang on to it. He was always in debt, liked
standing drinks. He could not understand the difficulties
publishers and editors, especially the latter, made about
advancing further sums.

'After all, it's not their own money. It's little or no
trouble to them. As a matter of fact the accountants, the
boys who are put to the ultimate bother, such as it is, of un-
locking the safe and producing the dough, are far easier to
deal with than the editor himself.'

Accountants, as described by Trapnel, would often leave
their offices after the money had been paid out, and join
him in a drink. Perhaps they thought they were living dangerously. It might be argued they were. Trapnel had made
a study of them.

'People who spend their time absorbed with money
always have a bright apologetic look about the eyes. They
crave sympathy. Particularly accountants. I always offer a
drink when specie changes hands. It's rarely refused.'

Bagshaw was unusually skilful in controlling this aspect

of Trapnel as a *Fission* contributor. Not at all inexperienced himself in the exertions of extracting money, he knew all the arguments why Trapnel should not be given any more until he produced the goods. Bagshaw would put on an immensely good-natured act that represented him as a man no less necessitous than Trapnel himself, if not more so. Trapnel did not have to believe that, but it created some sort of protection for Bagshaw. That was when Trapnel appeared in person. As time went on, these personal visits decreased in frequency.

Living as he did, there were naturally times when Trapnel was forced to apply for a loan. Widmerpool was a case in point. One of the principles dearest to Trapnel was that, as a writer himself, he did not care to borrow from another writer; anyway not more than once. At a party consisting predominantly of writers and publishers—publishers naturally unsuitable for rather different reasons—Widmerpool was a tempting expedient. A man of strong principle in his own particular genre, Trapnel appears to have observed this self-imposed limitation to the best of his ability, circumstances from time to time perforce intervening. The fulfilment of this creed must have been strengthened by practical experience of the literary profession's collective deficiencies as medium for floating loans.

However, almost everyone had their story of being approached by Trapnel at one time or another: Mark Members: Alaric Kydd: L. O. Salvidge: Evadne Clapham: Bernard Shernmaker: Nathaniel Sheldon: Malcolm Crowding: even Len Pugsley. All had paid up. Among these Alaric Kydd took it the hardest. The 'touch' had been one afternoon, when Kydd and Trapnel had met at the Quiggin & Craggs office. They were moving northwards together in the direction of Tavistock Square, according to Kydd, who was very bitter about it afterwards. He had been particularly outraged by Trapnel's immediate offer of a drink, a piece of good-fellowship received not at all in the spirit proffered. Quiggin, whose relations with Kydd were not entirely friendly, although proud of him as a capture, told the story after.

'Alaric had my sympathy. The money was at one moment resting frugally and safely in his pocket—the next, scattered broadcast by Trapnel. Alaric wasn't going to stand Trapnel a drink with it, it's therefore logical he should object to Trapnel wasting it on a drink for him.'

Kydd's never wholly appeased rancour implied abstraction of a somewhat larger sum than customary. A tenner was normal. Quiggin, whose judgment on such matters was to be respected, put it as high as twelve or fifteen—possibly even twenty. He may have been right. He had just signed a cheque for Kydd. There must have been a battle of wills. Trapnel did not on the whole prejudice his own market by gleaning the odd five bob or half-a-crown, though there may have been fallings by the wayside in this respect when things were bad; even descent to sixpences and pennies, if it came to that, for his unceasing and interminable telephone calls from the afternoon drinking clubs he liked to frequent. Such dives appealed to him chiefly as social centres, when The Hero and other pubs were closed, because Trapnel, as drinking goes, was not a great consumer, though he chose to speak of himself as if he were. An exceptionally excited or demoralized mood was likely to be the consequence of his 'pills', also apparently taken in moderation, rather than alcohol.

'The habit of words bestows adroitness on men of letters in devising formulae of excuse in evading onerous obligations. More especially when it comes to parting with hard cash.'

St John Clarke had voiced that reflection—chronologically speaking, before the beginning of years—when Mark Members had managed to oust Quiggin from being the well-known novelist's secretary; himself to be replaced in turn by Guggenbühl. Members had goodish stories about his former master, particularly on the theme of handling needy acquaintances from the past, who called in search of financial aid. Members insisted that the sheer artistry of St John Clarke' pretexts claiming exemption from lending were so ornate in expression that they sometimes opened fresh avenues of attack for the quicker-witted of his persecutors.

'Many a literary parasite met his Waterloo in that sitting-room,' said Members. 'There were crises when shelling out seemed unavoidable. St J. always held out right up to the time he was himself remaindered by the Great Publisher. I wonder what luck X. Trapnel would have had on that stricken field of borrowers.'

It was an interesting question. Trapnel was just about old enough to have applied for aid before St John Clarke's passing. His panoramic memory for the plots of twentieth-century novels certainly retained all the better known of St John Clarke's works; as of almost every other novelist, good, bad or indifferent, published in Great Britain since the beginning of the century. As to the United States, Trapnel was less reliable, though he could put up a respectable display of familiarity with American novelists too; anyway since the end of the first war. An apt quotation from *Dust Thou Art* (in the College rooms), *Match Me Such Marvel* (Bithel's favourite) or the much more elusive *Mimosa* (brought to my notice by Trapnel himself), might well have done the trick, produced at the right moment by a young, articulate, undeniably handsome fan; the intoxicating sound to St John Clarke of his own prose repeated aloud bringing off the miracle of success, where so many tired old leathery hands at the game had failed. In the face of what might sound damaging, even contradictory evidence, Trapnel was no professional sponge in the manner of characters often depicted in nineteenth-century novels, borrowing compulsively and indiscriminately, while at the same time managing to live in comparative comfort. That was the picture Members painted of the St John Clarke petitioners, spectres from the novelist's younger, more haphazard days, who felt an old acquaintance had been allowed too long to exist in undisturbed affluence. Members had paused for a phrase. 'Somewhere between men of letters and blackmailers, a largely forgotten type.'

No one could say Trapnel resembled these. He neither lived comfortably, nor, once the need to take taxis were recognized, borrowed frivolously. Indeed, when things were going badly, there was nothing frivolous about Trapnel's condition except the manner in which he faced it. He borrowed literally to keep alive, a good example of something often unrecognized outside the world of books, that a writer can have his name spread all over the papers, at the same time net perhaps only a hundred pounds to keep him going until he next writes a book. Finally, the battle against all but overwhelming economic pressures might have been lost without the support of Trapnel's chief weapon—to use the contemporary euphemism 'moral deterrent'—the swordstick. The death's head, the concealed blade, in the last resort gained the day.

I have given a long account of Trapnel and his ways in order to set in perspective what happened later. Not all this description is derived from first-hand knowledge. Part is Trapnel legend, of which there was a good deal. He reviewed fairly regularly for *Fission*, wrote an occasional short story, article or parody—he was an accomplished parodist of his contemporaries—and on the whole, in spite of friction now and then, when he lost his temper with a book or one of his pieces was too long or too short, the magazine suited him, he the magazine. His own volume of collected short stories *Bin Ends* was published. Trapnel's reputation increased. At the same time he was clearly no stranger to what Burton called 'those excrementitious humours of the third concoction, blood and tears'.

One day the blow fell. Alaric Kydd's *Sweetskin* appeared on the shelf for review. Even Quiggin was known to have reservations about the novel's merits. Several supposedly outspoken passages made him unwilling to identify himself with the author in his accustomed manner, in case there was a prosecution. In addition to that, a lack of humdrum qualities likely to appeal to critics caused him worry about its reception. These anxieties Quiggin had already transmitted to Bagshaw. *Sweetskin* was a disappointing book. Kydd had been coaxed away from Clapham's firm. Now he seemed to be only a liability. On the one hand, the novel might be suppressed, the firm fined, a director possibly sent to gaol; on the other, the alleged lubricities being in themselves not sufficient to guarantee by any means a large sale, *Sweetskin* might easily not even pay off its considerable advance of royalties. How was the book to be treated in *Fission*? Kydd was too well known to be ignored completely. That would be worse than an offensive review. Who could be found, without too hopelessly letting down the critical reputation of *Fission* itself, to hold some balance between feelings on either side of the backyard at the Quiggin & Craggs office?

Then an opportune thing happened. Trapnel rang up Bagshaw, and asked if he could deal with Kydd, in whose early work he was interested, even though he thought the standard had not been maintained. If he could see *Sweetskin*, he might want to write a longer piece, saying something about Kydd's origins and development, in which the new book would naturally be mentioned. Bagshaw got in touch with me about this. It seemed the answer. Trapnel's representative came round the same afternoon to collect the review copy.

The following week, when I was at *Fission* 'doing' the books, Trapnel rang up. He said he was bringing the *Sweetskin* review along himself late that afternoon, and suggested we should have a drink together. There was something he particularly wanted to talk about. This was a fairly normal thing to happen, though the weather was not the sort to encourage hanging about in pubs. I also wanted to get back to Burton. However, Trapnel was unusually pressing. When he arrived he was in a jumpy state, hard to say whether pleased or exasperated. Like most great egoists, a bad arriver, he lacked ease until settled down into whatever rôle he was going to play. Something was evidently on his mind.

'Would you object to The Hero? That's the place I'd feel it easiest to tell you about this.'

If the object of the meeting was to disclose some intimate matter that required dissection, even allowing for Trapnel's reasonably competent control of his creatures, few worse places could be thought of, but the venue was clearly demanded by some quirk of pub mystique. These fears were unjustified. The immoderate cold had kept most of the usual customers away. The place was almost empty. We sat down. Trapnel looked round the saloon bar rather wildly. His dark-lensed spectacles brought to The Hero's draught-swept enclaves a hint of warmer shores, bluer skies, olives, vines, in spite of the fact that the turn-ups of the tussore trousers were soaked from contact with the snow. He at once began a diatribe against *Sweetskin*, his notice of which had been left unread at the office.

'I warned you it wasn't much good.'

This would mean embarrassment for Quiggin, if Trapnel had been unremittingly scathing. Coming on top of the 'touch', unfavourable comment from such a source would make Kydd more resentful than ever. However, that was primarily Quiggin's worry. So far as I was concerned the juggernaut of critical opinion must be allowed to take its irrefragable course. If too fervent worshippers, like Kydd, were crushed to powder beneath the pitiless wheels of its car, nothing could be done. Only their own adoration of the idol made them so vulnerable. Trapnel was specially contemptuous of Kydd's attempts at eroticism. To be fair, *Sweetskin* was in due course the object of prosecution, so presumably someone found the book erotic, but Trapnel became almost frenzied in his expostulations to the contrary. It was then suddenly revealed that Trapnel was in the middle of a row with Quiggin & Craggs.

'I thought you got on so well with Ada?'

Ada Leintwardine dealt with Trapnel in ordinary contacts with the firm. She did not control disposal of money —there Quiggin was called in—but questions of production, publicity, all such matters passed through her hands. Book production, as it happened, owing to shortage of paper and governmental restrictions of one kind or another, was at the lowest ebb in its history at this period. A subject upon which Trapnel held strong views, this potential area of difference might have led to trouble. Ada always smoothed things over. After the honeymoon following the transfer of *Camel Ride to the Tomb*, Trapnel and Craggs scarcely bothered to conceal the lack of sympathy they felt for one another. It looked as if Quiggin had now been swept into embroilment by Trapnel's tendency to get on bad terms with all publishers and editors.

In this connexion, Ada was an example of Trapnel's exemption from the need to captivate every woman with whom he came in contact. He would not necessarily have captivated Ada had he tried. Nothing was less likely. The point was that he did not try. He always emphasized his amicable relations with her, how much he preferred these to be on a purely business basis. This proved no more than that Ada was not Trapnel's sort of woman, Trapnel not Ada's sort of man, but, for someone who liked running other people's lives so much as Ada, to get on with Trapnel, who liked running his own, was certainly a recommendation for tact in doing business.

'Ada's all right. She's a grand girl. It isn't Ada who gets me down. She's always on my side. It's Craggs who's impossible. I feel pretty sure of that. He makes trouble in the background.'

'What sort of trouble?'

'Influencing JG.'

'*Bin Ends* went quite well?'

'All right. They've been looking at the first few chapters of *Profiles in String*—provisional title. I want some money while I'm writing it. I can't live on air.'

'Surely they'll advance something on what you've shown them?'

'They've given me a bit already, but I've got to exist while I write the bloody book.'

'You mean they won't unbelt any more?'

'I may have to approach another publisher.'

'You're under contract?'

'They like the new book all right, what there is. Like it very much. If they won't see reason, I may have to put the matter in the hands of my solicitors.'

Trapnel tapped the skull against the table. Talk about his solicitors always meant a highly nervous state. Even at the time of the monumental entanglement of the *conte*, it was doubtful whether legal processes had ever been carried further than consultation with old Tim Clipthorpe, one of the seasoned habitués of The Hero, his face covered with crimson blotches, who had been struck off the roll in the year the *Titanic* went down, as he was always telling any adjacent toper who would listen. In any case, Trapnel gave the impression that, as publishing rows go, this was not a specially serious one. Even if it were, he could hardly have brought a fellow-writer, not a particularly close friend, to shiver in the boreal chills of The Hero's saloon bar merely to confirm the parsimony of publishers; still less to listen to a critical onslaught against the amateurish pornography and slipshod prose of Alaric Kydd. Even Trapnel's egotism was hardly capable of that. He was, in fact, obviously playing for time, talking at random while he tried to screw himself up to making some more or less startling confession. Again he tapped the swordstick against the table.

'Don't let's talk about all this rot anyway. One of the things I wanted to tell you was that Tessa's walked out on me.'

That was much more the sort of thing to be expected. Even so, Tessa seemed a rather slender pretext for bringing about a portentous meeting such as this one. An attractive girl, she had shown early signs of finding the Trapnel way of life too much for her. Her departure was not a staggering surprise. Sympathy seemed best expressed by enquiry, though the answer was not in much doubt.

'How did it happen?'

'Yesterday—just left a note saying she was through.'

'Things had been getting difficult?'

'There was rather a scene last week. I thought it had all blown over. Apparently not. As a matter of fact I'm not sorry. I was fond of Tessa, but things have to have an end —at least most do.'

'Dowson said something of the sort in verse.'

Trapnel brushed aside further condolences, admittedly rather feeble ones, on the subject of the vicissitudes of love. He was, to say the least, bearing Tessa's abdication with fortitude. I was surprised at quite such a show of indifference, thinking some of it perhaps assumed. Trapnel, although resilient, was not at all heartless in such matters.

'Now Tessa's gone I'm faced with a decision.'

'Giving up women altogether?'

Trapnel laughed with rather conscious bitterness.

'I mean Tessa kept me from making an absolute fool of myself. Now I'm left without that support.'

He did not have the appearance of having indulged in a recent drinking bout, nor too many pep-pills, but was in such an unusual state that I began to wonder whether, after all, Ada was at the bottom of all this; that I had been summoned to give advice on the uncommon situation of an author falling in love with his publisher. The suspicion became almost a certainty when Trapnel leant forward and spoke dramatically, almost in a whisper.

'Nick, I'm absolutely mad about somebody.'

'A replacement for Tessa?'

'No—nothing like that. Nothing like Tessa at all. This is love. The genuine thing. I've never known what it was before. Not really. Now I do.'

This was going a little far. He spoke with complete gravity, though he and I were not at all on the terms when revelations of that kind are volunteered. Trapnel's emotional life, if proffered at all, was as a rule dished up with a light dressing of irony or melancholy. He was never brutal; on the other hand, he was never severely stricken. From the outside he appeared a reasonably adoring lover, if not an unduly serious one. The attitude maintained that night in The Hero was different from anything previously handed out. I had made up my mind to leave very soon now, almost at once. If Trapnel wanted to make a statement, he must get on with the job, do it expeditiously. The night was too cold to hang about any longer, while he braced himself to set forth in detail this amatory crisis, whatever it might be.

'Why isn't this one like Tessa?'

Instead of answering the question, Trapnel opened *Sweetskin* again. He removed from its pages the review slip, which notes date of publication, together with the request (never in the history of criticism vouchsafed) that the publisher should be sent a copy of the notice when it appeared in print. This small square of paper had been inserted earlier by Trapnel to mark a passage of notable ineptitude to be read aloud as illustration of Kydd's inability to write with grace, distinction or knowledge of the ways of women. He had recited the paragraph a few minutes before. Now he took one of several pens from the outside breast pocket of the tropical jacket, quickly wrote something on the back of the slip of paper, and passed it across to me. On examination, this enigmatic missive disclosed two words inscribed in Trapnel's small decorative script, of which he was rather proud. I read them without at first understanding why my attention should be drawn to this name.

Pamela Widmerpool

The whole procedure had been so odd, I was so cold and bored, the final flourish so unexpected—although in one sense Trapnel at his most Trapnelesque—that I did not immediately grasp the meaning of this revealment, if revealment it were.

'What about her?'

Trapnel did not speak at once. He looked as if he could not believe he had heard the words correctly. I asked again. He smiled and shook his head.

'That's whom I'm in love with.'

No comment seemed anywhere near adequate. This was beyond all limits. Burton well expressed man's subjection to passion. To recall his words gave some support now. 'The scorching beams under the *Æquinoctial*, or extremity of cold within the circle of the *Arctick*, where the very Seas are frozen, cold or torrid zone cannot avoid, or expel this heat, fury and rage of mortal men.' No doubt that was just how Trapnel felt. His face showed that he saw this climax as the moment of truth, one of those high-spots in the old silent films that he liked to recall, some terrific consummation emphasized by several seconds of monotonous music rising louder and louder, until, almost deafening, the notes suddenly jar out of tune in a frightful discord: the train is derailed: the canoe swept over the rapids: the knife plunged into the naked flesh. All is over. The action is cut: calm music again, perhaps no music at all.

'Of course I know I'm mad. I don't stand a chance. That's one of the reasons why the situation's nothing like Tessa—or any other girl I've ever been mixed up with. I admit it's not sane. I admit that from the start.'

If things had gone so far that Trapnel could not even pronounce the name of the woman he loved, had to write it down on a review slip, the situation must indeed be acute. I laughed. There seemed nothing else to do. That reaction was taken badly by Trapnel. He had some right to be offended after putting on such an act. That could not be helped. He looked half-furious, half-upset. As he was inclined to talk about his girls only after they had left, there was no measure for judging the norm of his feelings when they were first sighted. Possibly he was always as worked up as at that moment, merely that I had never been the confidant. That seemed unlikely. Even if he showed the same initial excitement, the incongruity of making Pamela his aim was something apart.

'You didn't much take to her at the *Fission* party.'

'Of course I didn't. I thought her the most awful girl I'd ever met.'

'What brought about the change?'

'I was in Ada's room looking through my press-cuttings. Mrs Widmerpool suddenly came in. She's an old friend of Ada's. I hadn't known that. She didn't bother to be announced from the downstairs office, just came straight up to Ada's room. She wanted to telephone right away. I was standing there talking to Ada about the cuttings. Mrs Widmerpool didn't take any notice of me. I might just as well not have been there, far less chatted with her at a party. Ada told her my name again, but she absolutely cut me. She went to the telephone, at once began cursing the girl at the switchboard for her slowness. When she got the number, it was to bawl out some man who'd sent her a jar of pickled peaches as a present. She said they were absolutely foul. She'd thrown them down the lavatory. She fairly gave him hell.'

'That stole your heart away?'

'Something did. Nick, I'm not joking. I'm mad about her. I'd do anything to see her again.'

'Did you converse after the telephoning?'

'That's what I'm coming to. We did talk. Ada asked her if she'd read the *Camel*. My God, she had—and liked it. She was—I don't know—almost as if she were shy all at once. Utterly different from what she'd been at the party, or even a moment before in the room. She behaved as if she quite liked me, but felt it would be wrong to show it. That was the moment when the thing hit me. I didn't know what to do. I felt quite ill with excitement. I mean both randy, and sentimentally in love with her too. I was wondering whether I'd ask both her and Ada to have a drink with me before lunch—perhaps borrow ten bob from Ada and pay her back later in the afternoon, because I was absolutely cleaned out at the moment of speaking—then Mrs Widmerpool suddenly remembered she was lunching with some lucky devil, and had told him to be at the restaurant at twelve-thirty, it being then a good bit after one o'clock. She went away, but quite unhurried. She knew he'd wait. What can I do? I'm crazy about her.'

Trapnel paused. The story still remained beyond comment. However, it was apparently not at an end. Something else too was on Trapnel's mind. Now he looked a shade embarrassed, a rare condition for him.

'You remember I talked to her husband at that party? We got on rather well. I can never think of him as her husband, but all the same he is, and something happened which I wish had never taken place.'

'If you mean you borrowed a quid off him, I know—he told me.'

'He did? In that case I feel better about it. The taxi absorbed my last sixpence. I had to get back to West Kilburn that night by hook or crook. I won't go into the reason why, but it was the case. I'd walked there once from Piccadilly, and preferred not to do it again. That was why I did a thing I don't often do, and got a loan from a complete stranger. The fact was it struck me as I was leaving the party that Mr Widmerpool had been so kind in listening to me—expressed such humane views on housing and such things—that he wouldn't mind helping me over a temporary difficulty. I was embarrassed at having to do so. I think Mr Widmerpool was a bit embarrassed too. He didn't know what I meant at first.'

Trapnel laughed rather apologetically. It was possible to recognize a conflict of feelings. As a writer, he could perfectly appreciate the funny side of taking a pound off Widmerpool; the whole operation looked like a little exercise in the art, introducing himself, making a good impression, bringing off the 'touch'. He had probably waited to leave the party until he saw Widmerpool going down the stairs, instinct guiding him as to the dole that would not be considered too excessive to withhold. At the same time, as a borrower, Trapnel had to keep up a serious attitude towards borrowing. He could not admit the whole affair had been a prepared scheme from the start. Finally, as a lover, he had put himself in a rather absurd relation to the husband of the object of his affections. To confess that showed how far Trapnel's defences were down. He returned to the subject of Pamela.

'Ada says they don't get on too well together. She told me that when I dropped in again on the office the following day. A man who looks like that couldn't appreciate such a marvellous creature.'

'Did you tell Ada how you felt?'

'Not on your life. There's a lot of argument going on about the new novel, as I mentioned, quite apart from notices still coming in for *Bin Ends*. It was perfectly natural for me to look in again. As a matter of fact Ada began to speak of Mrs Widmerpool herself as soon as I arrived. I just sat and listened.'

'Ada's pretty smart at guessing.'

'She doesn't guess how I feel. I know she doesn't. She couldn't have said some of the things she did, if she had. I was very careful not to give anything away—you won't either, Nick, will you? I don't want anyone else to know. But how on earth am I to see her again.'

'Go and pay Widmerpool back his quid, I suppose.'

This frivolous, possibly even heartless comment was made as a mild call to order, a suggestion so unlikely to be followed that it would emphasize the absurdity of Trapnel's situation. That was not at all the way he took it. On the contrary, the proposal immediately struck him not only as seriously put forward, but a scheme of daring originality. No doubt the proposal was indeed original in the sense that repayment of a loan had never occurred to Trapnel as a measure to be considered.

'Christ, what a marvellous idea. You mean I'd call at their place and hand back the pound?'

He pondered this extravagant—literally extravagant—possibility.

'But what would Mr Widmerpool say if he happened to be there when I turned up? He'd think it a bit odd.'

'Even if he did, he'd be unlikely to refuse a pound. A very pleasant surprise.'

Even then it never occurred to me that Trapnel would take this unheard-of step.

'God, what a brilliant idea.'

We both laughed at such a flight of fancy. Trapnel's condition of tension slightly relaxed. Sanity seemed now at least within sight. All the same, he continued to play with the idea of seeing Pamela again.

'I'll get on the job right away.'

There seemed more than a possibility that the pound, so improbably required for potential return to Widmerpool, might be requested then and there, whether or not it ever found its way back into Widmerpool's pocket. The fact no such demand was made may have been as much due to Trapnel's disinclination to borrow in an obviously unornamental manner, as his rule that application to another writer was reluctant. His attack on such occasions was apt to be swift, imperative, self-assured, never less than correct in avoiding a precursory period of uneasy anticipation, often unequivocally brilliant in being utterly unexpected until the last second; at the same time never intrusive, even in the eyes of those perfectly conversant with Trapnel's habits. In the nature of things he met with rebuff as well as acquiescence—the parallel of seduction inevitably suggests itself—but there had been many successes. On this occasion probably Quiggin & Craggs, worsted in the current wrangle about advances, would pay up; anyway a pound. Paradoxical as that might seem, getting the money would be the least of Trapnel's problems, if, in the spirit in which he had first accosted Widmerpool, he wanted to add a grotesque end to the story by settling the debt.

'I can't thank you enough.'

He fell into deep thought, adopting now a different, rather dramatically conscious style. Having derived all that was needed from our meeting, his mind was devoted to future plans. I told him circumstances prevented my staying longer at The Hero. Trapnel nodded absently. I left him, his glass of beer still three-quarters full, rested precariously on the copy of *Sweetskin*. On the way home the whole affair struck me as reminiscent of Rowland Gwatkin, my former Company Commander, revealing at Castlemallock Anti-Gas School his love for a barmaid. Gwatkin's military ambition was narrow enough compared with Trapnel's soaring aspirations about being a 'complete man' and more besides. At the amatory level there was no comparison. Nevertheless, something existed in common, some lack of fulfilment, as Pennistone would say, 'in a higher unity'. Besides, if Trapnel's medical category—not to mention a thousand ineligibilities of character—had not precluded him from recommendation for a commission, no doubt he too would have shared Gwatkin's warlike dreams; a dazzling flying career added to the other personal targets.

After that night Trapnel disappeared. His work for *Fission* continued. The stooges came into play, delivering reviews or other pieces, collecting books and cheques, bringing suggestions for further items. Trapnel himself was no longer available. According to Bagshaw, he even ceased to pursue the question of further payment to assist the completion of *Profiles in String*. Use of surrogates did not prevent complicated negotiations taking place in relation to *Fission* contributions. For example, Trapnel suggested withdrawing what he had written about *Sweetskin*, and replacing the review with a parody. Bagshaw liked the idea. It was better for his own relations with Quiggin that Kydd's novel should not be torn to shreds; better, if it came to that, from my own standpoint too. Alaric Kydd himself might not be altogether pleased to be treated in this fashion, but, a prosecution now pending, he had other things to think about. In any case *Sweetskin* would enjoy more space than in a notice of normal length. Trapnel's lightness of touch in showing up Kydd's weak points as a novelist indicated that the hysterical feelings displayed at The Hero had calmed down; at least infatuation with Pamela had left his talent unimpaired. Possibly this hopeless passion had already been apportioned to the extensive storehouse of forgotten Trapnel fantasies.

Sweetskin was not the only book to cause Quiggin & Craggs worry. Bagshaw reported a serious row blowing up about *Sad Majors*. Here the complexities of politics, rather than those of sex, impinged on purely commercial considerations. Bagshaw was very much at home in this atmosphere. He talked a lot about the Odo Stevens manuscript, which he had been allowed to read, and described as 'full of meat'. However, although written in a lively manner, some of the material dealing with the Communist guerillas with whom Stevens had been in contact was at least as outspoken in its field as Kydd on the subject of sex.

'It appears a British officer operating with a rival Resistance group got rather mysteriously liquidated. Accidents will happen even with the best-regulated secret police. Of course a lot of Royalists were shot, and quite a fair number of people who weren't exactly Royalists, not to mention a crowd of heretical Communists too, the whole party ending, as we all know, in wholesale arrests and deportations. This is, of course, rather awkward for a firm of progressive tone. JG thinks it can be hoovered over satisfactorily. He wants to do the book, because it will sell, but Howard's against. He saw at once there'd be a lot of trouble, if the material appeared in its present form.'

'What will happen?'

'Gypsy won't hear of it.'

'What's Gypsy got to do with it?'

'It's her affair, isn't it, if what Stevens has said is damaging to the Party? She's bloody well consulted, apart from anything else, because Howard's afraid of her—actually physically afraid. He knows about one or two things Gypsy's arranged in her day. So do I. I don't blame him.'

'Have they turned the book down?'

'They're arguing it out.'

The weather was still unthawed when, a month or two later, I dined with Roddy Cutts at the House of Commons. Spring should have been on the way by then, but there was no sign. Our respective wives were both to give birth any day now. Roddy had suggested having a night out together to relieve the strain. A night out with Roddy carried no implications of outrageous dissipation. We talked most of the time about family affairs. He had seen Hugo Tolland the day before, who had been staying at Thrubworth, bringing back an account of how Siegfried, the German POW, was every day growing in local stature.

'Siegfried gives regular conjuring displays now in the village hall. There's talk of his getting engaged to one of Skerrett's granddaughters. He'll be nursing the constituency before we know where we are. Well, I suppose it's about time to be getting along. I'll just see how the debate's going before we make for home.'

Roddy Cutts's large handsome face always became drawn with anxiety when, at the close of any party at which he had been host, he glanced at the bill. This time the look indicated the worst; that he was ruined; parliamentary career at an end; he would have to sell up; probably emigrate. An extravagant charge would certainly have been out of place. Whatever the shock, Roddy made no comment. He dejectedly searched through pocket after pocket in apparently vain attempts to find a sum adequate to meet so severe a demand on a man's resources. The second round through, one of the waistcoat pockets yielded a five-pound note. He smoothed out its paper on the table.

'Give my love to Isobel, and hopes that all will be well.'

'And mine to Susie.'

The change arrived. Roddy sorted it lethargically, at the same time giving the impression that the levy might have been less disastrous than at first feared. His manner of picking up coins and examining them used to irritate our brother-in-law George Tolland. We rose from the table, exchanging the claustrophobic pressures of the hall, where the meal had been eaten, for a no less viscous density of parliamentary smoking-rooms and lobbies, suffocating, like all such precincts, with the omnipresent and congealed essence of public contentions and private egotisms; breath of life to their frequenters. Roddy's personality always took on a new dimension within these walls.

'If you'll wait for a minute in the central lobby, I'll just hear how National Assistance Payments are going.'

Callot-like figures pervaded labyrinthine corridors. Cavernous alcoves were littered with paraphernalia of scaffolding and ropes, Piranesian frameworks hinting of torture and execution, but devised only to repair bomb damage to structure and interior ornament. Roddy reappeared.

'Come along.'

We crossed the top of the flight of steps leading down into St Stephen's Hall, the stairs seeming to offer a kind of emergency exit from contemporary affairs into a mysterious submerged world of mediaeval shadows, tempting to explore if one were alone, in spite of icy draughts blowing up from these spectral depths. Suddenly, from the opposite direction to which we were walking, Widmerpool appeared. He was pacing forward slowly, deliberately, solemnly, swinging his arms in a regular motion from the body, as if carefully balancing himself while he trod a restricted bee-line from one point to another. At first he was too deep in thought to notice our advance towards him. Roddy shouted a greeting.

'Widmerpool, just the man I'm looking for.'

He could never resist accosting anyone he knew, and buttonholing them. Now he began a long dissertation about 'pairing'. Surprised out of his own meditations, Widmerpool seemed at first only aware that he was being addressed by a fellow MP. A second later he grasped the linked identities of Roddy and myself, our relationship, the fact that were brothers-in-law evidently striking him at once as a matter of significance to himself. He brushed aside whatever Roddy was talking about—conversation in any case designed to keep alive a contact with a member of the other side, rather than reach a conclusion—beginning to speak of another subject that seemed already on his mind, possibly the question he had been so deeply pondering.

'I'm glad to come on you both. First of all, my dear Cutts, I wanted to approach you regarding a little non-party project I have on hand—no, no, not the Roosevelt statue—it is connected with an Eastern European cultural organization in which I am interested. However, before we come to public concerns, there are things to be settled about the late Lord Warminster's letter of instructions. They are rather complicated—personal rather than legal bearings, though the Law comes in—so that to explain some of the points to you might save a lot of correspondence in the future. You could then pass on the information by word of mouth to your appropriate relatives, decisions thereby reached in a shorter time.'

Roddy showed attention to the phrase 'non-party project', but, with the professional politician's immediate instinct for executing a disengaging movement from responsibilities that promised only unrewarding exertion, he at once began to deny all liability for sorting out the problems of Erridge's bequests.

'Nicholas and I have no status in the matter whatsoever,

my dear Widmerpool, you must address yourself to Hugo or Frederica. They are the people. Either Hugo or Frederica will put you right in a trice.'

Widmerpool must have been prepared for that answer, actually expecting it, because he smiled at the ease with which such objections could be overruled by one of his long experience.

'Of course, of course. I perfectly appreciate that aspect, Cutts, that you and Nicholas are without authority in the matter. You are correct to stress the fact. The point I put forward is that the normal course of action would result in a vast deal of letter-writing between Messrs Turnbull, Welford & Puckering, Messrs Quiggin & Craggs, Messrs Goodness-knows-who-else. I propose to cut across that. I had quite enough of shuffling the bumf round when I was in the army. As a result I've developed a positive mania these days against pushing paper. Man-to-man. That's the way. Cut corners. I fear pomposity is not one of my failings. I can't put up with pompous people, and have often been in trouble on that very account.'

Roddy was determined not to be outdone in detestation of pomposity and superfluous formality. For a moment the two MPs were in sharp competition as to whose passion for direct- ness and simplicity was the more heartfelt, at least could be the more forcibly expressed. At the end of this contest Widmerpool carried his point.

'Therefore I suggest you forget the official executors for the moment, and accompany me back to my flat for the space of half an hour, where we can deal with the War- minster file, also discuss the small non-party committee I propose to form. No, no, Cutts, I brook no refusal. You can both be of inestimable help in confirming the right line is being taken regarding post-mortem wishes, I mean a line acceptable to the family. As a matter of fact you may both be interested to learn more of your late brother-in-law's system of opinion, his intellectual quirks, if I may use the phrase.'

Curiosity on that last point settled the matter. Roddy enjoyed nothing better than having a finger in any pie that happened to be cooking. Here were at least two. It was agreed that we should do as Widmerpool wished.

'Come along then. It's just round the corner. Only a step. We may as well walk—especially as there are likely to be no taxis.'

Along the first stretch of Victoria Street, dimly lighted and slippery, Roddy and Widmerpool discussed $2\frac{1}{2}\%$ Treasury Stock Redeemable after 1975; by the time we reached the flats, they had embarked on the topic of whether or not, as Governor of the Bank of England, Montagu Norman had adequately controlled the 'acceptance houses'. The entrance, rather imposing, was a high archway flanked by gates. This led into a small court-yard, on the far side of which stood several associated masses of heavy Edwardian building. It was a cheerless spot. I asked if Short still lived here.

'You know Leonard Short? He's just below us. Very convenient it should be so. He's a good little fellow, Short. My Minister has a high opinion of him.'

'Who is your Minister?'

Even Roddy was rather appalled by this ignorance, hastening to explain that Widmerpool had been appointed not long before Personal Private Secretary to a member of the Cabinet; the one, in fact, who had attended the Quiggin & Craggs party, the Minister responsible for the branch of the civil service to which Short belonged. Widmerpool himself showed no resentment at this lapse, merely laughing heartily, and enlarging on his own duties.

'As PPS one's expected to take an intelligent interest in the ministry concerned. The presence there of Leonard Short oils the wheels for me. We're quite an intellectual crowd here. I expect you've heard of Clapham, the publisher, who lives in another of the flats. You may even know him. He is a good type of the old-fashioned publishing man. I find his opinions worthy of attention now I have a stake in that business myself. There's nothing flashy about Clapham, neither intellectually nor socially. He was speaking to me about St John Clarke the other night, whom he knew well, and, so he tells me, still enjoys a very respectable sale.'

The hall was in darkness. There was a lift, but Widmerpool guided us past it.

'I must remind you electricity is now in short supply—shedding the load, as we have learnt to call it. The Government has the matter well in hand, but our lift here, an electric one, is for the moment out of action. You will not mind the stairs. Only a few flights. A surprisingly short way in the light of the excellent view we enjoy on a clear day. Pam is always urging a move. We have decided in principle to do so, inspected a great deal of alternative accommodation, but there is convenience in proximity to the House. Besides, I'm used to the flat, with its special characteristics, some good, some less admirable. For the time being, therefore, it seems best to remain where we are. That's what I'm always telling Pam.'

By this time we had accomplished a couple of flights.

'How is Mrs Widmerpool?' asked Roddy. 'I remember she was feeling unwell at the funeral.'

'My wife's health was not good a year ago. It has improved. I can state that with confidence. In fact during the last month I have never known her better—well, one can say in better spirits. She is a person rather subject to moods. She changes from one moment to the next.'

Roddy, probably thinking of the cipherine nodded heartily. Widmerpool took a key from his pocket. He paused before the door. Talk about Pamela had unsettled him.

174

'I don't expect Pam will have gone to bed yet. She does sometimes turn in early, especially if she has a headache, or it's been an exhausting day for her. At other times she sits up quite late, indeed long after I've retired to rest myself. We shall see.'

He sounded rather nervous about what the possibilities might be. The small hall was at once reminiscent of the flat—only a short way from here—where Widmerpool had formerly lived with his mother. I asked after her. He did not seem over pleased by the enquiry.

'My mother is still living with relations in the Lowlands. There's been some talk lately of her finding a place of her own. I have not seen her recently. She is, of course, not so young as she was. We still have our old jokes about Uncle Joe in our letters, but in certain other aspects she finds it hard to realize things have changed.'

'Uncle Joe?'

'My mother has always been a passionate admirer of Marshal Stalin, a great man, whatever people may say. We had jokes about if he were to become a widower. At the same time, she would probably have preferred me to remain single myself. She is immensely gratified to have a son in the House of Commons—always her ambition to be mother of an MP—but she is inclined to regard a wife as handicap to a career.'

Widmerpool lowered his tone for the last comment. The lights were on all over the flat, the sound of running water audible. No one seemed to be about. Widmerpool listened, his head slightly to one side, with the air of a Red Indian brave seeking, on the tail of the wind, the well-known, but elusive, scent of danger. The splashing away of the water had a calming effect.

'Ah, Pam's having a bath. She was expecting my return rather later than this. I'll just report who's here. Go in and sit down.'

He spoke as if relieved to hear nothing more ominous was on foot than his wife having a bath, then disappeared down the passage. Roddy and I entered the sitting-room. The tone of furniture and decoration was anonymous, though some sort of picture rearrangement seemed to be in progress. The central jets of a gas fire were lighted, but the curtains were undrawn, a window open. Roddy closed it. Two used glasses stood on a table. There was no sign of whatever had been drunk from them. From the other end of the passage a loud knocking came, where Widmerpool was announcing our arrival. Apparently no notice was taken, because the taps were not turned off, and, to rise above their sound, he had to shout our names at the top of his voice. Pamela's reactions could not be heard. Widmerpool returned.

'I expect Pam will look in later. Probably in her dressing-gown—which I hope you will excuse.'

'Of course.'

Roddy looked as if he could excuse that easily. Widmerpool glanced round the room and made a gesture of simulated exasperation.

'She's been altering the pictures again. Pam loves doing that—especially shifting round that drawing her uncle Charles Stringham left her. I can never remember the artist's name. An Italian.'

'Modigliani.'

'That's the one—ah, there's been a visitor, I see. I'll fetch the relevant documents.'

The sight of the two glasses seemed to depress him again. He fetched some papers. Kneeling down in front of the gas fire, he tried to ignite the outer bars, but they failed to respond. Widmerpool gave it up. He began to explain the matter in hand. Erridge, among other dispositions, had expressed the wish that certain books which had 'influenced' him should, if out of print, be reissued by the firm of Quiggin & Craggs. To what extent such republication was practicable had to be considered in the light of funds available from the Trust left by Erridge. Nothing was conditional. Widmerpool explained that the copyright situation was being examined. At present adjudication was not yet possible in certain cases; others were already announced as to be reissued elsewhere. Subsequent works on the same subject, political or economic—even more often events—had put Erridge's old favourites out of date. On the whole, as Widmerpool had promised, the answers could be effectively dealt with in this manner, though several required brief consideration and discussion. We had just come to the end of the business, Widmerpool made facetious reference to the propriety of canvassing Parliamentary matters, even non-party ones, in the presence of a member of the public, when the door bell rang. Widmerpool looked irritable at this.

'Who on earth can it be? Not one of Pam's odd friends at this hour of the night, I hope. They are capable of anything.'

He went to open the door.

'We don't need to waste any more time here,' said Roddy. 'The Erry stuff is more or less cleared up. The non-party project can be ventilated when Widmerpool and I next meet in the House. I don't want to freeze to death. Let's make a getaway while he's engaged.'

I was in agreement. Widmerpool continued to talk with whoever had come to the front door of the flat. Although he had left the door of the sitting-room open, the subject of their conversation could not be heard owing to the sound of the bath water, still running, or perhaps turned on again. It occurred to me that Pamela, with her taste for withdrawal from company, might deliberately have taken refuge in the bathroom on hearing the sound of our arrival; then turned on the taps to give the impression that a bath was in progress. Such procedure might even be a matter of routine on her part to avoid guests after a parliamentary sitting. The supposition was strengthened by Widmerpool's own lack of surprise at her continued absence. It was like a mythological story: a nymph for ever running a bath that never filled, while her husband or lover waited for her to emerge. Now Roddy was getting impatient.

'Come on. Don't let's hang about.'

We went out into the passage. The visitor turned out to be Short. He looked worried. Although only come from the floor below, apparently to deliver a message, he had taken the precaution of wearing an overcoat and scarf. Whatever the message was had greatly disturbed Widmerpool. One wondered if the Government had fallen, though scarcely likely within the time that had passed since we had left the House of Commons. Our sudden appearance from the sitting-room made Short even less at ease than he was already. He muttered some sort of a good evening. I introduced Roddy, as Widmerpool seemed scarcely aware that we had joined them. Before more could be said, evidently returning to the subject in hand, Widmerpool broke in again.

'How long ago did you say this was?'

'About an hour or two, as I told you. The message was just as I passed it on.'

Short was infinitely, unspeakably embarrassed. Widmerpool looked at him for a moment, then turned away. He walked hurriedly up the passage, lost to sight at the right-angle of its end. A door opened noisily from the direction of the running water. The sound of the flow ceased a moment later. The taps had been turned off sharply. Another door was opened. There came the noise of things being thrown about. Short blew his nose. Roddy got his overcoat and handed me mine. I asked Short what had happened.

'It was just a message left for Kenneth by his wife. She rang the bell of my flat about an hour ago, and asked me to deliver it.'

Short stopped. Whatever the message was had seriously upset him. That left us none the wiser. Short seemed for a moment uncertain whether or not to reveal his secret. Then it became too much for him. He cleared his throat and lowered his voice.

'As a matter of fact the message was—"I've left". We don't know each other at all well. I thought she must mean she was going to catch a train, or something of that sort. Had been delayed, and wanted her husband to know the time of her departure.'

'You mean left for good?'

Short nodded once or twice, almost to himself, in a panic-stricken manner. There could be no doubt that one side of his being had been immensely excited by becoming so closely involved in such a drama; another, appalled by all the implications of disorganization, wrongdoing and scandal. Before more could be told, Widmerpool returned.

'It was very thoughtless of her to have forgotten to turn the bath tap off. The hot one too. Nobody in the place will get any hot water for weeks. You know, Leonard, she must have made this arrangement to go away on the spur of the moment.'

'That's just what it looked like.'

Short spoke as if he saw a gleam of hope.

'She often acts like that. I deprecate it, but what can I do? I see she has taken both her suitcases. They must have been quite heavy, as most of her clothes have gone too. Did you help carry them down?'

'The man was carrying them.'

'Do you mean the porter? I thought he was having flu?'

'Not the regular porter. It might have been the taxi-driver or someone driving a hired car. Perhaps they have a temporary man downstairs.'

'I mean it was not just a friend?'

'He hardly looked like a friend.'

'What was he like?'

'He had a beard. He was carrying the two bags. Your wife had a stick or umbrella under her arm, and two or three pictures.'

This piece of information agitated Widmerpool more than anything that had gone before. Short appeared unable to know what to think. Before Widmerpool's return his words certainly suggested that he himself supposed Pamela had left for good; then Widmerpool's demeanour seemed almost to convince him that this was no more than a whim of the moment to go off and visit friends. Now he was back where he started.

'Repeat to me again exactly what she said.'

'"Tell him I'm leaving, and taking the Modigliani and the photographs of myself. He can do what he likes with the rest of my junk."'

'Nothing more?'

'Of course I supposed she was referring to some domestic arrangement you knew about already, that she wanted to inform you of the precise minute she had vacated the flat. I wondered if you had even taken another one. You have always talked of that. It looked as if she might be starting to move into it.'

Short sounded desperate. He must have been to talk like that. Roddy was desperate too, but only to get away. He was taking no interest whatever in the matter discussed. Now he could stand it no longer.

'Look, my dear Widmerpool, it's really awfully cold tonight. I think I'll have to be getting back, as I want to know how my wife is faring. She's expecting a baby, you know. Not quite yet, but you never can be certain with these little beggars. They sometimes decide to be early. We can have a word about your project in the smoking-room some time—over a drink perhaps.'

Widmerpool behaved very creditably. He accepted, probably with relief, that Roddy was not in the least interested in his affairs.

'Most grateful to you both for having looked in, and run over those points. All I want you to do now is to pass on the proposed decisions informally to the executors. If they have any objections, they can let me know. Then we can get the items sorted out. I'm sorry the evening has been interrupted in this way. We'll discuss the non-party matter on another occasion, Cutts. I must offer my apologies. There is nothing Pam enjoys more than mystifying people—especially her unfortunate husband. Goodnight, goodnight. Come into the flat for a moment, Leonard.'

What he was thinking was not revealed. Control of himself showed how far married life had inured him to sudden discomposing circumstances. If he believed that Pamela had deserted him without intention of return—it was hard to think anything else had happened—he kept his head. Perhaps her departure was after all a relief. It was impossible to guess; nor whether Trapnel was by now a figure known to him in his wife's entourage. Short did not look at all willing to enter the flat for yet another rehash of his encounter with Pamela, but Widmerpool was insistent. He would not accept a denial on account of work with which Short was engaged. Roddy and I took leave of them, and set off down the stairs. Neither of us spoke until we reached the street. Roddy then showed some faint curiosity as to what had been happening.

'What was it? I was too cold to take it in.'

'It looks as if his wife's gone off with a man called X. Trapnel.'

'Never heard of him.'

'He writes novels.'

'Like you?'

'Yes.'

'Is he one of her lovers?'

'So it appears.'

'I gather they abound.'

'All the same, this is a bit of a surprise.'

'God—there's a taxi.'

Not so very long after that evening, Isobel gave birth to a son; Susan Cutts, to a daughter. These events within the family, together with other comings and goings, not to mention the ever-pervading Burton, distracted attention from exterior events. Even allowing for such personal pre-occupations, the whole Widmerpool affair, that is to say his wife's abandonment of him, made far less stir than might be expected. There were several reasons for this. In the first place, that Widmerpool should marry a girl like Pamela Flitton had been altogether unexpected; that she should leave him was another matter. Nothing could be more predictable, the only question—with whom? A certain amount of gossip went round when it became known they were no longer under the same roof, but, the awaited climax having taken place, the question of the lover's identity was not an altogether easy one to answer; nor particularly interesting when answered, for those kept alive by such nourishment. Few people who knew Widmerpool also knew Trapnel, the reverse equally true. Besides, could it be stated with certainty that Pamela was living with Trapnel?

Everyone agreed that, even if Pamela had embarked on a romance with Trapnel, however unlikely that might be, nothing was, on the other hand, more probable than that she had left him immediately after. All that could be said for certain was that both had utterly disappeared from sight. That at least was definite. Accordingly, the physical presence of two lovers did not, by public appearance, draw attention to open adultery. In the circumstances, interest waned. The question of 'taking sides', in general so much adding to public concern with such predicaments, here scarcely arose, husband and lover inhabiting such widely separated worlds. There was some parallel to the time, years before, when Mona had left Peter Templer for J. G. Quiggin.

A further reason for the story to develop a strangely muffled character, almost as if leaked through a kind of censorship, was the hard work Widmerpool himself put in to lower the outside temperature. However he might inwardly regard the situation, as an MP he was understandably anxious to play down such a blemish on the life of a public man. Just as he had done to Short on the night of Pamela's departure, he emphasized through all possible channels his wife's undoubted eccentricity, circulating anecdotes about her to suggest that she was doing no more than taking a brief holiday from married life. She would return when she thought fit. That was Widmerpool's line. Her husband, knowing her strange ways, paid little attention. In the end more people than might be expected pretty well accepted that explanation. It was a trump card. At first that was not so apparent as it became later.

Of course a friend of Pamela's like Ada Leintwardine— a position in which Ada was, as a woman, probably unique —was thrown into a great state of commotion when the news, such as it was, broke. It was confirmed by L. O. Salvidge to the extent that two or three weeks before he had seen Trapnel in The Hero, accompanied by a very beautiful girl with a pale face and dark hair. They had stayed in the saloon bar only a few seconds, not even ordering drinks. Trapnel wanted to make some arrangement with one of the auxiliaries. Salvidge's information predated the night at Widmerpool's. Ada conceded not only that she had now lost all touch with Pamela, but—an unexampled admission on Ada's part—could claim no suspicion whatever as to what must have been going on. This amounted to confession that, however profound her own powers of intuition, they had fallen short of paramountcy in probing this particular sequence of emotional development. All she had supposed was that Trapnel had been 'rather intrigued' by Pamela; the notion that he should sufficiently flatter himself as to allow dreams of her mastery was something quite beyond credibility. Ada's alliance with Pamela had, in fact, never taken the form of frequentation of the Widmerpool household. They had just been 'girls together' outside Pamela's married life. Ada continually repeated her disbelief.

'It can't really be Trapnel.'

Not only did Trapnel himself no longer appear at the *Fission* office, his representatives now dropped off too. Bagshaw had recently retired to bed with flu. For once the new number was fully made up, left to be seen through the press by the latest secretary, a red-haired, freckled girl called Judy, whom Bagshaw himself had produced from somewhere or other, alleging that she was not at all stupid, but unreliable at spelling. Judy had just brought in a stack of advance copies of the magazine when in due course I arrived to carry out the normal stint with the books. These were being examined by Quiggin and Ada, who were both on the *Fission* side of the backyard.

Quiggin, possibly under the influence of Ada, had now for the most part abandoned his immediately post-war trappings suggesting he had just come in from skirmishing with a sten-gun in the undergrowth, though traces remained in a thick grey shirt. On the whole he had settled for a no-nonsense middle-aged intellectual's style of dress, a new suit in dark check and bow tie, turn-out better suited to his station as an aspiring publisher. Ada was laughing at what they were reading, Quiggin less certain that he was finding the contribution funny. He had taken his hands from the jacket pockets of the check suit, and was straightening the lapels rather uneasily.

'There's going to be a row,' said Ada.

She was pleased rather than the reverse by that prospect. Quiggin himself seemed not wholly displeased, though his amusement was combined with anxiety, which the *Sweetskin* case was sufficient to explain. An extract from Ada's own novel was to be included in this current number. Her work in progress had not yet been given a title, but it was billed as 'daring', so that in the cold light of print Quiggin might fear the police would now step in where *Fission* too was concerned.

'Are you going to be prosecuted, Ada?'

'I was laughing at X's piece. Read this.'

She handed me a copy of the magazine. It was open at Widmerpool's article *Assumptions of Autarchy v. Dynamics of Adjustment*. Since she had indicated Trapnel's piece as the focus of interest, I turned back to the list of contents to find the page. Ada snatched it from me.

'No, no. Where I gave it you.'

Another glance at the typeface showed what she meant. The page that at first appeared to be the opening of Widmerpool's routine article on politics or economics—usually a mixture of both—was in fact a parody of Widmerpool's writing by Trapnel. I sat down the better to appreciate the pastiche. It was a little masterpiece in its way. Trapnel's ignorance of matters political or economic, his total lack of interest in them, had not handicapped the manner in which he caught Widmerpool's characteristic style. If anything that ignorance had been an advantage. The gibberish, interspersed with *double ententes*, was entirely convincing.

'I do not assert . . . a convincing lead . . . cyclical monopoly resistance . . . the optimum factor . . .'

185

This was Bagshaw taking the bit between his teeth. However one looked at it, that much was clear. In the course of arranging subjects for Trapnel's parodies he had certainly included contributors to *Fission* before now. Alaric Kydd was not, as it happened, one of these, being somewhat detached from the *Fission* genre of writer, but Evadne Clapham, represented by a short story in the first number, had been one of Trapnel's victims. Always excitable, she had at first talked of a libel action. Bagshaw had convinced her finally that only the most talented of writers were amenable to parody, and she had forgiven both himself and Trapnel. All this was in line with Bagshaw's taste for sailing near the wind, whatever he did, but he had never spoken of setting Trapnel to work on Widmerpool. That was certainly to expose himself to danger. The temptation to do so, once the idea had occurred to an editor of Bagshaw's temperament, would, on the other hand, be a hard one to resist.

If, in the light of his business connexions with the publishing firm and the magazine, it were risky to parody Widmerpool, Widmerpool's lack of respect for Bagshaw's abilities as an editor did not make the experiment any less hazardous. For the parody to appear in print at this moment would certainly liven the mixture with new unforeseen fermentations. It was equally characteristic of Bagshaw to be away from the office at such a juncture. Quiggin himself certainly grasped that, at a moment when lurid theories about the elopement were giving place to acceptance of the Widmerpool version, there was a danger of a severe setback for such an interpretation of the story. He saw that circumstances were so ominous that the only thing to do was to claim the parody as a victory rather than a defeat.

'You have to look at things all ways. Kenneth Widmerpool is taking the line that no catastrophic break in his married life is threatened. Whether or not that is true, we have no reliable evidence how far, if at all, Trapnel is involved. In a sense, therefore, a good-natured burlesque by X of Kenneth's literary mannerisms suggests friendly, rather than unfriendly, relations.'

'Good-natured?'

Quiggin looked at Ada severely, but not without a suggestion of desire.

'Parodies are intended to raise a laugh. Perhaps you did not know that, Ada. If someone had taken the trouble to show me the piece before it was printed, I might have done a little sub-editing here and there. I don't promise it would have improved the whole, so perhaps it was better not.'

This speech indicated that Widmerpool might not have it all his own way, if he made too much fuss. It also confirmed indirectly the resentment of Widmerpool's domination that, according to Bagshaw, Quiggin had begun increasingly to show. Judy, the secretary, feeling that some of these recriminations were directed against herself, or, more probably envious of the attention Quiggin was devoting to Ada, now began to protest.

'How on earth was I to know one man had run away with the other man's wife? Books just handed the copy over to me, saying he had a temperature of a hundred-and-two, and told me to get on with the job.'

'Grown-up people always check on that particular point, my girl,' said Quiggin. 'Don't worry. We're not blaming you. Calm down. Take an aspirin. Isn't it time for coffee? I admit I could have done without Bagshaw arranging this just at the moment the *Sweetskin* case is coming on, and all the to-do about *Sad Majors*.'

I enquired as to Quiggin's version of the Stevens trouble.

'Odo's written an excellent account of his time with the Partisans. Adventurous, personal, but a lot of controversial matter. Readers don't want controversy. Why should they? Besides, it would be awkward for the firm to publish a book hinting some of the things Odo's does, with Kenneth Widmerpool on the board. All his support for societies trying to promote good relations with that very country. You want to keep politics out of a book like that.'

'Odo isn't very interested in politics, is he?'

'Not in a way, but he's very obstinate.'

I left them still in a flutter about the parody. There was not much Widmerpool could do. It would increase his opposition to Bagshaw, but Bagshaw probably had a contract of some sort. At the end of that, if the magazine survived, Widmerpool was likely to try and get him sacked anyway. It was a typical Bagshaw situation. Meanwhile, he showed no sign of returning to the office. The message came that his flu was no better. Some evenings later there was a telephone call at home. A female voice asked for me.

'Speaking.'

'It's Pamela Widmerpool.'

'Oh, yes?'

She must have known I was answering, but for some reason of her own preferred to go through the process of making absolutely sure.

'X is not well.'

'I'm very sorry—'

'I want you to come and see him. He needs some books and things.'

'But—'

'It's really the only way—for you to come yourself.'

She spoke the last sentence irritably, as if the question of my bringing Trapnel aid in person had already arisen in the past, and, rather contemptibly, I had raised objections to making myself available. Now, it seemed, I was looking for a similar excuse again. She offered no explanation or apology for thus emerging as representative of the Trapnel, rather than Widmerpool, ménage. In taking on the former

position there was not the smallest trace of self-conscious-
ness.

'This man Bagshaw has flu still. I can't get any sense out
of the half-witted girl left in charge at the *Fission* office.
That's why you must come.'

'I was only going to say that I don't know where you—
where X is living.'

'Of course you don't. No one does. I'm about to tell you.
Do you know the Canal at Maida Vale?'

'Yes.'

'We're a bit north of there.'

She gave the name of a street and number of the house.
I wrote them down.

'The ground-floor flat. Don't be put off by the look of the
place outside. It's inhabited all right, though you might not
think so. When can you come? Tonight?'

She added further instructions about getting there.

'What's wrong with X?'

'He's just feeling like hell.'

'Has he seen a doctor?'

'He won't.'

'Wouldn't it be wiser to make him?'

'He'll be all right in a day or two. He's got quite a store
of his pills. He just wants to talk to somebody. We don't
see anybody as a rule. You just happen to know both of us.
That's why you must come. Have you got a book to bring?
Something for him to review?'

I had taken some review copies from the *Fission* shelves
to look through at home. L. O. Salvidge's collection of
essays, *Paper Wine*, might do for Trapnel. I told Pamela I
would produce something. She rang off without comment.

'Don't get robbed and murdered,' said Isobel.

To visit Trapnel in one of his lairs was a rare experience
at the best of times. Once we had both been allowed to
have a drink with him at a flat in Notting Hill, within

range of the Portobello Road, where he liked to wander among the second-hand stalls. He was then living with a girl called Sally. The invitation had been quite exceptional, possibly intended to establish some sort of an alibi for reasons never revealed. The present expedition was more adventurous. The Paddington area, and north of it, supplied one of the traditional Trapnel areas of bivouac. It was surprising that he and Pamela were to be found no farther afield. Their total disappearance suggested withdrawal from such ground to less established streets. It was of course true to say that, even when not specifically retired to the outer suburbs, one rarely knew for certain where Trapnel was living. The absence of news about him from pub sources indicated experiment with hitherto unfrequented taverns. Such investigation would not be unwelcome; by no means out of character. A fresh round of saloon bars would hold out promise of new disciples, new eccentrics, new bores, new near-criminals. Pamela herself might well have objected to a really radical retreat from the approaches to central London. The part she played was hard to imagine.

At this period the environs of the Canal had not yet developed into something of a *quartier chic*, as later incarnated. Before the war, the indigenous population, time-honoured landladies, inveterate lodgers, immemorial whores, long undisturbed in surrounding premises, had already begun to give place to young married couples, but buildings already tumbledown had now been further reduced by bombing. The neighbourhood looked anything but flourishing. Leaving Edgware Road, I walked along the north bank of the Canal. On either side of the water gaps among the houses marked where direct hits had reduced Regency villas to rubble. The street Pamela had described was beyond this stucco colony. It was not at all easy to find. When traced, the exterior bore out the description of looking uninhabited.

The architecture here had little pretension to elegance. Several steps led up to the front door. No name was quoted above the bell of the ground floor flat. I rang, and waited. The door was opened by Pamela. She was in slacks. I said good-evening. She did not smile.

'Come in.'

Lighted only by a ray from the flat doorway left open, the hall, so far as could be seen in the gloom, accorded with the derelict exterior of the house; peeling wallpaper, bare boards, a smell of damp, cigarette smoke, stale food. The atmosphere recalled Maclintick's place in Pimlico, when Moreland and I had visited him not long before his suicide. By contrast, the fairly large room into which I followed Pamela conveyed, chiefly on account of the appalling mess of things that filled it, an impression of rough comfort, almost of plenty. There were only a few sticks of furniture, a table, two kitchen chairs, a vast and hideous wardrobe, but several pieces of luggage lay about—including two newish suitcases evidently belonging to Pamela—clothes, books, cups, glasses, empty Algerian wine bottles. The pictures consisted of a couple of large photographs of Pamela herself, taken by well-known photographers, and, over the mantelpiece, the Modigliani drawing. Trapnel lay on a divan under some brown army blankets.

'Look here, it's awfully good of you to come, Nick.'

One wondered, at this austere period for acquiring any sort of clothing to be regarded as of unusual design, where he had bought the dirty white pyjamas patterned with large red spots. The circumstances were in general a shade more sordid than pictured. Trapnel had been reading a detective story, which he now threw on the floor. A lot of other books lay about over the bedclothes, among them *Oblomov, The Thin Man, Adolphe,* in a French edition, all copies worn to shreds. Trapnel looked pale, rather dazed, otherwise no worse than usual. Before I could speak, Pamela made a request.

'Have you a shilling? The fire's going out.'

She took the coin and slipped it into the slot, reviving the dying flame, just going blue. As the gas flared up again, its hiss for some inexplicable reason suggested an explanation of why Pamela had married Widmerpool. She had done it, so to speak, in order to run away with Trapnel. I do not mean she had thought that out in precise terms—a vivid imagination would be required to predict the advent of Trapnel into Widmerpool's life—but the violent antithesis presented by their contrasted forms of existence, two unique specimens as it were brought into collision, promised anarchic extremities of feeling of the kind at which she aimed; in which she was principally at home. She liked—to borrow a phrase from St. John Clarke—to 'try conclusions with the maelstrom'. One of the consequences of her presence was to displace Trapnel's tendency to play a part during the first few minutes of any meeting. That could well have been knocked out of him by ill health, as much as by Pamela. He spoke now as if he were merely a little embarrassed.

'There were one or two things I wanted to talk about. You know I don't much like having to explain things on the telephone, though I often have to do that. Anyway, it's cut off here, the instrument was removed bodily yesterday, and I'm not supposed to go outside for the moment, owing to this malaise I've got. You and I haven't seen each other for some time, Nick. Such a lot's happened. As I'm a bit off colour I thought you wouldn't mind coming to our flat. It seemed easier. Pam was sure you'd come.'

He gave her one of those 'adoring looks', which Lermontov says mean so little to women. Pamela stared back at him with an expression of complete detachment. I thought of King Cophetua and the Beggar Maid, though Pamela was far from a pre-raphaelite type or a maid, and, socially speaking, the boot was, if anything, on the other foot. No doubt it was Trapnel's beard. He had also allowed his hair to grow longer than usual. All the same, he sitting up on the divan, she standing above him, they somehow called up the picture.

'I brought some essays by L. O. Salvidge.'

'*Paper Wine?*'

Trapnel, by some mysterious agency, always knew about all books before they were published. It was as if the information came to him instinctively. He laughed. The thought of reviewing Salvidge's essays must have made him feel better. One had the impression that he had been locked up with Pamela for weeks, like the Spanish honeymoon couples Borrit used to describe, when we were in the War Office together. To get back to the world of reviewing seemed to offer a magical cure for whatever Trapnel suffered. It really cheered him up.

'Just what I need—have we got anything to drink, darling?'

'A bottle of Algerian's open. Some dregs left, I think.'

'I don't want anything at the moment, thanks very much.'

Trapnel lay back on the divan.

'To begin with, that bloody parody of mine.'

'I mistook it at first for the real thing.'

That amused Trapnel. Pamela continued to stand by without comment or change of expression.

'I'm glad you did that. What's happened about it? Any reactions?'

'None I've heard about. There was some trepidation at the *Fission* office that trouble might arise from the obvious quarter. Books is away with flu.'

'What a bloody fool he is. I wrote the thing quite a long time ago at his suggestion. He said he'd have to talk to the others about it. I hadn't contemplated present circumstances then.'

'Nor did anyone else.'

'What about Books?'

'The evidence is that he didn't know.'

'Will Widmerpool believe that?'

'What can he do?' asked Pamela. 'He ought to be flattered.'

Even when she made this comment the tone suggested she was no more on Trapnel's side than Widmerpool's. She was assessing the situation objectively.

'That's what Books told Evadne Clapham,' said Trapnel. 'On that occasion I hadn't also run away with her husband. I suppose everything combined means I won't be able to write for *Fission* any longer. That's a blow, because it was one of my main sources of income, and I liked the magazine.'

'JG didn't seem unduly worried. He's got the *Sweetskin* prosecution on hand, and there's some trouble about Odo Stevens's book.'

'I don't want my publishing connexions messed up too. Quiggin & Craggs have their failings, but they aren't doing too badly with *Bin Ends*. I'm not under contract for the next novel. I'm getting near the end now. I don't want to have to hawk it round.'

At one moment Trapnel would give the impression that he was under contract with Quiggin & Craggs, and wanted to get rid of them; at the next, that he was not under contract, and wanted to stay. That was like him. He pointed to a respectably thick pile of foolscap covered with cuneiform handwriting. Although able to type, to use a typewriter was against Trapnel's principles. The books had to be written by his own hand. This talk about the novel seemed to displease Pamela. She began to frown.

'How's my husband?' she asked.

'I've not seen him lately—not since the night you left.'

'You saw him then?'

'I'd been dining with another MP. We came back to the Victoria Street flat to discuss some things.'

'Which MP?'

'Roddy Cutts—my brother-in-law.'

'That tall sandy-haired Tory?'

'Yes.'

'Were you there when Short delivered the message?'

'Yes.'

'How was it taken?'

'What do you mean?'

'Well or badly?'

'There was no scene.'

A slight flush had come over her face when she asked these questions. There could be no doubt she derived some sort of sensual satisfaction from dwelling on what had happened. Trapnel, acute enough to recognize, and resent, this process of exciting herself by such means, looked uneasy. The manner in which she managed to maintain a wholly unchanged demeanour in these very changed surroundings was notable; yet after all why should she become different just because she had decided to spend a season with Trapnel? With him, with Odo Stevens, with Allied officers, for that matter with Widmerpool, she remained the same, as individuals mostly do within a more intimate orbit; at home; with a lover; under unaccustomed stress. To suppose otherwise is naïve. At the same time, some require action, others are paralysed by action. That dissimilarity recognized, people stay themselves. Pamela did not give an inch. She was not rattled. She did the rattling.

The same could not be said of Widmerpool. He was obstinate, not easily deflected from his purpose, but circumstances might rattle him badly. He was not, like Pamela, consistent in never adapting his behaviour to others. Her constant search for new lovers made the world see her as existing solely in the field of sex, but the Furies that had driven her into the arms of Widmerpool by their torments —no doubt his too—at the same time invested her with the magnetic power that mesmerized Trapnel, operated in a manner to transcend love or sex, as both are commonly regarded. Did she and Widmerpool in some manner supplement each other, she supplying a condition he lacked—one that Burton would have called Melancholy? Now she showed her powers at work.

'I'm not satisfied with X's book.'

That was the first aesthetic judgment I had ever heard her make. When she had earlier changed the subject from Trapnel's writing, I thought she found, as some women do, concentration on a husband's or lover's work in some manner vexing. That she should return to his writing of her own volition was unexpected. It looked as if this were another manner of keeping Trapnel on his toes, because he reacted strongly to the comment.

'I'm going to alter the bits you don't like. You know, Nick, Pam's got a marvellous instinct for a sequence that has gone a shade wrong technically. I can't put it all right in five minutes, darling. These things take time and hard work. It'll all be done in due course, when I've thrown off this bloody thing that's playing such hell with work.'

'This is *Profiles in String*?'

'I can't get the *feel* of the end chapters. Most of the bad criticism you read is lack of understanding of what it feels like to get the wheels working internally when you're writing a novel. Not one reviewer in a thousand grasps that.'

Pamela showed no interest in subtleties of literary feeling.

'I'd rather you burnt it than published it as it stands. In fact you're not going to.'

Trapnel sighed. It was unlike him to accept criticism so humbly. On the face of it, there seemed no more reason to suppose Pamela knew how a novel should be written—

from Trapnel's point of view—than did the reviewers. In general, if he allowed himself to seek another opinion about how to deal with some matter in what he was writing—a short story, for example— he was accustomed to argue hard all the way in favour of whatever treatment he himself had in mind. Pamela showed contempt for the abject manner in which her objections had been received. Once more she switched the subject to her own situation.

'What are people saying about us?'

'No one knows quite what has happened.'

'How do you mean?'

She pouted. At that moment the bell rang. Trapnel groaned.

'God, it's the man trying to collect the money for the newspapers. He's come back.'

Pamela made a face.

'Take no notice. He'll go away after a while.'

'He'll see the light. It was daytime when he came before, and he thought we weren't in.'

Pamela turned to me.

'You answer the door. Tell him we're away—that we've lent you the flat.'

I showed unwillingness to undertake this commission. Trapnel was apologetic.

'We're being dunned. It always happens if you allow people to know your address. It's like hotels insisting on cleaning the room out from time to time. There's always some inconvenience, wherever you live. I couldn't help giving the address this time, otherwise we wouldn't have had any papers delivered.'

'Perhaps it's for the other people in the house.'

'They've gone away—decamped, I think. Do deal with it.'

'But what can I say to the man, if he is the newspaper man?'

'Tell him—'

The bell rang again. Pamela showed signs of getting cross.

'Look, X can't get up in his present state. Do go. If you had ten bob—twelve at the most—that would keep him quiet.'

There seemed no way of avoiding the assignment. I took ten shillings from my notecase, in so far as possible to cut short discussion, and went into the hall. To see the way, it was necessary to leave the flat door ajar. Even so, the place was inconveniently dark, and the front door required a certain amount of negotiating to open. It gave at last. The figure waiting on the the doorstep was not the newspaper-man, but Widmerpool. He did not seem in the least sur-prised that I should be the person to admit him.

'I expect you're here on business about the magazine, Nicholas?'

'Delivering a book to be reviewed, as a matter of fact.'

'I'm rather glad to find you on the premises. Don't go away from a mistaken sense of delicacy. Matters of a rather personal nature are likely to be discussed. I am quite glad to have a witness, especially one conversant with the circumstances, connected, I mean, by ties of business, albeit literary business. Where is Trapnel? This way, I take it?'

The light shining through the sitting-room door showed Widmerpool where to go. He took off his hat, crossed the boards of the hall, and over the threshold of the flat. It had at least been unnecessary to announce him. In fact he announced himself.

'Good evening. I have come to talk about some things.'

Pamela, hands stuck in the pockets of her trousers, was still standing, with her peculiar stillness of poise, in front of the gas fire. If Widmerpool had shown lack of surprise at my opening the door to him, he had at least expressed what seemed to him an adequate explanation as to why I should be with Trapnel. I arranged reviewing at *Fission*; Trapnel reviewed books. That was sufficient reason for my presence. The fact that Trapnel had run away with Widmerpool's wife had nothing to do with the business relationship between Trapnel and myself. To disregard it was almost something to approve. That view was no doubt more especially acceptable in the light of propaganda put about by Widmerpool himself.

Pamela, on the other hand, except insomuch as having left her husband, he might, in one sense, be expected to come and look for her, in another, could scarcely have been prepared for his arrival. So far from showing any wonder, she made no sign whatever of being even aware that an additional person had entered the room. She did not permit herself so much as a glance in Widmerpool's direction. Her expression, one of slight, though not severe displeasure, did not alter in the smallest degree. She seemed to be concentrating on a tear in the wallpaper opposite that ran in a great jagged parabola through a pattern of red parrots and blue storks, freak birds of the same size.

Widmerpool did not speak immediately after his first announcement. He went rather red. He put his hat on top of Trapnel's manuscript, where it lay on the table. Trapnel himself was now sitting bolt upright on the divan. This must, in a way, have been the moment he had been awaiting all his life: a truly dramatic occasion. That he was determined to rise to it was shown at once by the tone of his voice when he spoke.

'Would you oblige me by removing your hat from off my book?'

Widmerpool, whatever else he had taken in his stride, was astonished by this request. No doubt it presupposed an altogether unforeseen, alien area of sensibility. Picking up the hat again, he replaced it on one of the suitcases.

Trapnel maintained a tone of dramatically cold politeness. His voice trembled a little when he spoke again.

'I'm sorry. I must have sounded rude. I did not mean to be that. I have a special thing about my manuscripts— that is, I hate them being treated like any old pile of waste paper. Please take your coat off and sit down.'

'Thank you, I prefer to stand. I shall not be staying long, so that it is not worth my taking off my coat.'

Widmerpool gazed round the room. It was clearly worse, far worse, than he had ever dreamed; if he had thought at all about what he was likely to run to earth. His face showed that, considered in the light of housing insufficiencies inspected in his own constituency, the flat was horrific. Trapnel, possibly remembering the talk they had exchanged on such deplorable conditions, noticed this survey. He almost grinned. Then his manner changed.

'How did you find the house?'

This time Trapnel spoke with the hollow faraway voice of a horror film. He was determined to remain master of the situation. Widmerpool was quite equal to the manoeuvring.

'I came by taxi.'

'I mean how did you discover where I was living?'

'There are such aids as private detectives.'

Widmerpool said that with disdain. Trapnel laughed. The laughter too was of the kind associated with a horror film.

'I always wanted to meet someone who employed a private detective.'

Widmerpool did not answer at once. He appeared to be jockeying for position, taking up action stations before the contest really broke into flame. He cleared his throat.

'I have come here to clarify the situation. By arrival in person, some people might judge that I have put myself in a false position. Such is not my own opinion. A person of your kind, Trapnel, has neither the opportunity to observe, nor capacity to understand, the demands laid on a man who takes up the burden of public life. It is therefore necessary that certain facts should be plainly stated. The best person to state them is myself.'

Trapnel listened to this with the air of an accomplished actor. His 'hollow' laughter was now followed by a 'grim' smile. It was still a performance. Widmerpool had not got him, so to speak, out in the open yet.

'First,' said Widmerpool, 'you borrow money from me.'

Trapnel's defiance had not been geared to that particular form of attack at that moment. He dropped his acting and looked very angry, quite unsimulated rage.

'Then you lampoon me in a magazine of which I am one of the chief supporters.'

Trapnel began to smile again at that. If the first accusation put him in a weak position, the second to some extent restored equilibrium.

'Finally, my wife comes to live with you.'

Widmerpool paused. He too was being melodramatic now. Trapnel had ceased to smile. He was very white. He had lost command of his rôle as actor. Pamela watched them, still showing no change of expression. Widmerpool must have been to some extent aware that by making Trapnel angry, dislodging him from playing a part, he was moving towards ascendancy.

'You can keep my pound. Do not bother, when you are next paid for some paltry piece of journalism, to make another attempt to return it—which was, so I understand, your subterfuge for insinuating yourself into my house. The pound does not matter. Forget about it. I make you a present of it.'

Trapnel did not speak.

'Secondly, I want to express quite clearly my own indifference to your efforts to ridicule my economic theories.

Some people might have thought that an act of ungrateful-
ness on your part. Your own ignorance of the elementary
principles of economics makes it not even that. Your so-
called parody is a failure. Not funny. Several people have
told me so. And at the same time I recognize it as a deliberate insult. That is a matter between the board and Bagshaw—'

Trapnel burst out.

'You're trying to get Books sacked—'

'Don't interrupt me,' said Widmerpool. 'Bagshaw has a
contract.'

He made a half turn about in order, more unmistakably,
to include Pamela in whatever he was now about to announce. She went so far as to raise her eyebrows slightly.
Widmerpool still primarily addressed himself to Trapnel.

'You may fear that I am going to institute divorce pro-
ceedings. Such is not my intention. Pamela will return in
her own good time. I think we understand each other.'

Widmerpool paused.

'That is what I came to tell you,' he said. 'That—and to
express my contempt for the way you live and the way you
have behaved.'

Trapnel threw back the army blankets. He rose quite
slowly from the divan. His body, seen through the spotted
pyjamas, was desperately thin. He retied their cord; then,
in his bare feet, walked very deliberately to where the huge
wardrobe stood in the corner of the room. Against it was
propped the death's-head sword-stick. Trapnel picked up
the stick, and pressed the spring at the back of the skull.
The blade was released. He threw the sheath on top of
Oblomov, *The Thin Man*, *Adolphe*, and the several other
books lying on the bedclothes.

'Get out.'

Trapnel did not actually threaten Widmerpool with the
sword. He held the point to the ground, as if about to raise

the weapon in formal salute before joining combat in a duel. It was hard to estimate where exactly his actions hovered between play-acting and loss of control. Widmerpool stood firm.

'No dramatics, please.'

This calmness was to his credit. He knew little of Trapnel, but what he knew certainly gave no guarantee that a man of Trapnel's sort would not be capable of eccentric violence. If it came to that, I felt no absolute assurance on that matter myself. Whatever his merits as a writer, Trapnel could not be regarded as a well-balanced personality. Anything might be looked for from him. Besides, there were his 'pills'. One had the impression that, as such stimulants go, they were fairly mild. At the same time, he could easily have moved on to stronger stuff. Pamela might have encouraged that course; living with her almost necessitated it. Even the pills in their accustomed form might be sufficient to induce indiscreet conduct, especially when the question posed was evicting from a lover's flat the husband of his mistress.

'Are you going?'

'I have no wish to stay.'

Widmerpool picked up his hat from the suitcase. He brushed the felt with his elbow. Then he turned once more towards Pamela.

'I shall be abroad for some weeks in Eastern Europe. As a Member of Parliament I have been invited to enjoy the hospitality of one of the new Governments.'

'I said get out.'

Trapnel raised the sword slightly. Widmerpool took no notice. He continued raspingly to brush the surface of the hat. This time he addressed himself to me.

'The visit should make an interesting *Fission* article. Some apologists for the Liberal and Peasant leaders have suggested that concessions to the Soviet point of view have been too all-embracing. What I always tell people, who are not themselves in the know, is that our own brand of social-democracy, for better or worse, is not always exportable.'

He reorientated himself towards Pamela.

'When I return I shall not be surprised to find that you have reconsidered matters.'

She looked straight at him. Otherwise she gave no sign that she had heard what he said. Widmerpool went very red again. He passed through the door into the hall. The front door slammed, but did not shut. Trapnel in his bare feet ran out of the flat. He could be heard to pull the front door violently open again. From the steps he shouted into the night.

'Coprolite! Faecal débris! Fossil of dung!'

A minute later he returned to the sitting-room. He took the sheath-half of the swordstick from the bed, replaced the blade and returned it to the corner by the wardrobe. Then he climbed under the blankets again, and lay back. He looked quite exhausted. Pamela, on the other hand, now showed signs of life. A faint colour had come into her face, a look of excitement I had never before seen there. She smiled. Something unexpected was afoot. She came across the room, and sat down on the bed. Trapnel took one of her hands. He did not speak. Comment came from Pamela this time.

'I'm glad you were here, Nicholas. I'm glad it all happened in front of someone. I wish there had been a lot more people. Hundreds more. Now you know what my life was like.'

Trapnel patted her hand. He was much shaken. Not well in any case, he was likely to be dissatisfied with the scene that had taken place. He could scarcely be said to have dominated it in the manner of one of his own screen heroes, even if it were better not to have run Widmerpool through, or whatever was in his mind.

'I do apologize for getting you mixed up with all this, Nick. It wasn't my fault. How the hell could I guess he was going to turn up here? I thought there wasn't a living soul knew the address, except one or two shops round here. Private detectives? It makes you think.'

The idea of private detectives obviously fascinated Trapnel's *roman policier* leanings, which were highly developed. He was also worried.

'Will you be awfully good, and keep quiet about all this, Nick? Don't say a word, for obvious reasons.'

Pamela shook back her hair.

'Thank you so much for coming, and for bringing the book. I expect we shall see you again here, as we aren't going out much, as long as X isn't well. I'll ring you up, and you can bring another book some time.'

She spoke formally, like a hostess saying goodbye to a visitor she barely knows, who has paid a social call, and now explains that he must leave. A complete change had come over her after the impassivity she had shown until now. Before I could reply, she spoke again, this time abandoning formality.

'Bugger off—I want to be alone with X.'

5

I left london one saturday afternoon in the autumn to make some arrangement about a son going to school. Owing to the anomalies of the timetable, the train arrived an hour or so early for the appointment. There was an interval to kill. After a hot summer the weather still remained warm, but, not uncommon in that watery region, drizzle descended steadily, while a feeble sun shone through clouds that hung low over stretches of claret-coloured brick. It was too wet to wander about in the open. For a time I kicked my heels under a colonnade. A bomb had fallen close by. One corner was still enclosed by scaffolding and a tarpaulin. Above the arch, the long upper storey with its row of oblong corniced windows had escaped damage. The period of the architecture—half a century later, but it took little nowadays to recall him—brought Burton to mind; Burton, by implication the art of writing in general. On this subject he knew what he was talking about:

''Tis not my study or intent to compose neatly . . . but to express myself readily & plainly as it happens. So that as a River runs sometimes precipitate and swift, then dull and slow; now direct, then winding; now deep, then shallow, now muddy, then clear; now broad, then narrow; doth my style flow; now serious, then light; now comical, then satirical; now more elaborate, then remiss, as the present subject required, or as at the time I was affected.'

Even for those with a prejudice in favour of symmetry, worse rules might be laid down. The antithesis between satire and comedy was especially worth emphasis; also to write as the subject required, or the author thought fit at the moment. One often, when writing, felt a desire to be 'remiss'. It was good to have that recommended. An important aspect of writing unmentioned by Burton was 'priority'; what to tell first. That always seemed one of the basic problems. Trapnel used to talk about its complexities. For example, even to arrange in the mind, much less on paper, the events leading up to the demise of *Fission* after a two-year run, the swallowing up (by the larger publishing house of which Clapham was chairman) of the firm of Quiggin & Craggs, demanded an effective grasp of narrative 'priorities'.

Looking out between the pillars at the raindrops glinting on the cobbles of a broad open space, turning the whole thing over in the mind, much seemed to me inevitable, as always contemplating the past. At the same time, although many things had gone wrong, several difficulties had been successfully surmounted. For instance, the prosecution of *Sweetskin* had been parried; the verdict, 'Not Guilty'. Nevertheless, the case had cost money, caused a lot of worry to the directors. Alaric Kydd himself had been so certain that he would be sent to prison for uttering an obscene work that he let his flat on rather good terms for eighteen months; later finding difficulty in obtaining satisfactory alternative accommodation. He was also wounded by the tone of voice—certainly a very silly one—in which prosecuting counsel read aloud in court certain passages from his novel.

More damaging to the firm in a way, though morally rather than financially, was the *Sad Majors* affair. Bagshaw leaked an account of that. He had come back to the office in a restless, resentful mood after his bout of flu, according to Ada, spending the first forty-eight hours of convalescence drinking, then retiring to bed again for a further day before settling down. Whether or not he had deliberately kept the Trapnel parody 'on the spike' for use at the most appropriate occasion was never cleared up. Most probably, as in previous episodes of Bagshaw's history, an infallible instinct for causing trouble had brought guidance without need of exact knowledge. Widmerpool appeared to have made no complaint to the board. He remained out of touch with Quiggin & Craggs long after the Court Circular announced his return from the People's Republic, where he had been paying his visit. No doubt he was busy with parliamentary affairs. There was in any case not much he could do. If *Fission* had not ceased publication, Bagshaw's contract would in any case have run out. He had dropped hints that he himself wanted to move. No one was going to stand in his way. The fact was that Bagshaw was by now attracted by the promise of helping to open up the still mainly unexplored eldorado of television.

Bagshaw took pleasure in elaborating the Odo Stevens story. He did not like Stevens as a man, but admired him as an adventurer. They used to meet when Stevens from time to time looked into the *Fission* office to see if there were a book to review. Stevens had developed an additional contact with the magazine on account of his association with Rosie Manasch. Never backward at publicizing his successes, he did not at present convey more than that he had an ally in that quarter. If Rosie had decided she needed relaxation with a man considerably younger than herself, she was agreed to have had a distressing time in many ways, and Stevens, whatever his failings, had the advantage of being a figure not to be taken too seriously. Both parties were judged well able to look after themselves. That was how it seemed at the time. However, even at an early stage the relationship was sufficiently strong to play a part in the

Quiggin & Craggs upheaval. This came about when the *Sad Majors* controversy, simmering for some little while, took aggressive shape. Bagshaw, always interested in a row of this sort, was ravished by a move now made.

'You can't help admiring the way Gypsy does things. Good old hard-core stuff. You know the trouble about the Stevens book—thought to bring discredit on the Party. Gypsy's performed one of those feats that most people don't think of on account of their ruthless simplicity. She has quite simply liquidated the manuscript. Both copies.'

'Aren't there more than two copies?'

'Apparently not.'

'How did she get hold of them?'

'After much argument, the original MS had been sent to the printer to be cast off. It was to be allowed to go ahead anyway as far as proof. Then Howard said he'd like to re-read the book in peaceful surroundings, so he borrowed the carbon, and took it home with him. A day or two later, Gypsy, that's her story, thought it was another manuscript Howard had asked her to post to Len Pugsley—who sometimes does reading for the firm, he poked Gypsy briefly—and Len says the parcel never arrived. He was moving house at the time. Stevens's carbon seems to have gone astray between the Oval and Chalk Farm. Meanwhile, the printers got a telephone message, the origins of which no one can trace, to send back the MS they were to cast off. There was some question about it to be settled editorially. Now that copy can't be found either.'

'Stevens will have to write it again?'

'That's where the neatness of the sabotage comes in. Re-writing will take a longish time. By the time it's finished the poor impression Stevens gives of the Comrades and their behaviour will, with any luck, be out of date—any-way in the eyes of the reading public. At worst, all ancient history.'

'How's Stevens taking the loss?'

'He's pretty cross. Can you blame him? The more interesting point is that Rosie Manasch is very cross too. In fact she's withdrawn her support from the mag in consequence of her crossness with Quiggin & Craggs as a firm. That's awkward, because—though personally I think a lot of unnecessary fuss was made about the Trapnel parody— the rest of the board don't feel it a good moment to stir up Widmerpool.'

'Is Stevens getting compensation?'

'You haven't studied the writing paper. The greatest care is taken of manuscripts, but no responsibility. However, they've allowed the contract to be cancelled.'

'That was handsome.'

Compared with the Stevens row, the disappointment caused by Sillery's Diary, after all the haggling about terms, and high advance, was a minor blow, though again there were repercussions. The extracts were called *Garnered at Sunset: Leaves from an Edwardian Journal.*

'A masterpiece of dullness,' said Bagshaw. 'JG read it. Howard read it. For once they were in complete agreement. The only thing to do will be to publish, and hope for the best. I'm surprised at Ada. She's strung them along over Sillery.'

Ada's policy in the matter, as not seldom, was enigmatic, probably dictated by a mixture of antagonistic considerations. The Diary, seen as one of the paths to a career, had not been truly subjected to her usually sharp judgment. Its lack of interest had been obscured by inner workings of the curious kind of flirtation she and Sillery had shared. Those elements might be put forward as excuse for the recommendation. It was also possible, knowing Sillery as she did, that Ada had genuinely found *Garnered at Sunset* absorbing. Publishers' readers, as Quiggin remarked, are no less subjective than other animals. It might be thought that this critical lapse on Ada's part would have prejudiced her position in the firm. On the contrary, nothing more retributive was visited on her than that Quiggin proposed marriage.

Bagshaw suggested that an emotional scene contingent on some sort of reprimand on the subject of the Sillery Journal, had brought things to a head, but there can be no doubt an offer of marriage was already at the back of Quiggin's mind. The fact that the firm was moving towards a close had nothing to do with it. He was accepted. As a married man, the place he had found on the board of Clapham's firm would be advantageous; on the whole a step forward in a publishing career. The two of them were quietly married one August afternoon before the Registrar; Mark Members and L. O. Salvidge, witnesses. Craggs and Gypsy were not asked. Craggs had announced he was going into semi-retirement when the firm closed down, but it seemed likely that he would continue his activities, at least in an inconspicuous manner, with many little interests of a political sort that had always engrossed him. All these things played a part, others too, in the winding up of Quiggin & Craggs, representative of common enough impediments to running a publishing house; exceptional, in as much as they were exceptional, only on account of the individuals concerned. The climax, in an odd way, seemed to be the night spent with Trapnel and Bagshaw. That had been rather different. By then, in any case, both magazine and publishing business had received the death sentence. All the same that night—the symbolic awfulness of its events—was something to put a seal on the whole affair. It confirmed several other things too.

Matters had begun with a telephone call from Bagshaw at about half-past nine one evening four or five weeks before. From the opening sentences it was clear he was drunk, less clear what he wanted. At first the object seemed no more than a chat about the sadness of life, perhaps a long one, but entailing merely a sympathetic hearing. That was too good to be true. It soon grew plain some request was going to be made. Even then, what the demand would be became only gradually apparent.

'As the mag's closing down, I thought a small celebration would be justified.'

'So you said, Books. You've said that twice.'

'Sorry, sorry. The fact is everything always comes at once. Look, Nicholas, I want your help. I'd already decided on this small celebration, when Trappy got in touch with me at the office. He rang up himself, which, as you know, he doesn't often do. He's in a lot of trouble. This girl, I mean.'

'Pamela Widmerpool?'

It was as well to make sure.

'That's the one.'

The fact that Pamela might be Widmerpool's wife had made, from his tone of voice, little or no serious impact on Bagshaw. He clearly thought of her as one, among many, of Trapnel's girls . . . Tessa . . . Pat . . . Sally . . . Pauline . . . any of the Trapnel girls Bagshaw himself had known in the course of their acquaintance.

'What's happened?'

'They've had some row about his novel—you know the one—what—can't quite—'

He made a tremendous effort, but I had to intervene.

'*Profiles in String*?'

'That's the book. He's tremendously pleased with it, but can't decide about an ending. He wants one, she wants another.'

'Trapnel's writing the bloody book, isn't he?'

Bagshaw was shocked at this disregard for authority conferred by a love attachment.

'Trappy was upset. They had a row. Now he doesn't want to go back and find she's left. She may have done. He wants someone to go back with him. Soften the blow. I said I'd do that.'

'Look, Books, why are you telling me all this?'

'I was quite willing to do that. See him home, I mean. Trappy and I went to the pub to talk things over. You know how it is. I'm not quite sure I can get him back unaided.'

'Do you mean he's passed out?'

Bagshaw was insulted at the suggestion that such a fate might have overtaken any friend of his.

'Not in the least. It's just he's in a bit of a state. Sort of nervous condition. That's what I'm coming to. It's really an awful lot to ask. Would it be too great an infliction for you to come along and lend a hand?'

'Is it those pills?'

'Might be.'

'Where are you?'

'Not far from Trappy's flat. Once we've got him under way there'll be nothing to it.'

Bagshaw named a pub I had never heard of, but, from the description of its locality, evidently not far from Trapnel's base, assuming that unchanged from the night I had visited him. Since that night I had heard nothing of him or Pamela. She had not rung up to ask for further books to review. The L. O. Salvidge notice had never been sent in. Salvidge was aggrieved. Trapnel ceased altogether to be a contributor to *Fission* in its latter days.

'Can he walk?'

'Of course he can walk—at least I think so. It's not walking I'm worried about, just I don't know how he'll behave when he gets into the open. After all, which of us does? You'd be a great support, Nicholas, if you could manage to come along. You always get on all right with Trappy, which is more than some do. I'm full of apologies for asking this.'

Although in most respects quite different, the situation

213

seemed to present certain points in common with conducting Bithel, collapsed on the pavement, back to G Mess; restoring Stringham to his flat after the Old Boy dinner. In some sense history was repeating itself, though incapacity to walk seemed not Trapnel's disability.

'All right, I'll be along as soon as I can.'

Isobel was unimpressed by this call for help. There was much to be said for her view of it. Now that Bagshaw was off the line, compliance took the shape of moral weakness, rather than altruism or benevolence.

'Looking after Trapnel's becoming monotonous. Is Mrs Widmerpool still his true-love?'

'She's what the trouble's about.'

The pub turned out to be another of Bagshaw's obscure, characterless drinking places, this time off the Edgware Road. It was fairly empty. Bagshaw and Trapnel were at a table in the corner, both perfectly well behaved. Closer investigation showed Bagshaw as drunk in his own very personal manner, that is to say he would become no drunker however much consumed. There was never any question of going under completely, or being unable to find his way home. Trapnel, on the other hand, did not at first show any sign of being drunk at all. He had abandoned his dark lenses. Possibly he only wore them in hard winters. He was sitting, quietly smiling to himself, hunched over the death's-head stick.

'Hullo, Nick. I've just been talking to Books about a critical work I'm planning. It's to be called *The Heresy of Naturalism*. People can't get it right about Naturalism. They think if a writer like me writes the sort of books I do, it's because that's easier, or necessary nowadays. You just look round at what's happening and shove it all down. They can't understand that's not in the least the case. It's just as selective, just as artificial, as if the characters were kings and queens speaking in blank verse.'

'Some of them are queens,' said Bagshaw.

'Do listen, Books. You'll profit by it. What I'm getting at is that if you took a tape-recording of two people having a grind it might truly be called Naturalism, it might be funny, it might be sexually exciting, it might even be beautiful, it wouldn't be art. It would just be two people having a grind.'

'But, look here, Trappy—'

'All right, they don't have to be revelling in bed. Suppose you took a tape-recording of the most passionate, most moving love scene, a couple who'd—oh, God, I don't know —something very moving about their love and its circumstances. The incident, their words, the whole thing, it gets accidentally taped. Unknown to them the machine's been left on by mistake. Anything you like. Some wonderful *objet trouvé* of that sort. Do you suppose it would come out as it should? Of course it wouldn't. There are certain forms of human behaviour no actor can really play, no matter how good he is. It's the same in life. Human beings aren't subtle enough to play their part. That's where art comes in.'

'All I said was that Tolstoy—'

'Do keep quiet, Books. You've missed the point. What I mean is that if, as a novelist, you put over something that hasn't been put over before, you've done the trick. A novelist's like a fortune-teller, who can impart certain information, but not necessarily what the reader wants to hear. It may be disagreeable or extraneous. The novelist just has to dispense it. He can't choose.'

'All I said was, Trappy, that personally I preferred Realism—Naturalism, if you wish—just as I've a taste for political content. That's how Tolstoy came in. It's like life.'

'But Naturalism's only "like" life, if the novelist himself is any good. If he isn't any good, it doesn't matter whether he writes naturalistically or any other way. What could be less "like" life than most of the naturalistic novels that appear? If he's any good, it doesn't matter if his characters talk like Disraeli's, or incidents occur like Vautrin, smoking a cigar and dressed up as a Spanish abbé, persuades Lucien de Rubempré not to drown himself. Is *Oliver Twist* a failure as a novel because Oliver, a workhouse boy, always speaks with exquisite refinement? As for politics, who cares which way Trimalchio voted, or that he was a bit temperamental towards his slaves?'

'Trappy—no, wait, let me speak—all this started by my saying that, just as masochism's only sadism towards yourself, revolutions only reconcentrate the centre of gravity of authority, and, if you wish, of oppression. The people who feel they suffer from authority and oppression want to be authoritative and oppressive. I was just illustrating that by something or other I thought came in Tolstoy.'

'But, Books, you said Tolstoy wrote "like" life, because he was naturalistic. I contend that his characters aren't any more "like"—in fact aren't as "like"—as, say, Dostoevsky's at their craziest. Of course Tolstoy's inordinately brilliant. In spite of all the sentimentality and moralizing, he's never boring—at least never in one sense. The material's inconceivably well arranged as a rule, the dialogue's never less than convincing. The fact remains, *Anna Karenin*'s a glorified magazine story, a magazine story of the highest genius, but still a magazine story in that it tells the reader what he wants to hear, never what he doesn't want to hear.'

'Trappy, I won't have you say that sort of thing about Tolstoy, though of course Dostoevsky's more explicit when it comes to exhibiting the Marxist contention that any action's justified—'

'Do stop about Marxism, Books. Marxism has nothing to do with what I'm talking about. I'm talking about Naturalism. I'm in favour of Naturalism. I write that way myself. All I want to make clear is that it's just a way of writing a novel like any other, just as contrived, just as selective. Do you call Hemingway's impotent good guy naturalistic? Think what Dostoevsky would have made of him. After all, Dostoevsky did deal with an impotent good guy in love with a bitch, when he wrote *The Idiot*.'

Bagshaw was silenced for the moment. Trapnel was undoubtedly in an exceptionally excited state, unable to stop pouring out his views. He took a gulp of beer. The pause made comment possible.

'We don't know for certain that Myshkin was impotent.'

'Myshkin was as near impotent as doesn't matter, Nick. In any case Hemingway would never allow a hero of his to be made a fool of. To that extent he's not naturalistic. Most forms of naturalistic happening are expressed in grotesque irrational trivialities, not tight-lipped heroisms. Hemingway's is only one special form of Naturalism. The same goes for Scott Fitzgerald's romantic-hearted gangster. Henry James would have done an equally good job on him in non-naturalistic terms. Most of the gangsters of the classic vintage were queer anyway. James might have delicately conveyed that as an additional complication to Gatsby's love.'

Before literary values could be finally hammered out in a manner satisfactory to all parties, the pub closed. We moved from the table, Trapnel still talking. In the street his incoherent, distracted state of mind was much more apparent. He was certainly in a bad way. All the talk about writing, its flow not greatly different from the termination of any evening in his company, was just a question of putting off the evil hour of having to face his own personal problems. No doubt he had gone into these to some extent with Bagshaw earlier. They had then started up the politico-literary imbroglio in progress when I arrived at the pub. Now, even if nothing were said about Pamela, the problem of getting him home was posed. He was, as Bagshaw so positively believed, perfectly able to walk. There was no difficulty about that. His manner was the disturbing element. An air of dreadful nervousness had descended on him. Now that he had ceased to argue about writing, he seemed to have lost all powers of decision in other matters. He stood there shaking, as if he were afraid. This could have been the consequence of lack of proper food, drinking, pills, or the mere fact of being emotionally upset. Burton had noticed such a condition. 'Cousin-german to sorrow is fear, or rather sister, *fidus Achates*, and continual companion.' That was just how Trapnel looked, a man weighed down by sorrow and fear. Suddenly he reeled. Bagshaw stepped towards him.

'Hold up, Trappy. You're tight.'

That was a fatal remark. Not only did open expression of that opinion make Trapnel very indignant, it also had the effect of physically increasing, anyway for the moment, the lack of control that was overcoming him. Trapnel always hated any suggestion that limits existed to his own powers of alcoholic assimilation. Bagshaw must already have known that. The fact that his comment was true made it no more excusable, except for being equally applicable to Bagshaw himself.

'Tight? I'm always being asked by people how it is I'm never drunk, however much I put back. They can't make it out. I can finish a bottle of brandy at a sitting, get up sober as when I started. Drink just doesn't have any effect on me. You don't suppose the few halves of bitter we've had tonight made me drunk, Books, do you? It's you who are a little tipsy, my boy. You've rather a weak head.'

He waved his stick. If the contrast had to be made, this described their capacities in reverse. Bagshaw took it well, having made the initial error by his comment.

'Drunk or sober, we can none of us stand here all night. Shall we head for your place, Trappy?'

This suggestion had a steadying, immediately subduing effect on Trapnel. He seemed to remember suddenly all he had been trying to forget. The outward appearance of drunkenness left him at once. He might have swallowed an instant sedative. The state of utter dejection returned. He spoke to Bagshaw quietly, almost humbly.

'Does Nicholas know what's happened?'

'Roughly.'

'I'd like to be a bit clearer about what's up.'

'There's been some trouble with Pam. It was all over my new book. We never seem to agree about writing, especially my writing. It's almost as if she hates it, doesn't want me to do it, and yet she thinks about my work all the time, knows just where the weak places are. We have a lot of rows about it. We had one this morning. I left the house in a rage. I told her she was mad on Naturalism. That's why the subject was on my mind. Books and I began talking about it. I'm for it too. I told her I was. I've told everyone, and written it. What I can't stand is people giving it their own exclusive meaning. That's what Pam does. She just uses it to pick on the way I write. She brings up all my own arguments against me. Then when I half agree, she takes an absolutely opposite line. It's like Pavlov's dogs. I think sometimes I'll go up the wall.'

'Why discuss your work with her?' said Bagshawe inconsistently. 'Tell her to get on with the washing-up.'

'It's not the first row we've had by a long chalk. Christ, I don't want her to leave me. I know it's pretty awful living the way we do, but I can't face the thought of her leaving. You know I'm not sure there isn't going to be a film in *Profiles in String*. It was the last thing I thought about when I started, but now I believe there might be. It would go over big, if it went over at all.'

At one moment it looked as if Trapnel were going to break down, at the next, that he was about to indulge in

one of his fantasies about making money, which over-
whelmed him from time to time. These sudden changes of
gear were going to require careful handling, if he were to be
conveyed back to the flat. It was much more likely that he
would want to go to a drinking club of some sort. He
usually knew the address of one that would admit him.
Bagshaw, grasping the fact that Trapnel needed soothing,
now took charge quite effectively. He must have had long
experience in persuading fellow-drunks to do what he,
rather than they themselves, wanted. He was ruthless about
getting his own way when he thought that necessary,
showing total disregard for other people's wishes or convenience. That was now all to the good.

'We know what you feel, Trappy. Come on. We'll go
back and see how things are. She's probably longing to see
you.'

'You don't know her.'

'I admit that, but I've seen her. They're all the same.'

'There's not a drop to drink.'

'Never mind. Nick and I will just see you home.'

'Will you really? I couldn't face it otherwise.'

Trapnel was like a child who suddenly decides to be fret-
ful no longer. Now he was even full of gratitude. We
reached Edgware Road with him still in this mood. There
was a small stretch of the main highway to negotiate before
turning off by the Canal. The evening was warm, stuffy,
full of strange smells. For once Trapnel seemed suitably
dressed in his tropical suit. We turned down the south
side of the Canal, walking on the pavement away from the
houses. Railings shut off a grass bank that sloped down to
the tow-path. Trapnel had now moved into a pastoral
dream.

'I love this waterway. I'd like to have a private barge,
and float down it waving to the tarts.'

'Do you get a lot down here?' asked Bagshaw, interested.

'You see the odd one. They live round about, but tend to work other streets. What a mess the place is in.'

Most of London was pretty grubby at this period, the Canal no exception. On the surface of the water concentric circles of oil, undulating in the colours of the spectrum, were illuminated by moonlight. Through these luminous prisms floated anonymous off-scourings of every kind, tin cans, petrol drums, soggy cardboard boxes. Watery litter increased as the bridge was approached. Bagshaw pointed to a peculiarly obnoxious deposit bobbing up and down by the bank.

'Looks as if someone's dumped their unit's paper salvage. I used to have to deal with that at one stage of the war. Obsolete forms waiting to be pulped and made into other forms. An internal reincarnation. Fitted the scene in India.'

Trapnel stopped, and leant against the railings.

'Let's pause for a moment. Contemplate life. It's a shade untidy here, but romantic too. Do you know what all that mess of paper looks like? A manuscript. Probably someone's first novel. Authors always talk of burning their first novel. I believe this one's drowned his.'

'Or hers.'

'Some beautiful girl who wrote about her seduction, and couldn't get it published.'

'When lovely woman stoops to authorship?'

'I think I'll go and have a look. Might give me some ideas.'

'Trappy, don't be silly.'

Trapnel, laughing rather dementedly, began to climb the railings. Bagshaw attempted to stop this. Before he could be persuaded otherwise, Trapnel had lifted himself up, and was halfway across. The railings presented no very serious obstacle even to a man in a somewhat deranged state, who carried a stick in one hand. He dropped to the other side without difficulty. The bank sloped fairly steeply to the lower level of the tow-path and the water. Trapnel reached the footway. He paused for a moment, looking up and down the length of the Canal. Then he went to the water's edge, and began to poke with the swordstick at the sheets of paper floating about all over the surface.

'Come back, Trappy. You're not the dustman.'

Trapnel took no notice of Bagshaw. He continued to strain forward with the stick, until it looked ominously as if he would fall in. The pieces of paper, scattered broadcast, were all just out of reach.

'We shall have to get over,' said Bagshaw. 'He'll be in at any moment.'

Then Trapnel caught one of the sheets with the end of the stick. He guided it to the bank. For a second it escaped, but was recaptured. He bent down to pick it up, shook off the water and straightened out the page. The soaked paper seemed to fascinate him. He looked at it for a long time. Bagshaw, relieved that the railings would not now have to be climbed, for a minute or two did not intervene. At last he became tired of waiting.

'Is it a work of genius? Do decide one way or the other. We can't bear more delay to know whether it ought to be published or not.'

Trapnel gave a kind of shudder. He swayed. Either drink had once more overcome him with the suddenness with which it had struck outside the pub, or he was acting out a scene of feigned horror at what he read. Whichever it were, he really did look again as if about to fall into the Canal. Abruptly he stopped playing the part, or recovered his nerve. I suppose these antics, like the literary ramblings in the pub, also designed to delay discovery that Pamela had abandoned him; alternatively, to put off some frightful confrontation with her.

'Do come back, Trappy.'

Then an extraordinary thing happened. Trapnel was still standing by the edge of the water holding the dripping sheet of foolscap. Now he crushed it in his hand, and threw the ball of paper back into the Canal. He lifted the sword-stick behind his head, and, putting all his force into the throw, cast it as far as this would carry, high into the air. The stick turned and descended, death's-head first. A mystic arm should certainly have risen from the dark waters of the mere to receive it. That did not happen. Trapnel's Excalibur struck the flood a long way from the bank, disappeared for a moment, surfaced, and began to float downstream.

'Now he really has become unmoored,' said Bagshaw.

Trapnel came slowly up the bank.

'You'll never get your stick back, Trappy. What ever made you do it? We'll hurry on to the bridge right away. It might have got caught up on something. There's not much hope.'

Trapnel climbed back on to the pavement.

'You were quite wrong, Books.'

'What about?'

'It was a work of genius.'

'What was?'

'The manuscript in the water—it was *Profiles in String*.'

I now agreed with Bagshaw in supposing Trapnel to have gone completely off his head. He stood looking at us. His smile was one of the consciously dramatic ones.

'She brought the MS along, and chucked it into the Canal. She knew I should be almost bound to pass this way, and it would be well on the cards I should notice it. We quite often used to stroll down here at night and talk about the muck floating down, french letters and such like. She must have climbed over the railings to get to the water. I'd like to have watched her doing that. I'd thought of a lot of things she might be up to—doctoring my pills, arranging for me to find her being had by the milkman, giving the bailiffs our address. I never thought of this. I never thought she'd destroy my book.'

He stood there, still smiling slightly, almost as if he were embarrassed by what had happened.

'You really mean that's your manuscript over there in the water?'

Trapnel nodded.

'The whole of it?'

'It wasn't quite finished. The end was what we had the row about.'

'You must have a copy?'

"Of course I haven't a copy. Why should I? I told you, it wasn't finished yet.'

Even Bagshaw was appalled. He began to speak, then stopped, something I had never seen happen before. There was certainly nothing to say. Trapnel just stood there.

'Come and look for the stick, Trappy.'

Trapnel was not at all disposed to move. Now the act had taken place, he wanted to reflect on it. Perhaps he feared still worse damage when the flat was reached, though that was hard to conceive.

'In a way I'm not surprised. Even though this particular dish never struck me as likely to appear on the menu, it all fits in with the cuisine. Christ, two years' work, and I'll never feel the same as when I was writing it. She may be correct in what she thinks about it, but I'll never be able to write it again—either her way or my own.'

Bagshaw, in spite of his feelings about the manuscript, could not forget the stick. The girl did not interest him at all.

'You'll never find a swordstick like that again. It was a great mistake to throw it away.'

Trapnel was not listening. He stood there musing. Then all at once he revealed something that had always been a mystery. Being Trapnel, an egotist of the first rank, he supposed this disclosure as of interest only in his own case, but a far wider field of vision was at the same time opened up by what was unveiled. In a sense it was of most interest where Trapnel was concerned, because he seems to have reacted in a somewhat different fashion to the rest of Pamela's lovers, but, applicable to all of them, what was divulged offered clarification of her relations with men. Drink, pills, the strain of living with her, the destruction of *Profiles in String*, combination of all those, brought about a confession hardly conceivable from Trapnel in other circumstances. He now spoke in a low, confidential tone.

'You may have wondered why a girl like that ever came to live with me?'

'Not so much as why she ever married that husband of hers,' said Bagshaw. 'I can understand all the rest.'

'I doubt if you can. Not every man can stand what's entailed.'

'I don't contradict that.'

'You don't know what I mean.'

'What do you mean?'

Trapnel did not answer for a moment. It was as if he were thinking how to phrase whatever he intended to say. Then he spoke with great intensity.

'It's when you have her. She wants it all the time, yet doesn't want it. She goes rigid like a corpse. Every grind's a nightmare. It's all the time, and always the same.'

Trapnel said this with absolute simplicity. Irony, melodrama, narcissism, fantasy, all his accustomed tendency to play a rôle had been this time completely eliminated. The curtain was at least partially drawn aside. A little light had been let in, Stevens had not told all the truth.

'I could take it, because—well, I suppose because I loved her. Why not admit it? I'm not sure I don't still.'

Bagshaw could not stand that. Excessive displays of amative sensibility always disturbed him.

'Even Sacher-Masoch drew the line somewhere, Trappy
—true we don't know where. What did her husband think
about this, I'd like to know.'

'She told me he only tried a couple of times. Gave it up
as a bad job.'

'So that's how things are?'

'For certain reasons it suited him to be married to her.'

'And her to him?'

'She stopped that, if ever true, when she came to live with
me.'

Even after what had taken place, Trapnel spoke defensively.

'It gave him a kind of prestige,' he said.

'Not much prestige the way she was carrying on.'

'You don't understand.'

'I don't.'

'It's not what she does, it's what she is.'

'You mean he's positively flattered?'

'That's what she seemed to think. She may be right.
That's a form of masochism too. It's not my sort. Not that
I can explain my sort, if that's what it is. It doesn't feel un-
natural to me. As I said, I love her—at least used to. I don't
think I do now. She'll always go on like this. She's a child,
who doesn't know any better.'

'Oh, balls,' said Bagshaw. 'I've heard men say that sort
of thing about women before. It's rubbish, the scrapings of
the barrel. You must rise above that, Trappy. Let's get back
to your place anyway.'

I had never seen Bagshaw so agitated. This time Trapnel
came quietly. When we reached the bridge, he insisted that
he did not want to look for the stick.

'It's a sacrifice. One of those things you dedicate to the
Gods. I remember reading about a sacred pool in an Indian
temple, where good writing floated on the water, bad
writing sank. Perhaps the Canal has the same property,
and Pam was right to put my book there.'

Those words meant that he was getting back his normal form. Panache was coming into play. I sympathized with Bagshaw's sentiments as to the deliberate throwing away of a good swordstick, but Trapnel's manner of dealing with the situation had not been without its lofty side. Nothing unexpected was found in the flat. Pamela had packed her clothes, and left with the suitcases. The Modigliani and her own photographs were gone too. No doubt she had strolled down to the Canal, disposed of *Profiles in String*, then returned with a taxi to remove her effects. Trapnel glanced for a second at the spaces left by the pictures.

'She can't have been gone more than a few hours. She must have done it after dark. If only I'd come back earlier in the day she'd still have been here.'

He took off the tropical jacket, slipped it on to a wire coat-hanger pendant from a hook in the door, loosened his tie. After that he stretched. That seemed to give him an idea. He began to look about the room, opening drawers, examining the shelf at the top of the inside of the wardrobe, even searching under the bed. Doubtless he was looking for 'pills' of one sort or another. Pamela might well have taken them away with her. He talked while he hunted round.

'I warned you hospitality would be rather sparse if you came back. Not a drop of Algerian left. I'm sorry for that. It was a great help when you're seeing things through. I'll just have to have a think now as to the best way of tackling life.'

'Will you be all right, Trappy?'

'Absolutely.'

'Nothing we can do?'

'Not a thing—ah, here we are.'

Trapnel had found the box. He swallowed a couple of examples of whatever sustaining globules were kept inside it. Possibly they were no more than sleeping pills. There was now no point in our staying a moment longer.

Both Bagshaw and I tried to say something more of a sympathetic sort. Trapnel shook his head.

'Probably all for the best. Who can tell? Still, losing that manuscript takes some laughing off. I'll have to think a lot about that.'

Bagshaw still hung about.

'Are you absolutely cleaned out, Trappy?'

'Me? Cleaned out? Good heavens, no. Thanks a lot all the same, but a cheque arrived this morning, quite a decent one, from a film paper I'd done a piece for.'

Whether or not that were true, it was a good exit line; Trapnel at his best. Bagshaw and I said goodnight. We passed again along the banks of the Canal, its waters still overspread with the pages of *Profiles in String*. The smell of the flat had again reminded me of Maclintick's.

'Will he really be all right?'

'I don't know about being all right exactly,' said Bagshaw. 'It's hard to be all right when you've not only lost your girl, but she's simultaneously destroyed your life work. I don't know what I'd feel like in the same position. I've sometimes thought of writing another novel—a political one. Somehow there never seems time. I expect Trappy'll pull through. Most of us do.'

'I mean he won't do himself in?'

'Trappy?'

'Yes.'

'God, no. I'd be very surprised.'

'People do.'

'I know they do. There was a chap in Spain when I was there. An anarcho-syndicalist. He'd talk about Proudhon by the hour together. He shot himself in a hotel room. I don't think Trappy will ever take that step. He's too interested in his own myth. Not the type anyway. He'd have done it before now, if he were going to.'

'He says something about suicide in the *Camel*.'

'The *Camel*'s not an exact description of Trappy's own life. He is always complaining people take it as that. You must have heard him. There are incidents, but the novel's not a blow-by-blow account of his early career.'

'I've heard X say that readers can never believe a novelist invents anything. He was at least in Egypt?'

'Do you mean to say he's never told you what he was doing there?'

'I'd always imagined his father was in the Consular, or something of the sort—possibly secret service connexions. X is always very keen on spying, says there's a resemblance between what a spy does and what a novelist does, the point being you don't suddenly steal an indispensable secret that gives complete mastery of the situation, but accumulate a lot of relatively humdrum facts, which when collated provide the picture.'

Bagshaw was not greatly interested in how novelists went to work, but was greatly astonished at this ignorance of Trapnel's life when young.

'A spy? Trapnel *père* wasn't a spy. He was a jockey. Rode for the most part in Egypt. That's why he knew the country. Did rather well in his profession, and saved up a bit. Married a girl from one of those English families who've lived for three or four generations in the Levant.'

'But all this is good stuff. Why doesn't X write about it?'

'He did talk of an article for the mag. Then he thought he'd keep it for a book. Trappy has mixed feelings. Of course he got through whatever money there was, as soon as he laid hands on it. He's not exactly ashamed. Rather proud in a way. All the same, it doesn't quite fit in with his own picture of himself. Hints about the secret service seem more exciting. The other was just ordinary home life, therefore rather dull.'

By this time Bagshaw was all but sober. Our paths lay in

different directions. We parted. I made my way home. A great deal seemed to have happened in a comparatively short time. It was still before midnight. A clock struck twelve while I put the key in the door. As if from a neighbouring minaret, a cat muezzin began to call other cats to prayer. The aberrations of love were incalculable. Burton, I remembered, supposed the passion to extend even into the botanic world:

'In vegetal creatures what sovereignty Love hath by many pregnant proofs and familiar example may be proved, especially of palm trees, which are both he and she, and express not a sympathy but a love-passion, as by many observations have been confirmed. *Constantine* gives an instance out of *Florentius* his Georgicks, of a Palm-tree that loved most fervently, and would not be comforted until such time her love applied himself unto her; you might see the two trees bend, and of their own accords stretch out their bows to embrace and kiss each other; they will give manifest signs of mutual love. *Ammianus Marcellinus* reports that they marry one another, and fall in love if they grow in sight; and when the wind brings up the smell to them, they are marvellously affected. *Philostratus* observes as much, and Galen, they will be sick for love, ready to die and pine away . . .'

Now, considering these matters that autumn afternoon under the colonnade, vegetal love seemed scarcely less plausible than the human kind. The damp cobblestones in front gave the illusion of quivering where the sunlight struck their irregular convexities. Rain still fell. The Library presented itself as a preferable refuge from the wet. I was uncertain whether rules permitted casual entry. It was worth trying. At worst, if told to go away, one could remain in the porch until time to move on. It would be no worse than where I was. Abandoning the colonnade, I crossed the road to a grey domed Edwardian building. Beyond its threshold, a parabola of passage-way led into a high circular room, rising to the roof and surrounded by a gallery. The place, often a welcome oasis in the past, seemed smaller than remembered. A few boys were pottering about among the bays of books, with an absent-minded air, or furiously writing at a table, as if life itself depended on getting whatever it was finished in time. A librarian presided at his desk.

Hoping to remain unobserved, I loitered by the door. That was not to be. The librarian looked up and stared. He took off his spectacles, rubbed his eyes, chose another pair from several spectacle-cases in front of him, put them on his nose and stared again. After a moment of this, he beckoned me. Recognizing that I was not to be allowed to kill five or ten minutes in peace, I prepared for expulsion. No doubt there was a regulation against visitors at this hour. The thing to do would be to delay eviction as long as possible, so that a minimum of time had to be spent in the porch. The librarian's beckonings became more urgent. He was a man older than normal for the job, more formally dressed. In fact, this was clearly an assistant master substituting for a regular librarian. Professional librarians were probably unprocurable owing to shortage of labour. I went across the room to see what he wanted. Tactics could be decided by his own comportment. This happy-go-lucky approach was cut short. Sitting at the desk was my former housemaster Le Bas. He spoke crossly.

'Do I know you?'

Boyhood returned in a flash, the instinct to oppose Le Bas —as Bagshaw would say—dialectically. The question was unanswerable. It is reasonable for someone to ask if you know him, because such knowledge is in the hands of the questioned party. How can it be asserted with assurance whether or not the questioner knows one? Powers of telepathy would be required. It could certainly be urged that five years spent under the same roof, so to speak under Le Bas's guidance, gave him a decided opportunity for knowing one; almost an unfair advantage, both in the superficial, also the more searching sense of the phrase. That was the primitive, atavistic reaction. More mature consideration brought to mind Le Bas's notorious forgetfulness even in those days. There was no reason to suppose his memory had improved.

'I was in your house—'

Obviously it would be absurd to call him 'sir', yet that still obtruded as the only suitable form of address. What on earth else could he be called? Just 'Le Bas'? Certainly he belonged to a generation which continued throughout a lifetime to use that excellently masculine invocation of surname, before an irresponsible bandying of first names smothered all subtleties of relationship. In any case, to call Le Bas by a christian name was unthinkable. What would it be, in effect, if so daring an apostrophe were contemplated? The initials had been L. L. Le B.—Lawrence Langton Le Bas, that was it. No one had ever been known to call him Lawrence, still less Langton. Among the other masters, some—his old enemy Cobberton, for example—used once in a way to hail him as 'Le B.' There was, after all, really no necessity to call him anything. Le Bas himself grew impatient at this procrastination.

'What's your name?'

I told him. That made things easier at once. Direct enquiry of that sort on the part of a former preceptor was much to be preferred to Sillery's reckless guessing. Confessed ignorance on the point—as on most points—showed a saner attitude towards life. Le Bas had learnt that, if nothing else. He was probably older than Sillery, a few years the wrong side of eighty. Like Sillery, though in a different manner, he too looked well; leathery, saurian; dry as a bone. Taking off the second pair of spectacles, he again rubbed in the old accustomed fashion the deep, painfully inflamed sockets of the eyes. Then he resumed the earlier pair, or perhaps yet a third reserve.

'What's your generation, Jenkins?'

This was like coming up for sentence at the Last Judgment. I tried to remember, to speak more exactly, tried to decide how best to put the answer clearly to Le Bas.

'Fettiplace-Jones was captain of the house when I arrived ... my own lot ... Stringham ... Templer ...'

Le Bas glared, as if in frank disbelief. Whether that was because the names conveyed nothing, or my own seemed not to belong amongst them, was only to be surmised. It looked as if he were about to accuse me of being an impostor, to be turned away from the Library forthwith. I lost my head, began to recite names at random as they came into my mind.

'Simson ... Fitzwith ... Ghika ... Brandreth ... Maiden ... Bischoffsheim ... Whitney ... Parkinson ... Summers-Miller ... Pyefinch ... the Calthorpes ... Widmerpool ...'

At the last name Le Bas suddenly came to life.

'Widmerpool?'

'Widmerpool was a year or so senior to me.'

Le Bas seemed to forget that all we were trying to do was approximately to place my own age-group in his mind. He took one of several pens lying on the desk, examined it, chose another one, examined that, then wrote 'Widmerpool' on the blotting paper in front of him, drawing a circle round the name. This was an unexpected reaction. It seemed to have nothing whatever to do with myself. Le Bas now sunk into a state of near oblivion. Could it be a form of exorcism against pupils of his whom he had never much liked? Then he offered an explanation.

'Widmerpool's down here today. I met him in the street. We had a talk. He told me about a cause he's

233

interested in. That's why I made a note. I shall have to try and remember what he said. He's an MP now. What happened to the others?'

It was like answering enquiries after a match—'Fettiplace-Jones was out first ball, sir' . . . 'Parkinson kicked a goal, sir' . . . 'Whitney got his colours, sir'. I tried to recollect some piece of information to be deemed of interest to Le Bas about the sort of boys of whom he could approve, but the only facts that came to mind were neither about these, nor cheerful.

'Stringham died in a Japanese prisoner-of-war camp.'

'Yes, yes—so I heard.'

That awareness was unexpected.

'Templer was killed on a secret operation.'

'In the Balkans. Somebody told me. Very sad.'

Once more the cognition was unforeseen. Its acknowledgment was followed by Le Bas taking up the pen again. Underneath Widmerpool's name he wrote 'Balkans', drew another circle round the word, which he attached to the first circle by a line. It looked more than ever like some form of incantation.

'Now I remember what it was Widmerpool consulted me about. Some society he has organized to encourage good relations with one of the Balkan countries. Now which one? Simson was drowned. Torpedoed in a troopship.'

He mentioned Simson as another relevant fact, not at all as if he did not wish to be outdone in consciousness of widespread human dissolution in time of war.

'What are you doing yourself, Jenkins?'

'I'm writing a book on Burton—the *Anatomy of Melancholy* man.'

Le Bas took two or three seconds to absorb that statement, the aspects, good and bad, implied by such an activity. He had probably heard of Burton. He might easily know more about him than did Sillery. Dons were not necessarily better informed than schoolmasters. When at last he spoke, it was clear Le Bas did know about Burton. He was not wholly approving.

'Rather a morbid subject.'

He had used just that epithet when he found me, as a schoolboy, reading St John Clarke's *Fields of Amaranth*. He may have thought reading or writing books equally morbid, whatever the content. To be fair to Le Bas as a critic, *Fields of Amaranth*—if you were prepared to use the term critically at all—might reasonably be so described. I now agreed, even if on different grounds. The admission had to be made. Time had been on Le Bas's side.

We were interrupted at this moment by a very small boy, who had come to stand close by where we were talking. It would be fairer to say we were inhibited by his presence, because no direct interruption took place. Dispelling about him an aura of immense, if not wholly convincing goodness, his intention was evidently to accost Le Bas in due course, at the same time ostentatiously to avoid any implication that he could be so lacking in good manners as to break into a conversation or attempt to overhear it. Le Bas, possibly not unwilling to seek dispensation from further talk about the past, distant or immediate, with all its uncomfortably realistic—Trapnel might prefer, naturalistic—undercurrents, turned in the boy's direction.

'What do you want?'

'I can wait, sir.'

This assurance that his own hopes were wholly unimportant, that Youth was prepared to waste valuable time indefinitely while Age span out its senile conference, did not in the least impress Le Bas, too conversant with the ways of boys not to be for ever on his guard.

'Can't you find some book?'

'Sir—the *Dictionary of Phrase and Fable*.'

'Brewer's?'

'I think so, sir.'

'You've looked on the proper shelf?'

'Of course, sir.'

'What's your name?'

'Akworth, sir.

Le Bas rose.

'It will be the worse for you, Akworth, if Brewer turns out to be on the proper shelf.'

I explained to Le Bas why I had come; that it was time to move on to my appointment.

'Good, good. Excellent. I'm glad we had a—well, a chat. Most fortunate you reminded me of that society of Widmerpool's. I don't know why he should think I am specially interested in the Balkans—though now I come to think of it, Templer's . . . makes a kind of link. You know, Jenkins, among my former pupils, I should never have guessed Widmerpool would have entered the House of Commons. Fettiplace-Jones, yes—he was another matter.'

Le Bas paused. He had immediately regretted this implied criticism of Widmerpool's abilities.

'Of course, they need all sorts and conditions of men to govern the country. Especially these days. Sad about those fellows who were killed. I sometimes think of the number of pupils of mine who lost their lives. Two wars. It adds up. Come along, Akworth.'

The boy smiled, conveying at once apology for disruption of our talk, and his own certainty that its termination must have come as a relief to me. As he hurried off towards one of the shelves, beside which he had piled up a heap of books, he gave the impression that quite a complicated intellectual programme for ragging Le Bas had been planned. Le Bas himself sighed.

'Goodbye, Jenkins. I hope the school will have acquired a regular librarian by your next visit.'

It was still wet outside, but, by the time my appointment

was at an end, the rain had stopped. A damp earthy smell filled the air. The weather was appreciably colder. In spite of that a man in a mackintosh was sitting on the low wall that ran the length of the further side of the street in front of the archway and chapel. It was Widmerpool. He looked in great dejection. I had not seen him since the night at Trapnel's flat, when he had, so to speak, expressed his confidence in Pamela's return. Now that had come about. He had prophesied truly. Isobel, about a month before, soon after the destruction of *Profiles in String*, had pointed out a paragraph in a newspaper listing guests at some public function. The names 'Mr Kenneth Widmerpool MP and Mrs Widmerpool' were included. It was just as predicted. In the Governmental reshuffle at the beginning of October Widmerpool had received minor office. In spite of these two matters, both showing himself undoubtedly in the ascendant, he sat lonely and cheerless. I should have been tempted to try and slip by unnoticed, but he saw me, and shouted something. I crossed the road.

'Congratulations on your new parliamentary job.'

'Thanks, thanks. What are you doing down here?'

I told him, adding that I had been talking with Le Bas.

'I ran into him too. I took the opportunity of giving him some account of my Balkan visit. Whatever one may think of Le Bas's capabilities as a teacher, he is supposedly in charge of the young, and should therefore be put in possession of the correct facts.'

'How did your trip go?'

'We hear a lot about what is called an "Iron Curtain". Where is this "Iron Curtain", I ask myself? I found no sign. That was what I told Le Bas. You might think him a person to hold reactionary views, but I found that was not at all the case, now that the idea of world revolution has been dropped. By the way, how are you employed since *Fission* has closed down?'

I mentioned various concerns that involved me. Widmerpool showed no embarrassment in mentioning the magazine. He even asked if it were true that Bagshaw had secured a job in television. However, when I enquired why, on such a damp and increasingly cold evening, he should be sitting on the wall, apparently just watching the world go by, he shifted uneasily, stiffening at the question.

'Pam and I came down for the day.'

He laughed.

'She's got a young friend here whom she met somewhere during his holidays, and he invited her to tea. She's having tea in his room now. I'm waiting for her.'

'A boy, you mean?'

'Yes—I suppose you'd call him a boy still.'

'I meant still at the school?'

'He was leaving, but stayed on for some reason—to captain some team, I think. Son or nephew of one of the Calthorpes. Do you remember them? Pam thought it would be an amusing jaunt. She insisted I mustn't spoil the party by coming too. Rather a good joke.'

All the same, he did not look as if he found it specially funny. Blue-grey mist was thickening round us. I had a train to catch. The Widmerpools had come by car. They had no fixed plan about getting back to London. Pamela hated being tied down by too positive arrangements. She was going to pick her husband up hereabouts when the tea-party was over. I thought of what Trapnel had said of her couplings.

'I must be off.'

'I don't believe I ever sent you details about that society I was telling Le Bas about. My secretary will forward them. I received Quiggin & Craggs's Autumn List recently—their last. There were some interesting titles. Clapham has asked me to continue my association with publishing by joining his board.'

I too had received the list; later heard Quiggin's comments on it. Sillery's *Garnered at Sunset*, unexciting as the selection might be, had been noticed respectfully. Shernmaker, for example, was unexpectedly approving. Sales were not too bad, even if the advance was never recouped. Sillery might be said to have successfully imposed his will in this last fling. So did Ada Leintwardine. *I Stopped at a Chemist* upset several of the more old-fashioned reviewers who had survived the war, but they admitted a novel-writing career lay ahead of her. Even Evadne Clapham was impressed. In fact, *Golden Grime* was the last of Evadne Clapham's books in her former style. Her subsequent manner followed Ada's. *Engine Melody*—truncated title of *The Pistons of Our Locomotives Sing the Songs of Our Workers*—believed to be not too well translated, was by no means ignored, Nathaniel Sheldon's mention including the phrase 'muted beauty'. Vernon Gainsborough's *Bronstein: Marxist or Mystagogue?*, with seven other books on similar subjects, was favourably noticed in a *Times Literary Supplement* 'front'.

'It's a real *apologia pro vita sua*,' said Bagshaw. 'Conversion from Trotskyism expressed in such unqualified terms must have warmed Gypsy's heart after her reverses.'

The last reference was to *Sad Majors*. Odo Stevens had dealt effectively with efforts, such as they were, to suppress his book. He had enjoyed exceptional opportunities for knowing about such things. That may have put him at an advantage. As usual, he also had good luck. So far from being inconvenient, the whole matter worked out in his best interests. Having already grasped that he might have done better financially by going to some publisher other than Quiggin & Craggs, he at once recognized that the loss of the two typescripts would give a potent reason for requiring release from his contract. He did not mention the third typescript, which had been all the time in the hands of Rosie Manasch. Rosie had apparently suggested that her former Fleet Street contacts might be useful in exploiting serial possibilities. She was right. *Sad Majors* was serialized on excellent terms. It was published in book form in the spring.

L. O. Salvidge, rather an achievement in the light of current publishing delays, got out a further volume of essays to follow up *Paper Wine*. The new one, *Secretions*, was much reviewed beside Shernmaker's *Miscellaneous Equities*. It was a notable score for Salvidge to have produced two books in less than a year. After the unsuccessful prosecution, Kydd's *Sweetskin* at first failed to recover from the withdrawal at the time of the injunction, but, given a new wrapper design, Kydd himself alleged that it picked up relatively well. That season also appeared David Pennistone's *Descartes, Gassendi, and the Atomic Theory of Epicurus*, the work of which he used to speak so despairingly when we were in the army together. I busied myself with Burton, even so only just managing to see *Borage and Hellebore: a Study* in print by the following December.

The scattered pages of *Profiles in String*, with the death's-head swordstick, floated eternally downstream into the night. It was the beginning of Trapnel's drift too, irretrievable as they. He went underground for a long time after that night. When at last he emerged, it was to haunt an increasingly gruesome and desolate world. There were odds and ends of film work, stray pieces of journalism, an occasional short story. In the last, possibly some traces reappeared of what had gone into *Profiles in String*, though in a much diminished form. Something of it may even have emerged on the screen. Another novel never got written. Trapnel himself always insisted that a novel is what its writer is. The definition only opens up a lot more questions. Perhaps he had taken a knock from which he never recovered; perhaps he had used up already what was in him, in the way writers do. In these sunless marshlands of existence, a dwindling reserve of pep-pills, a certain innate inventiveness, capacity for survival, above all the mystique of panache—in short, the Trapnel method—just about made it possible to hang on. That was the best you could say.

I once asked Dicky Umfraville—whose own experiences on the Turf made his knowledge of racing personalities extensive—whether he had ever heard of a jockey called Trapnel, whose professional career had been made largely in Egypt.

'Heard of him, old boy? When I was in Cairo in the 'twenties, I won a packet on a French horse he rode called Amour Piquant.'

A Selected List of Classics Available from Mandarin

While every effort is made to keep prices low, it is sometimes necessary to increase prices at short notice. Mandarin Paperbacks reserves the right to show new retail prices on covers which may differ from those previously advertised in the text or elsewhere.

The prices shown below were correct at the time of going to press.

☐	7493 0325 5	**Cannery Row**	John Steinbeck	£3.50
☐	7493 0326 3	**East of Eden**	John Steinbeck	£4.99
☐	7493 0327 1	**Grapes of Wrath**	John Steinbeck	£3.50
☐	7493 0328 X	**Long Valley**	John Steinbeck	£3.50
☐	7493 0329 8	**Once There Was a War**	John Steinbeck	£3.99
☐	7493 0330 1	**The Pearl**	John Steinbeck	£2.50
☐	7493 0331 X	**To a God Unknown**	John Steinbeck	£3.50
☐	7493 0332 8	**Tortilla Flat**	John Steinbeck	£3.50
☐	7493 0333 6	**Travels with Charley**	John Steinbeck	£3.99
☐	7493 0334 4	**Log from Sea of Cortez**	John Steinbeck	£4.99
☐	7497 0194 3	**The Red Pony**	John Steinbeck	£2.50
☐	7493 0371 9	**The English Teacher**	R. K. Narayan	£3.99
☐	7493 0370 0	**The Financial Expert**	R. K. Narayan	£3.99
☐	7493 0305 0	**The Bachelor of Arts**	R. K. Narayan	£3.99
☐	7493 0304 2	**The Dark Room**	R. K. Narayan	£3.99
☐	7493 0461 8	**The Balkan Trilogy**	Olivia Manning	£7.99
☐	7493 0414 6	**A Town Like Alice**	Nevil Shute	£3.99
☐	7493 0408 1	**On the Beach**	Nevil Shute	£3.99
☐	7493 0341 7	**Requiem for a Wren**	Nevil Shute	£3.99
☐	7493 0413 8	**No Highway**	Nevil Shute	£3.99
☐	7493 0412 X	**Trustee from the Toolroom**	Nevil Shute	£3.99
☐	7493 0410 3	**Slide Rule**	Nevil Shute	£3.99

All these books are available at your bookshop or newsagent, or can be ordered direct from the publisher. Just tick the titles you want and fill in the form below.

Mandarin Paperbacks, Cash Sales Department, PO Box 11, Falmouth, Cornwall TR10 9EN.

Please send cheque or postal order, no currency, for purchase price quoted and allow the following for postage and packing:

UK	80p for the first book, 20p for each additional book ordered to a maximum charge of £2.00.
BFPO	80p for the first book, 20p for each additional book.
Overseas including Eire	£1.50 for the first book, £1.00 for the second and 30p for each additional book thereafter.

NAME (Block letters) ....

ADDRESS ....

....

....